BROT & SAINTS

BROTHERS & SAINTS

EDGAR RAC

TATE PUBLISHING
AND ENTERPRISES, LLC

Published by Tate Publishing & Enterprises, LLC
127 E. Trade Center Terrace | Mustang, Oklahoma 73064 USA
1.888.361.9473 | www.tatepublishing.com

Tate Publishing is committed to excellence in the publishing industry. The company reflects the philosophy established by the founders, based on Psalm 68:11,
"The Lord gave the word and great was the company of those who published it."

Book design copyright © 2016 by Tate Publishing, LLC. All rights reserved.
Cover design by Joshua Rafols
Interior design by Richell Balansag

Published in the United States of America

ISBN: 978-1-68187-455-5
Fiction / Christian / General
15.11.05

Thanks to God, his unconditional Love and Mercy, which inspired me to write this book;

To my dear mother, Rolanda;
And to my late grandparents, Rita and Michail. You are always in my heart.

1

There were not many people in the viewing room; only a few closest friends and a widow, weeping humbly, holding her two boys by the hand. The man resting in a coffin was Michael Preston. Five days ago, he went to sleep early in the evening and never woke up. His heart stopped beating when he was only thirty-three years old.

"Take the children," said the widow, named Deborah, to one of her friends. Then she took out a white handkerchief from her pocket and came closer to the man she loved with all her heart. She touched his cold hands and started weeping even more. Michael's eyes were forever closed as well as the door leading to hope of growing old side by side. The widow could not say a single word—her speechlessness was covered with tears; painful thoughts that had turned into nothing but ashes were flashing before her weary eyes.

A couple of minutes later, she sat down on a chair next to the coffin, lowered her head, closed her eyes, and tried to think only of the time they had spent together. She remembered how they first met each other at a bus station, how they fell in love, and kissed for the first time. She also saw the moment when a man she loved kneeled down before her and asked if she would marry him. This happened nearly ten years ago on a beach in the middle of the night; it was summer and the sky was starry. The loud waves of cold ocean were as the most romantic music of all, for when the beautiful and most precious ring was on Deborah's finger, the time seemed to have stopped, and nothing save eternity and universe of love seemed to exist. Now, her bitter tears were humbly dropping on her black dress—it was as though for the first time in her life, she didn't want to wipe them. "Here we are, my beloved," murmured Deborah, eyeing her teardrops falling down. "Inside what we have never dared to think of. Death has separated us, but now eternity to me seems closer than ever. Wait for me, sweet prince. Wait for me in the everlasting kingdom. My heart will forever be yours."

After the funeral, the priest of their local church came up to Deborah and her two boys—Russell, who was seven, and Ludwig, who was nine years old—and took her by the hand. She looked at him with hope in her eyes, though all the priest could see was weariness and pain.

"I know this probably is not the best time for a conversation, Deborah," said the priest, "but I would sure like to have a word with you someday. Everything is not as sad as it looks."

"You're right, Father John, I can't talk right now," replied the woman. "I just want to go home. My boys need some rest."

"I understand. God is with you, Deborah. You are certainly not alone."

At this, Deborah Preston only glanced at the man standing in front of her and was able to say not a single word more. She turned around and left, holding her two boys by the hand.

Four days later, alone in her agony and indescribable longing, she came to visit her husband for the first time after his funeral. She brought neither flowers nor anything what could honor those glorious memories surrounding the tombstone Deborah was now standing before. Her heart started beating faster as her eyes stopped on her husband's name engraved on that intimidating piece of stone. She could never have imagined that standing in front of a tombstone could be so terrifying and even somewhat challenging. She took hold of her emotions, however, and managed to smile as her tears were falling down.

"You were the one to teach me how to overcome fears, my dear Michael," she said barely in a whisper. "Remember when you told me to smile at them? You also said that

that's what fears hate the most." After a brief moment, she wiped her tears and continued rather bravely. "I cannot put it into words how deep is the pain in my heart, my beloved. Our dreams, our faith, and love—everything is still in my mind, but my heart is empty because I don't have anyone to share it with. Our boys miss you too, but I don't want you to worry—I promise you will be proud of them. They will be strong Christian warriors, and I will do everything in my power to accomplish God's will in them. We pray together every evening, and I read the Bible to them every Sunday after dinner. They always listen with wonder and question with curiosity afterwards," said Deborah, smiling. "I am sorry for not bringing them here today. I thought this would be too difficult for them. I promise you will see our boys next time."

Minutes later, the priest of their church came to Deborah and tenderly touched her shoulder. The woman startled a little, but after seeing that it was the priest who had been leading their church for more than twenty years now, she only hugged him and said, "Thank you for coming. I am sorry for being rude the other day."

"You weren't rude, Deborah," said the fifty-year-old priest named John. "I saw you coming here, so I hope you don't mind if we talk a little. Unless, of course, you don't want to," he rushed to add.

"No, I could use some encouragement right now," replied the widow, looking at the tombstone. "I never thought this life could be that tragic. I thought such drama existed only in movies."

"Drama? Birth is no drama, my daughter. It is nothing but joy and gladness."

"Yes, I understand." She smiled comprehensibly. "For God, Michael is now alive. But for me, he is only a memory and a hope that maybe someday his face will once again be enlightened before my weary eyes. He's not here to hold my hand or to be a shoulder to lean upon. His birth is God's joy, and certainly not mine."

"I know it is difficult to find at least frailest of comforting words, but we, my child, have to be strong in our faith that death is exactly what leads us to our eternal home. One day, we—who live and die in Christ—will also be in that land of eternity and love, and we will be able to hug Michael once more."

"You really think so?"

"The day will come, Deborah, when all these tears will be wiped from your eyes. Also tears of all those who believe."

"Thank you," muttered the widow with a smile. Then she kneeled down on a wet grass, touched the tombstone gently and sighed.

2

Less than thirteen years had passed since Michael Preston's death. Russell and Ludwig were raised in love, warmth, and care. Owning a small flower business, Deborah spent most of her time educating her boys, teaching them about God, life, and spiritual mountains, hills and walls within it. They lived in a small village out of town, where only one supermarket was barely existing. Many people in the place were as lazy as human beings could be; having many acres of lands, the citizens of that village did nothing but complain about being forgotten and abandoned by people in charge of order. Most people there had little, though what they needed was even less than that. Wars, troubles, and scandals seemed to be far away from that peaceful place where literally nothing special was happening. There was one church shepherded by the same pastor for many decades now; the sacred institution was the only place where people could find themselves talking about something more than just weather forecast or that time of year. It was the twenty-first century, though it often seemed that this huge and revolutionary fact had passed by their little village of unseen routine and hardly describable pace. In general, people lived rather peacefully in there, each day dully staring through their open windows into each other's. There was no bigger delight for those people but to day by day try to find out what their neighbors, friends, and even strangers from next door were doing. Perhaps the happiest people living in the village were teenagers, because they were always most likely to leave that place forever. Pursuit of education and a better life somewhere else was their only pretext, which, in fact, helped many young men and women abandon the godforsaken place forever. The life there was wonderful and precious only for those who were eager enough to spend their lives in laziness, peace, and absolute carelessness. Nevertheless, not all people there were miserably living in their unnoticeable world of vanity.

Many years ago, Deborah Preston, after being shaken and changed by the death of her beloved husband, decided to invest her lifetime savings into a flower business. She bought a suitable field not far away from their humble house and planted many sorts of flowers there. With time, she was able to afford to hire a jobless friend of hers, who was planting flowers for her. All she had to do was sell them in the markets, which was also changed in time. Soon enough, she hired another person who could sell those flowers instead of her, and thus she fully dedicated herself and her time to raising her children. Flower business in big cities was growing, along with which Preston family's life was gaining more colors and light. Most of their income was spent on books, sports, and things that were able to bring more happiness to their daily lives. Though they lived in a very small and humble wooden house, they never thought of moving somewhere else; instead, they renovated their fortress as well as they could so that life in there could be nothing but enjoyment. This, of course, was not without the constant awareness and presence of their neighbors' eyes— it is never possible to hide oneself in a small village like that. Since changes and something yet unseen was strange and rather unacceptable in that lonely and small part of the world, Deborah's renovated house was a thrilling and fascinating story, which was discussed even long after the house was renewed. News in each other's lives was always something warmly welcomed into their daily routines. The pleasure of gossiping about someone's uncommon behavior or way of life was always beyond comprehension.

What also brought colors and made everyone feel elated as far as gossips were concerned was television and radio. Newspapers were not that popular since intellectual way of widening one's mind and knowledge was a long forgotten fable, having in mind that there were no libraries or bookshops of any kind. TVs and radios, on the other hand, were in each house treated with dignity and respect.

Politics, economy, sports, and even entertainment news—it was discussed with great curiosity every single day. People would just gather for breakfast or dinner in each other's houses and simply go through all the news they had heard of hours ago. There were some who were daily trying to leave their houses as quickly as possible in order not to be the host of that day's routine—it was as if an unwritten rule which every single soul in that village was well aware of. Sometimes it occurred that those who had bought a new TV or had something new and special in their homes to brag about were often even inviting their neighbors to come to visit. Surely, pride was always cruelly punished afterwards, but the enjoyment of making others jealous was greater than any gossips that would wander around the village for weeks to follow.

Besides all that, there was no way of increasing intellectual treasures or making their miserable and temporary existences more significant. Out of a couple of hundred of people living there, only few had more than five books in their homes—it was a taboo which was never mentioned as the time went by. The only sources of literature that existed in the village were provided only in the elementary school.

During late evenings, when even rhyming rumors happened to be boring and blindly staring at the TV screens of no use, villagers would simply light up a few candles and sit in their comfortable couches, covering themselves in as many warm blankets as they could find. Those given an honor and a blessing of having families were usually either cooking dinners together or telling their offsprings some old tales about their ancestors and their pious lives. Evenings, especially in winters, were always quiet and mysterious; thoughts of mice could often be heard better than any kind of proof of life in the village. Only lights in their windows were alive, and nothing but stillness leading to tomorrow was surrounding the entire place. Though the villagers were always fond of singing their traditional songs, the music was needless at such moment of peace. Perhaps such evenings, when streets are empty and each door in the village is closed, was the only beautiful mystery happening more often than any of those people were able to notice.

This time of year was winter, and the entire land was utterly covered in snow. Nothing save wooden huts with lights coming through the windows were visible in the land drowning in white. The weather there was usually cold in winters, and rarely did someone dare to step outside their cozy homes without any particular reason. Merely a couple of weeks were left till Christmas, and the significance and very essence of this time of year was highly honored and valued by those people, whose spiritual lives were entirely based on the traditions they lived by and believed in. They lived in a land that acknowledged only Catholic customs, and no other perspectives were considered or accepted. There were only a few small Christian groups in the entire country, and even those were dying lights. In a small village like that, there had never arisen any other ideas or doubtful questions concerning different spiritual point of views; if one wasn't a Catholic (not depending on whether he was a strict one or not), he was considered a stranger and an outcast. In fact, there has never been such incident in this small village that is now completely immersed into white color and starry sky, which as if whispers that the holy night is drawing near.

"And remember, my boys—don't tell anyone that you are Christians. People may not understand you," told Deborah to her children many years ago when they were just kids. She didn't know where all this began, but as a child she was always raised under Christian traditions, believing in the Word of God and worshipping Jesus only. She met her future husband, Michael Preston, in one of those few Christian communities; and in just a couple of years, they moved to this little village as a married couple, seeking peace and happy life together.

Disguising their Christian faith wasn't an easy task. Letting anyone know about their standpoints would lead to an uncomfortable and rather shameful position, upon which everyone looked with hatred and great disrespect. Yet, Deborah and her family lived happily under the protection of God Almighty; they read the Bible and prayed every single day. Worries about what their neighbors would think was what they least cared about. They knew very well what religious system they were living in; however, they could neither understand nor make themselves accept those peculiar regulations and questionable priorities. Nonetheless, the eternal antagonism between Catholicism and Christianity never bothered the Preston family. They peacefully and happily lived their humble Christian life, not worrying about what Catholic world thought of their position and beliefs. Once in a while, they even attended masses in their local church, where they often were considered very irresponsible believers. In the eyes of other churchgoers, attending holy mass at least once a week was the least what a Catholic could do.

"It is better to attend Catholic masses than not to go to a church at all," was how Deborah often explained it. Her boys were not against it, especially when they went to the church not more than thrice a year.

Unsurprisingly, what they heard and saw in that church was always opposite to their realization of what Christianity was. Instructed by their mother, however, none of the boys paid much attention or tried to memorize the order of the rites and when one had to kneel down, stand up, or make a sign of a cross, which the Prestons never did. Every mass was like a lecture taught in a foreign language, which even echoes didn't sound familiar. Scenes they saw and preachings they heard were nothing but a mystery, being understood by every kneeling soul in the church except for the Prestons. Nevertheless, they were never bothered by the fact. Instead of trying to catch the sparks of Christianity and fellowship in Christ, they simply, with humbled hearts and thanksgiving on their minds, worshipped Christ along with others, though the constant sense of difference was never allowing the hardly breakable spiritual walls to fall.

Sometimes, especially before Christmas, Deborah was often questioned whether she and her boys fasted before the holy celebration. It was as if mandatory to refuse eating meat or (this concerns more strict Catholics) even dairy products. Many faithful Catholics observed this tradition, and, what is more amazing, frequently checked on each other to see if it was followed uprightly. It could happen in a form of a question or a simple visit at home. Indeed, although the village was small and hardly noticeable at all, the traditions and local rules of unwritten significance were always observed and cherished as if their last connection to the world from which it often seemed to have been isolated.

Catholicism was the only escape the little village had—though to some it was uncomfortable and seldom didn't match one's desires or dreams, still it was something people considered sacred and precious. There was no religious education, and people truly knew little of the purpose of this life and of the eternity of the one to come. The church was all they had in the aspect of salvation, and few had any idea about other religions or ways of life. They were simple villagers believing in any saint or priest who came to visit or preach for a few Sundays. That was all they had as well as all they held on to. Strangers like Deborah, whose life seemed suspicious and rather odd, were always treated with certain amount of carefulness mingled with displeasure and dissatisfaction. Ironically, most of those judgmental opinions were based more on their misunderstanding and unwillingness to even try rather than their stubbornness not to accept any peculiar and doubtful Christian dogmas.

The thick walls between different religious point of views and intense uncertainty surrounding the entire conflict was not what reigned among the people or inside their daily rumors. Everything in that village was far away from even the idea of the controversy behind the foolish battlefield of Christian perspectives. It was as if they lived in their own temporal paradise, where hardly imaginable existence would be impossible without traditions and customs set by those who probably were aware of more than others. Despite the lifeless atmosphere with no air in it, it satisfied people and that was enough, for opening new doors and trying new tastes was intimidatingly insane in the eyes of routine.

3

One Saturday evening, less than a couple of weeks away from Christmas, Deborah and her son Russell were sitting at a dinner table. This was no ordinary feasting—roasted chicken, fried potatoes, vegetables, and various souses were on the table. Tiny bottles of different spices were also there, not to mention mother's favorite salads that her entire family adored. Old rock 'n' roll music was on the radio and that perfectly suited the evening's cheerful atmosphere. Snow, which was as sun enlightening the darkness of the late evening, was all around the village, and frost on their tiny windows somehow managed to bring coziness and warmth into their little wooden house. With beautifully decorated Christmas tree standing next to the fireplace, and with no worries disturbing either the instant or anything easily reachable, the air was somewhat light and everything surrounding them made them feel as though inside the enjoyment and bliss of Christmas morning already.

"Ludwig, where are you?" shouted Deborah in a voice mingled with sounds of laughter. Meanwhile, Ludwig was upstairs in his room, putting on a colorful shirt for such a special occasion. He was one of those young men to whom outward looks meant a great deal; everything had to be perfect as far as his appearance was concerned. His shoes were always polished, and never did he leave the house before judging himself in front of the mirror. Ludwig, as well as his younger brother, was a tall and rather handsome man—looking at him one could easily take him for a professional basketball player. Both brothers were well-built, and habits like push-ups or weightlifting exercises took big parts of their Christian lives. Strength and confidence in their bodies and physical abilities were what they cherished and considered valuable and inevitable in aspect of manhood.

"Coming, Mother!" Ludwig said loudly.

"Probably staring at the mirror and marveling at his dashing smile," remarked Russell while his mother was simply enjoying the beauty of Elvis Presley song that was playing on the radio.

"Don't say that, Russell," she said, tittering. "He does well, you know. Taking care of himself, I mean."

"Anything done in excess is opposite to good, Mother."

"I agree," she said with a warm smile.

"Did anyone miss me?" Ludwig gloriously declared, entering the sitting room a couple of minutes later.

"I believe I hear a familiar voice," Russell said calmly.

"Yes, we did," Deborah added, standing up. "Please have a seat, my dear. Who would like to say grace today?"

"I am sorry, Mother, I don't look handsome enough to do that this evening," Russell remarked again, teasing his brother.

"Okay, I think I will, then," said Deborah. Then she sat down again and they took each other's hand. "Dear Jesus, we thank you for this blessed evening and for these gifts we have received from your grace and mercy. We thank you, Lord, for everything you give us. Also for your protection and forgiveness. Bless us, dear Jesus, in every step of our lives. We are yours. Thank you. Amen."

"Amen," said both boys, after that they all began eating the dishes which were as though impregnated with the unmistakable scent of Deborah's motherly hands. Indeed, mother's warmth was perhaps the most important ingredient in their everyday meals.

"Just out of mere curiosity, is that strange man coming here tonight?" Russell asked, looking at his mother.

"What strange man?" Deborah asked in reply. Seconds later, someone knocked at the door.

"Perhaps that one," Russell murmured, at which Ludwig chuckled, putting his fork aside. As Deborah rushed to the door, both boys sighed deeply and neither started eating without her. "If someone else comes here tonight or if you decide to brush your teeth, our chicken and potatoes will be cold and our dinner destroyed," he added, looking at his empty plate.

"I begin to dislike that suspicious admirer."

"No worries. Our mother's not that naive."

When Deborah opened the door, she saw a man in his late forties, standing with a bouquet of flowers in his hand and hardly imaginable hope lively glowing in his eyes. "Good evening, Deborah," he said, smiling widely.

"Good evening, Alexander," Deborah replied, respectfully hiding the weariness of the sight in front of her behind a modest smile.

"Oh, please! Call me Alex," he said humbly, eyeing the woman's face as some divine flower given to humankind by God himself.

"He says that every single time they meet," Russell whispered with a chuckle, hoping not to be heard for the front door was not that far away from their dinner table.

"I am sorry to interrupt your dinner," Alexander continued, barely breathing. "Here, this is for you." He handed the bouquet and added as a child trying to make an impression. "I believe it's warmth what those flowers need now. It's freezing outside."

"Thank you, Alexander. It is very kind of you." She took the flowers, and speechlessly looked at the man who, tirelessly using such gestures of sympathy, had been trying to win her heart for more than a year now. Alexander was also standing speechless, naively hoping to be invited inside.

"Well, I guess I had better go," he said an instant later, feeling rather uncomfortable. This, however, was something he was unwillingly getting used to.

"Thank you, Alexander, I really appreciate the flowers. I am sorry, but I am sort of busy right now. It's now my family time, and I…"

"Yes, sure! no problem, Debby. I understand," the man said humbly. "I am sorry for disturbing you."

"Have a nice evening, Alexander. I am truly grateful for the flowers."

"Sure. Besides," he quickly added as Debby was about to close the door, "if you ever need something, help or anything else, I live in a house next to the post office. There are no other houses around it, so it's easy to find."

"Thank you, Alexander. That is very kind of you. I'll keep that in mind."

"Yes, good night."

"Good night," she said, closing the door.

"How do you think, would it be helpful if we wrote a note that Alexander is not welcome anywhere near our house and hung it on our front door?" Russell said jokingly.

Deborah, speechlessly allowing her boys to enjoy the amusement, put the beautiful flowers in a vase and looked at them all as if saying hello, introducing to them both herself and their new home.

"I think it's not our house he needs," remarked Ludwig in reply.

"Besides, did he call you Debby?" Russell said, looking at his mother. "Who does that man think he is?"

Both boys tittered a little when their mother left the vase on a small commode next to the TV and rejoined them at the table. A smile was on her face, for any spoken word would bring forth even more comments and amusingly creative ideas about Deborah's admirer, who was a single and humble man, seeking for family happiness as everyone in this madly wonderful world.

"Mom, why do you purposely call him Alexander each time he asks you to address him in a more informal manner?"

"I just don't want him to imagine something what doesn't exist, boys," she replied rather thoughtfully.

"Doesn't he have a chance?"

Instead of answering, Deborah glanced at Russell with eyes that told it all. There was both seriousness and a kind plea not to ask that question ever again.

"I see," Russell said again, friendly trying to amuse everyone at the table. "Poor fella, he doesn't even know his efforts are vain."

"Okay, enough!" Deborah exclaimed, laughing a little herself.

This was not the first time Alexander came with a bouquet of flowers in his hands, and it was certainly not the last. Sometimes the boys laughed at it, though there were other times when they were really annoyed by the fact, knowing that their mother was not interested in anything beyond the relationship which usually lasted less than two minutes. The brothers always tried to protect their mother for she was all they had, and such desperate men like Alexander were never welcome near their mother. Ironically, some men on the streets would perhaps dare to approach Deborah and introduce themselves, were it not for the two tall and well-built young men, whose figures immediately made those men change their minds and hope for a better and luckier tomorrow. Russell and Ludwig were always as protective shields, guarding their mother from anything what could cause her harm and sadness. The brothers were as a fortress in which Deborah was always treated like a princess, like a queen; she was respected, loved, and always protected under the wings of the two angels whom she herself had raised.

The evening and their dinner continued; they ate, talked, and laughed at various matters beginning with anecdotes and ending with hilarious happenings and accidents in their daily lives and church.

"I also remember," said Russell, barely breathing through his uncontrollable laughter, "when one time during church service—I believe it was last year before Christmas—one man started snoring so loudly that even the priest stopped talking and chuckled. Unfortunately, he was woken up afterwards. I remember how I thought I'd die from laughter."

"Yes, you also ran outside the same moment that snoring man was woken up," said Ludwig, laughing.

"What could I do? I couldn't breathe whatsoever! That was the only time I thought my laughter would literally kill me."

"Did you return afterwards? I don't recall."

"No, I didn't dare to. Besides, if I looked at the man that had snored, I would probably had to leave the church again."

"Yes, but at least the villagers had something to talk about for many weeks afterwards."

"They always talk. That's why the village life is unlike any other," said Deborah, wiping her tears of laughter. "People's tongues here are like continuous howling of wind. It never ceases, and even when it does, the echo of it remains for days until tongues are loosed again and the usual repertoire continues."

"Somehow I don't mind living here, Mother. The most important thing is to stay together, no matter where and under what circumstances," said Russell with sounds of gratitude sparkling inside his voice.

"It is true, boys, but you have to think about your future and education. There are plenty wonderful universities in this country, and you have to decide what you want to do in this life. Family will always be the most precious thing this world has ever seen, but men must not forget that they must take good care for their families, both financially and spiritually."

"Yes, I have given that a fair amount of thought, Mother," said Russell, while Ludwig was deeply immersed into his thoughts. "You are absolutely right," he added, nodding.

"Think about it, boys, because it's time you continued your lives outside this little village, getting an education and a future."

Later, they carried on talking about matters which did nothing but amuse them. Both boys were somewhat touched deep inside their hearts, though it couldn't be said they hadn't thought about their future before. Mother's encouragement and support was what they greatly needed from time to time, although youthful ignorance was sometimes blocking even the lightest of lights and the kindest of intentions.

4

On one memorable day, when only a week was left until miraculous and magical Christmas morning, Ludwig was asked by his mother to go to their church and donate some money. It was a Monday afternoon, and at this time of day, the church was usually empty. Deborah always enjoyed donating big sums of money when no one was there to witness it. Usually, Russell was the one to do this sort of annual chore, but this time, since the younger brother was busy working with some business partners of his mother's (he had entirely embarked on his mother's work, which was profitable and easy to run), Ludwig was asked to do what only Deborah considered important and necessary. When Mother handed him two hundred euros, Ludwig looked at her in astonishment and sort of fear which comes whenever consciousness fails to handle too difficult situations and is surrounded by doubts.

"We've never donated this much, Mother."

"I know, but it is Christmas. There are people who are in need of food more than we, and I certainly don't believe that absence of these bills will change something in our lives."

"Catholics are rich enough. Look at their churches, their priests, and religious industry that they have. I believe their pope sells more books than Dickens nowadays."

"Don't say that. There are some nice people too. Just let's do what we do every year before Christmas, and please, save me from these boring and vain discussions about how horrible Catholics are. We go to their church simply because we don't have anywhere else to go, and we, as obedient and pious Christians, must support them and help them."

"Mother, I reckon they won't even notice these two hundred euros among their wealth and other donations which they receive daily from their believers," said Ludwig rather humbly.

"Please don't argue with me," responded Deborah, turning around and resuming reading some book, which looked as ancient as time. "Just please do this, my boy. Thanks to the Lord, we don't lack money, and thereby we can afford donating more than usually."

That was the point at which the conversation was over. Ludwig put on his shoes, his black coat, and was off.

Going to the Catholic church was always a painful task for him to do. Without any specific reason, he disliked both the believers and the hierarchy of the religion; listening to their teaching during masses on Sundays (which the

Prestons attended only twice a year before Christmas), and watching them performing different mysterious rituals was something he literally couldn't stand. Surely, Ludwig couldn't have called himself an enemy of Catholicism, and that was mainly based on his respect for his mother's opinion—she never criticized, judged, or condemned other people for believing in the same God only in a different form of fellowship. Both boys never dared to argue with their mother, and her standpoints were as commandments to the obedient sons. Just as now, when Ludwig was kindly asked to do something he wasn't much fond of, he nonetheless took the money, and went to the church, which he hoped to leave even before he entered it.

When he finally arrived, he went in through a huge wooden door with old and cold metal handles, and seconds later found himself in a church where, as always, he saw more things than holiness. Right next to the door, there was holy water in a ceramic bowl hanging on a wall; it was for people to dip their fingers in it and then make a sign of a cross afterwards. Ludwig only looked at it and went forward, firmly staying in that peculiar state of ignorance. Then he approached a statue of St. Joseph; there was a donation chest below it into which he was supposed to put the envelope with two hundred euros in it.

Each year before Christmas and Easter, the priest of the church allowed the believers to do kind angelic works; many years ago, he came up with an idea to create a chest of good deeds, where people could put some food, clothes, things they didn't need anymore, and even money in order to help the poor and needy. With time, this had become quite a popular custom, which also involved a huge amount of pride and pompousness. That was one of those reasons why Ludwig was never fond of the idea of putting something into the chest and secretly becoming the part of Catholic traditions. The chest was always kept closed; there was only a hole on top of it through which good deeds entered their fate. It was opened only on Christmas Eve, and the entire proof of how much kind deeds mattered were taken out and supposedly given to the needy, hungry, and homeless.

Ludwig, now standing before the chest, was holding the envelope in his hand and trying to imagine what would happen if the chest had a mouth and could speak out. He thought of what it could say about people's kindness, about the essence of hypocrisy, and the very nature of good deeds. Perhaps that poor chest knew more than all the clouds of the world, under which hardly explainable things tend to happen every sacred hour. Then he looked at the statue of St. Joseph, and somewhat shook his head as if trying to shake all the bad thoughts off. Unwillingly and with an aching heart, he dropped the envelope into the box, sighed rather sadly, and turned around to leave.

"What are you doing here, Ludwig?" asked a beautiful girl who was quickly approaching the young man, whose only wish at the moment was to leave the place in order to avoid to be trapped in there forever. At least that's what he thought of at the moment.

The girl of about twenty years old came out of nowhere, and that startled Ludwig a great deal, since he also believed that Catholic churches were full of wandering ghosts and shadows of the dead. However, when he heard the girl's voice, he stopped and couldn't help but dumbly gaze upon the truly indescribably beautiful girl, whose white hair were like wings of angels being gently tossed by the northern wind.

"You are Ludwig, right?" she said, finally reaching the boy. "I've seen you in this church before, haven't I? Do you remember me?"

As her fast talking seemed to have awakened him from that instant enchantment of beauty, he smiled and answered, "Yes, I am Ludwig. I apologize, but I don't remember we've met."

"Of course, you don't. We've never talked before!" She laughed. "I am Monica." She stretched forth her hand, and Ludwig gently shook it. "What were you doing in here? The evening mass will start only in three hours."

"Yes, I know," he said, though he didn't know the daily schedule of masses, "but I am not here for that. As a matter of fact, I was about to leave."

"Praying in loneliness? Perhaps you're right. Every Christian needs some time alone with God."

"Christian?" echoed Ludwig in misunderstanding.

"Yes, even Jesus often prayed alone, don't you remember?"

"Sure," muttered Ludwig, trying to end the awkward conversation, though the girl's beauty was something he could stare at for many long hours.

"Are you in a hurry, Ludwig?" she asked suddenly, reading the answer on his face.

"Actually…well…no, I guess."

"That's great!" exclaimed the girl in fake surprise. "Would you like to come to our prayer group where we talk about God and pray together? That's actually the reason why I came here. We always meet here twice a week. Not many come but still at least a few believers is better than one, don't you agree?"

"Yes, I guess," muttered Ludwig, thinking of how to politely run away from the present moment, which seemed to make Ludwig more curious with every single word spoken by the girl.

"It would be great if you could join us," continued Monica. "The more of us pray as one, the stronger the prayer. As you know, it can heal, perform miracles, and do unimaginable things which most of us are not even aware of."

"Yes, of course," nodded Ludwig, noticing that a couple more teenagers had just entered the church. Somehow Ludwig came to realize that he will not be able to avoid what was to come. Regrets that he had come there in the first place started glowing in his eyes, though a forced smile on his face was trying to make him look polite and kind.

"Is this your friend, Monica?" asked one of the young men, who had just approached them. He then stretched forth his hand and introduced himself. "I am Martin."

"Nice to meet you," said Ludwig, shaking his hand.

"And I am Niccolo," introduced the other young man, who was about twenty-five and looked like an Italian. "I don't think we've met you here before, Ludwig," he said with a slight accent. "First time here?"

"No, I just don't come here too often."

"Will you join us in our prayer group?" asked Martin hopefully.

Not being able to handle the tension of being stared at by three young people, Ludwig got somewhat confused and said rather frightfully, as if being afraid of some horrible consequences. "Sure, I have time now."

"Great! Follow us then!" exclaimed Monica and they all were off.

To Ludwig's surprise, they left the church through the back door and went to the priest's office, which was in the same building only with the entrance from the outside. Ludwig knew about the place, for Deborah visited the priest a couple of times there after their father passed away. The office now was empty; nothing but hundreds of different books and some supposedly holy relics were there.

"Here, sit down, brother," said Niccolo, giving Ludwig a chair.

"Does the priest approve this?" Ludwig asked frightfully, looking around with wonder and curiosity.

"You mean Father John?" asked Martin with a giggle. "Sure he does! He is the one who created this group!" After all of them took their chairs and sat around a cozy table under the light of a lamp above them, Martin continued, "He once said after one Sunday mass that whoever wished to unite in prayer and learn more about Catholicism or the Bible could join his prayer group, as he called it. At first, many brothers and sisters came, but by and by only a few of us left. We come here to pray for peace in the world and for prosperity of the Catholic Church. We also pray for other people, for those who are in hunger and need of love and a loaf of bread. There are some who even come here and ask us to pray for them. Such brothers usually write their prayer intentions down on a paper and give it to Father John, who afterwards hands it to us. Thus, in secret and unity, we try to make this world a better place."

"It's marvelous," commented Ludwig, being sincerely keen on what his new friends were telling him.

"Yes, many support this group. Sometimes we even travel to bigger towns and preach Jesus there also. We have a lot of booklets, different events in our church, praying evenings, and every now and then, we organize Christian music festivals. It may sound crazy, but only until you see how many believers actually come to pray together and listen some blessed Christian music. It is unbelievable how powerful prayers are, brother. That's actually why we gather here twice a week—to pray for the world to become a more Christian place."

"I believe you're doing a wonderful job," said Ludwig in absolute amazement and wonder. "I never even thought this group and such Christian events exist here at all."

"How did you happen to be here this afternoon, Ludwig?" inquired Niccolo, smiling sincerely.

Among his many thoughts about why they considered that question to be so important, Ludwig quickly glanced at the young believers, and, seeing their smiles and eyes glowing with sacred faith, he found himself in a queer state of peace and spiritual safety. He didn't feel discomfort sitting among Catholics and getting ready to even pray with them. On the contrary, he had utterly forgotten that young men sitting before him were Catholics whatsoever. At the moment, they were his brothers and sisters in Christ.

After a moment of silence, Ludwig told them about the envelope and why he was there, to which they all reacted with marvel. The way they accepted the story was as though they had heard about some divine revelation or unheard message from above.

"Amazing!" shouted Monica, almost jumping off her seat.

"Now that's what I call God's plan and guidance," remarked Niccolo.

"Can't you see the beauty of the picture?" said Monica, again whose astonishment seemed to be increasing every second. "God brought you here this afternoon!" Here, Ludwig wanted to correct her and say that it was his mother, but he didn't dare. "He brought you into this group by leading you to that chest! Some may call it fate, but I say it's pure guidance of God."

"She is right, Ludwig. Do you see it now?"

"Yes, now I do after you revealed it to me," he confessed modestly.

"It was no accident that you met Monica," said Martin, evidently astonished at what they thought was a pure miracle and an act of God's guiding hand. At the time, Ludwig didn't have much time and eagerness to contemplate on whether it was what they said or it was something else. Either way, it had already happened and perhaps the final result was not that intimidating as Ludwig imagined it to be. By the time they took each other's hand, lowered their heads, and were about to start praying, he even found himself pleased and grateful to be there.

"First, let's pray the Our Father, Hail Mary, and Glory Be," said Martin. "Then we will pray the rosary."

"Sounds good, Martin," said Monica, and they all began to pray in one voice and echo.

When he finally had a second to turn his consciousness back on, Ludwig was more than surprised to realize that he was actually sitting in the same room with Catholics and trying to pray their traditional prayers. The only prayer he knew was the Our Father prayer, and it didn't took a long time for others to notice that Ludwig didn't know the words of the other two. While they were praying Hail Mary and Glory Be, Ludwig was just listening and pretending to be murmuring every second word. Perhaps if someone had told him that the day would come when he would be trying to pray Catholic prayers and holding hands with Catholics themselves, he would've probably gone crazy and needed some fresh air. Nonetheless, he wasn't bothered by his ignorant and firm beliefs at the moment, for trying to pass that prayer time unnoticed was his biggest task. His eyes were closed and he feared to open them, even after the third and last prayer was said, already floating in the air as a feather of freedom and light.

"I can see our brother doesn't know his prayers very well!" said Martin after they let go each other's hands and opened their eyes.

"Yes, well, I'm not much of a churchgoer," confessed Ludwig, fearing the judgment that might come. Feeling like a stranger in an unknown and mysterious land, he knew not how to behave, what to say, or whether certain things were right or wrong. Catholicism was not only something Ludwig always disliked and consciously ignored; to him, it was also an enigma surrounded by secrets both dark and light.

"You mean to tell you don't know the Hail Mary prayer?" asked Monica.

"I'm afraid I don't," he replied humbly, making a short pause after each word. He was afraid of the reaction that might follow, though what he witnessed exceeded his expectations and calmed the waves in his mind.

"No worries, brother," said Martin, standing up and going to some bookshelf hanging on the wall.

"Yes, we are all here to learn and help others," added Niccolo with a smile.

"Here," said Martin, returning to the table. He handed Ludwig a booklet of prayers, which included those three which they had just prayed. It was a booklet of all traditional Catholic prayers, and it was something Ludwig had held in his hands for the first time in his life. "This will help you memorize our prayers. Besides, I am sure you can find them on the internet, too."

"Thank you," said Ludwig, quickly looking through the booklet.

"Now you can read along if you want. If you don't feel ready, you can follow us with your thoughts. I am pretty sure that counts," said Monica, admiring Ludwig with a smile on her face.

"Thank you. I never thought Catholics could be this friendly," said Ludwig, being completely unaware of the circumstances he was in.

"Really?" asked Martin with a laugh. "Well, I guess we learn something new every day, don't we?"

At this, all three teenagers laughed, but as for Ludwig, he seemed to have realized what he had just said. His smile disappeared, and he thought it would be better if he didn't say anything more. His cheeks turned red, and the only way he could hide his shame was to look down at the booklet and wait for others to continue their prayers.

"I love people with a sense of humor," said Martin, tapping Ludwig on a shoulder.

"Okay, let's proceed, shall we," said Monica seriously this time. "Now we will pray the holy rosary. Ludwig, all you need to do is read the second part of each prayer. You see, there is a mark where to begin." Then she pointed at the booklet to show where to start reading and continued, "I will be reading the first part of each prayer, and you, boys, need to finish them. Don't worry if you don't get what I'm saying. You'll understand soon before we reach our second mystery."

In fact, Ludwig had not a slightest idea what Monica had just said. He just nodded a couple of times, and thought he would comprehend with time.

They began praying, and whatever the three young Catholics did or said, Ludwig tried his best to do the same. It wasn't as difficult as it seemed, though the entire point of rosary's mysteries holding the periods of the life of Jesus, and prayers said in repetition without any specific reason at first appeared to be a complete nonsense and a waste of time. Sometimes, somewhere in the middle of ten Hail

Mary prayers, which contained one rosary mystery, Ludwig closed his eyes and attempted to realize what exactly it was that they were doing. The faces of his new friends were glowing as stars in the middle of dark skies, and that was perhaps the only inspiration and encouragement for him to believe that there was something greater behind the recitations and different announcements during the prayer.

By the end, Ludwig was at least glad for being able to memorize the Hail Mary, though how it could help to make the world a better place was still a riddle to him. They all, even poor Ludwig, made the sign of the cross and thanked each other for such a powerful prayer.

"So, how was it?" asked Monica, putting her rosary, which she used during the recitation, into her jeans pocket. "This was your first time, wasn't it?"

"Yes, it was. I feel pretty great, and I must thank you all for that."

"No need to thank us, brother," said Martin, with his thick and manly voice. "We're more than happy that God led you here today! Seeing our bothers and sisters living in Jesus is one of the most beautiful masterpieces of art you can find in this world."

"Indeed," agreed Niccolo, taking some sheet of paper from out of his pocket. "These here are the intentions. Would you mind if we began?" Then he put the paper in the middle of the table and waited for others to give him an answer.

All this time, Niccolo looked rather modest, as though afraid of saying an additional word or standing up when everyone was supposed to be seated. Ironically enough, Ludwig managed to find his own figure in the eyes of the Italian believer, whose presence in their small village was still a mystery to him. Ludwig perceived that Niccolo was also as if afraid of being there—he was clearly afraid of saying a wrong prayer, of making a sign of a cross when it wasn't necessary, and also of being asked to say anything in addition to their intentions and various pleas to God, most of which were made up spontaneously. This entire observation, however, made Ludwig feel a little better. He was glad to know he wasn't the only believer there who didn't wish to be somewhere else every second instant. It must be noted that the Christian, whose true faith was now comfortably disguised under the slightly appealing mask of Catholicism, with every minute coming and going, began feeling pretty good about the situation he was in. He started noting only positive and holy features in their behavior, prayers, and perspective. At the moment, he didn't dare to think of his family's opinion concerning what he now found holy and true. What his mind was filled with when they began praying for some lady named Victoria and her health were ways how he could memorize those wonderful prayers from the booklet as soon as possible. He was also interested in the rosary prayer, and in the fact of contemplating on Jesus's life during the recitation of one prayer. He would lie if he said he didn't wish to know more; to be precise, as much as there was to know.

They continued praying for their neighbors, friends, sellers at the market, and even for poor old man named Albert—a seventy-year-old man who had been cleaning the streets of their little village for more than forty decades now. Their intentions and pleas lasted around twenty minutes, after what Martin turned to Ludwig and said, "I hope to see you here more often, brother! We will also meet this Thursday, same time. Will you come?"

"I don't know," he said after a hesitation. "I would really like to, but—"

"We'd be more than happy; we lack believers like you. The more of us gather here, the stronger the prayer!" said Monica with excitement flashing in her eyes.

"I will do my best," replied Ludwig finally, now remembering his mother and brother. The smile disappeared from his face, and he stood up and said, "Thank you so much for everything here. It was really a pleasure praying with you."

"Take care, Ludwig," said Martin, also standing up. He brotherly embraced Ludwig afterwards, as did the others. "We will be praying for you."

"Thank you. And I will be praying for you as well."

5

The following Thursday came along with intensity and thoughtfulness. Ludwig never told anything about his new interest in Catholicism to his family; considering that to be rather unwise, he enjoyed having some secrets of his own—something no one else in the world could see or be aware of. He liked the feeling of having a private life, of being able to make some decisions on his own. Surely deep inside, he was a conscientious soul, but this time his mind was entirely blinded by the number of opened doors. It was as some sort of revolutionary road that could lead him straight into the Christian perfection and a meaningful life. It wasn't that he didn't feel content with his simple Christian faith, which his mother taught him since he was a little boy, but what Catholicism and the research he did on it offered him was beyond anything poor Ludwig could ever imagine. He was so confused in his happiness about the revelation of a new religion; that sometimes it took some time for him to calm down and be able to believe that such a treasury of prayers, rites, and holiness that Catholicism contained could indeed be real without any falsehood. Many long hours were spent reading different articles and Catholic testimonies. He found out that there had been many appearances of Jesus's mother in different parts of the world, and also that even Jesus's face has been revealed to a few chosen ones. Ludwig was more than surprised to find out about things he never knew existed. As a matter of fact, he never had any idea the world had been given certain instructions and guidance by Mary, Mother of Christ. He also read about scapular, which Mary gave to be worn around the neck, about different medals, chaplets, and sacred images of both Jesus and Mary. Eventually, the more he read and searched for more information, the more he understood that Catholicism was like an interminable path, which was doubtlessly holy and divine. Above all, having found out enough to reconsider his beliefs again, Ludwig seriously thought of why he had never known about such things before and what was it that Christians had against such purity and sacredness of Catholic traditions. He couldn't firmly claim he hadn't been aware of their notorious rites during masses, which he considered to be nothing but hypocritical and vain. Nonetheless, after reading all that information about Catholic truths and certain relics, he was quick to change his mind and brave enough to resolve to rethink his spiritual life from a Catholic perspective.

Surprisingly even for him, he had no qualms whatsoever about whether to go to the next meeting of the prayer group or not. When Russell was off to work (he temporarily helped Mother in her office, which was twenty minutes away from their home), and Deborah went to do some shopping, which was a common thing to see before Christmas, Ludwig quickly went into his room, locked it in case anyone returned unexpectedly, and recited the prayers from his booklet one more time. By then, he knew them practically by heart, but he thought that another recitation would do him no harm. When the noon came, he started feeling a little anxious and impatient, willing to go to the meeting as soon as possible. Another hour later, he, out of pure habit, took his Bible with the booklet of prayers and was off.

He was walking deep in thought, contemplating only about Catholic values, their church, and philosophy of life, which he found incredibly attractive and holy. At some point, he even felt sorry for his mother and Russell, which were simple Bible-believing Christians. A wide smile was on his face as he tried to at least imagine what deep meaning every single detail (including the relics which many Catholics wore around their necks as some divine shield) had in the religion. Priests didn't look that frightening and hypocritical to him anymore, as well as their churches, which he immediately recalled with all its statues of saints and paintings reflecting the life of Christ hanging on cold walls. What caused such a sudden change of heart and mind, even Ludwig himself did not know. He was as blinded by the happiness of being as if born anew as he was enlightened by the perspective of what awaited him ahead. His old Christian being was as though dead and buried somewhere deep inside his past—Ludwig was feeling as a new person with a new faith, ready to live a decent Christian life and be a worthy follower of Jesus.

When he came to Father John's office (a place where they met last time), he knocked, and after a few prolonged minutes, the door was finally opened. However, the one who opened the door was more of a surprise to reborn Ludwig than the fact that his heart had been entirely changed in just a couple of short days. Father John himself was now standing before him. Both being equally surprised, neither of the men knew how to begin the conversation or what to say.

"I am sorry, but I thought this is where the meeting of a prayer group would take place," said Ludwig, rather intimidated by the rare fact that he was actually talking to a Catholic priest.

"This is the place, young man. Do I know you? Your eyes look familiar," answered the old man, looking happy and satisfied with everything there was to find under the sky full of stars and past. His eyes were glowing with gratitude, and though his hands were somewhat shaking, he looked full of energy and willingness to do God's will. Father John appeared in Ludwig's eyes as a man ready to help, support, donate, and sacrifice whatever was necessary. His figure and deep face features reflected a picture of man who had nothing to lose in this world, since his entire treasury was kept safely in the hands of God.

"I am not sure," said Ludwig hesitantly, though feeling a little bit better seeing nothing but light in the eyes of the priest. "Our family attend your services once in a while."

"Two or three times a year is not in a while, my son." Father John chuckled, remembering where he had seen the boy before. Ludwig only frowned a little, though a smile also appeared on his face. "You are Ludwig, Deborah's son, correct?" Ludwig nodded. "Ha! I knew your eyes looked familiar! You see—though old, still have something to boast about!" He chuckled again as a small child. "Yes, I remember those eyes." He continued seriously, looking straight into Ludwig's blue eyes. Now Father John recalled every tiniest detail of Michael Preston's funeral. As memories kept uncontrollably flowing into his mind, he also recollected Deborah, her tears, and of course two boys standing by her side. It somewhat saddened the old man's heart, though seeing that the day had come when one of those two little boys miraculously knocked at his doors momentarily drew a smile on his face.

"Am I too early or too late, Father?" said Ludwig slowly, hesitating before finishing the question.

"For what, my son?" replied the priest, whose mind was somewhere far away at the moment. It was as if his consciousness had traveled around the world in a matter of five seconds or more.

"Well, I think there is supposed to be—"

"Yes, of course!" exclaimed Father John suddenly. "The meeting! Come in, come in! Are you thirsty?"

"Frankly, I am," said Ludwig, entering the office, which was as if impregnated with fragrance of something sacred and divinely mysterious. That was how he felt whenever Catholicism was passing through his thoughts.

Later, while drinking some hot chocolate, they discussed how Ludwig happened to become a part of their faintly known prayer group, and how exactly he came to know the path of Catholicism. At some points of their conversation, Father John was quite astonished, which increased his interest even more. After Ludwig unfolded to the Father the things he had learned about Catholicism, the priest only smiled interestingly and said afterwards, "Yes, many think that Catholicism is but a list of obligations and religious duties."

"I used to think so, too."

"Indeed? It's funny how people find service to the Lord an obligation and something one is forced to do against one's will. Besides, during your research, did you find out about such things as confession, the importance of Eucharist, and significance of masses?"

"I must say I have read a little bit about things you've mentioned, but I don't think I know very much."

Then, strangely enough for Ludwig to draw his attention at it, Father John unexpectedly took a newspaper from his table behind him and looked at it indifferently, obviously caring little about what the news were. In fact, Ludwig was even quick to suspect that the newspaper could be at least two years old.

"I like newspapers," said the Father, surveying the front page, making it clear that he wasn't interested in reading it. "So much junk here is made so popular and appealing that readers are actually forced to believe that that's what life contains of. I like talking wisely," he said, smiling cheeky, though the humbleness and simplicity in the silhouette of his soul could never be hidden. "Don't you find that true?"

"I don't know," shrugged Ludwig. "Maybe."

"Do you read newspapers?"

"Not too often, Father."

"Why not? Don't you enjoy having your mind corrupted and filled with nothing but vanity and trash?"

"I wouldn't like to know how that feels." The boy chuckled.

"Lucky you," said the Father and dropped the newspaper back on the table behind him. Turning to Ludwig, he frowned and said, "Why do you call me Father? I don't remember having children."

"I am sorry, I don't know how to address a priest correctly," answered Ludwig, feeling uncomfortable and somewhat guilty.

"What makes you think I am a priest?" Father John asked again, being clearly interested in their conversation.

"Well, you're dressed like one, and I've seen you at masses."

"Suppose you're right, but does that make me your father?"

"I feel quite confused right now," said the boy with sigh coming out of his smile. The priest also smiled which consoled Ludwig's feelings a little.

"You're father is up there," said the priest, pointing up. "He is your Heavenly Father who will always be there for you, Ludwig. He will never give you a stone instead of bread, and he never wishes you any harm. He loves you as a father loves his children."

"Then what does that make you?"

"John," answered the priest, whose smile was as though beseeching for the conversation to continue.

"Is that it?"

"Well, I also share bread and wine on the Lord's table from time to time."

Ludwig laughed, and Father John liked seeing that.

"Catholicism is not as bad as it looks, Ludwig," continued Father John. "Besides, our lives are not about what religion we choose, but about how strong we love our Savior, Jesus Christ. We can be obedient, dutiful, and pure Catholics or Baptists our entire lives, but if we don't sincerely fall in love with God, then we are certainly not worth more than a handful of dust, which now is and seconds later is blown away. Religion is not what draws us closer to God." The priest laughed. "It is what helps us to love him stronger. We cannot find salvation in religious rites, churches or traditions, whether those are Catholic or Lutheran.

Salvation lies only in Jesus Christ, my son. I've seen many people make mistakes at this point of their lives. They come to church seeking for help in statues and engravings on stones. I laugh at them when I see that, and they surely get mad at me afterwards. Some have even called me a heretic without any comprehension what the word means. Perhaps they'd heard it in some movie and thought this was a proper way of talking in order to look religions and pious. I don't know. Still, later I explained to them the things I am explaining to you know, and many people changed their attitude the very same minute. In fact, this is a very serious matter, but I think I've made the picture clear, haven't I?"

"What you say is indeed interesting. I've never thought of it, and I certainly didn't expect to hear this for a Catholic priest."

"From John." The priest corrected. "Nice to meet you, Ludwig," he said, stretching forth his hand. "My name is John."

"Nice to meet you, John." The boy chuckled, shaking the priest's old and weary hand.

"Well, since we know each other better now, how about some more hot chocolate? Or would you like something better?"

"Better?"

"Yes, I also have some tea, coffee, and even some wine!" exclaimed the priest joyously. "How about that! Who would've thought you could find a brand-new bottle of wine in a priest's office?" He then looked at the bottle, at the boy, and later at the bottle again, thinking of whether to open it or not. "No, I had better save that for the masses. Can you imagine what happened if one Sunday morning we realized we're all out of wine? Those old ladies which like to talk much would literally destroy my reputation! And what I need in the last place is people talking about how unworthy priest I am."

"Are you?" asked Ludwig, playing along with Father John's sense of humor.

"Only after Christmas and Easter," he replied, putting two hot cups of green tea on the table. "I hope you like tea. You didn't say what you wanted, so I thought I'd make what I could enjoy in case you refused to drink it." After a while, Father John thought to keep the discussion alive, and he said, "So, how many prayers do you know, boy?"

"Only three. I've learned them from this booklet." He showed his booklet, but what the priest's sight fell on was Ludwig's Bible.

"Yes, this booklet contains many marvelous prayers," said the old man, gently taking the Bible. "Is this booklet yours?"

"This is not a booklet." The boy chuckled. "This is my Bible."

"I see. How well do you know it?"

"I've been reading it since the very day I learned how to read, and I must say I know it very well, John."

"Indeed? What book is your favorite?"

"Ecclesiastes," answered Ludwig with holy pride and self-esteem. "I could read it over and over again without even a pause."

The priest looked rather surprised; his eyes widened, and his chin dropped down. He was looking through the book as if checking if every page was in its place.

"Ecclesiastes, eh?"

"Yes. I remember it always helped me during hard times. Somehow I find a lot of hardly explainable power in those pages."

"Interesting," muttered the priest, frowning a little. "Many find this book too complicated to be understood by an ordinary mind. Nonetheless, I, too, find Ecclesiastes a mighty book, which contains much more than wisdom. We can be grateful that the Lord has touched you through those marvelous words. Besides," the priest said quickly, closing the book and giving it back to Ludwig, "do you have a rosary?"

"I am afraid I don't."

"Well, that's not a problem, but fear sure is." Then the old man opened the drawer of the table behind him and took something rattling. "This is what's called a rosary, Ludwig."

He gave the boy something what looked more like an unordinary bracelet that was made out of tiny rope and wooden beads. Besides its weird structure and ideal synchronicity, Ludwig also managed to notice a very beautiful wooden crucifix at the end of the entire bracelet.

"Do you know how it is prayed?" asked the priest, looking at he boy with curiosity.

"Yes, I've prayed it once," replied the boy, still looking at the rosary with amazement and sincere gratitude.

"Wonderful. Monica will give you the book where Mysteries of the Rosary are enlisted with detailed explanations what they mean. Praying blindfolded is like driving a car without any wheels! We don't want that, do we?"

"I guess not." The boy tittered.

Later, several minutes after they finished drinking their tea, the same three believers, whom Ludwig saw last time in their prayer group, entered the room. Afterwards, they all sat around the same table, made some more hot green tea, and, after discussing certain matters touching Ludwig's blessed path, they began praying for the prosperity and peace for the entire world beginning with their small village where they were as a lighthouse, secretly shining their light for the ships of grace and mercy to safely arrive.

Ludwig was given an honor to read some inspirational verses from his Bible, while others listened with seriousness and depth of sublimity and holiness. The listeners' ears and the echo of Ludwig's voice were surrounded by a complete silence—the kind which could never be imagined or understood without witnessing it. Then they all prayed the holy rosary, pleading God to help the sick, comfort the oppressed, and save the unfaithful. They prayed for many, including Father John, whose sacrificial service and life were helping others to keep standing on their feet and believing in something greater than the world's temporary miseries. They firmly believed their prayers were making life of others easier and more joyful; and indeed, it did. The amount of light, sacred will, and piousness that all those believers put into their prayers was something what could not only inspire or simply encourage, but also heal and help to believe. Ludwig was among those who felt it deep in his heart, and during each prayer they recited with faith, all he could do was give thanks to his Creator for bringing him here. His joy knew no boundaries, and his willingness to serve could not be hidden for long.

6

The Christmas day was drawing nigh, and the grace and blessings in Ludwig's new spiritual life were hourly increasing. It had become a common thing to see Ludwig with a rosary, which Father John had given him, around his wrist or certain Catholic prayers coming out from his mouth. The boy started praying more, eating less and even forgetting his daily Bible-reading habit. What he found himself interested in the most, however, was the treasury and richness that Catholicism offered and shared. In Ludwig's eyes, it was like a well of living water—the kind of water after which one was never thirsty again. With new knowledge and understanding, Ludwig also became more humble, obedient, and modest. With time, he knew that without these features, a Catholic believer was like an angel of light without any wings. In fact, he learned much more than that, but to apply it all to his life and soul would take time.

Deborah and Russell were still not aware of Ludwig's sudden change of heart. Russell was still too busy to notice his brother's spiritual life and his perspectives, but as for their mother, she obviously wasn't that blind not to detect certain secrets in Ludwig's eyes which lately had been shining with gladness. His emotions and feelings were ill-concealed and easy to notice, especially for those who were there to spot it. Nevertheless, Deborah never said a word about things she saw in her son's life, for she was well aware that soon her beloved firstborn would come to her himself.

That happened on Christmas Eve, when bells of joy were getting ready to ring, and the entire world seemed to be immersed into the most mysterious silence of all. There were no guests coming that evening—weeks ago, they'd decided to spend the holidays alone, as it usually happened for the last ten years. The only guest who was expected to come was poor and lonely man named Alexander, though not even Deborah was thinking of him that day.

A couple of hours prior to the holy evening celebration, when Russell was in his room, wrapping presents to his family in red and green papers, and Deborah was in the kitchen, making final adjustments for the dishes which smell often reached even the farthest corner of their village (which often was the reason why Alexander came in hope and attempt to make an impression), Ludwig asked his mother if she needed any help. He was so afraid and easily nervous that he had to put his hands into his pants pockets in order to hide the slightly shivering hands. He dreaded that his mother could misunderstand the entire subject he wanted to share with her right now. He thought it was high time he told her the entire truth about what had been happening to him for the last seven days. She was his closest friend and the likeliest person to understand his feelings and newly reborn beliefs.

"No, thank you, my dear," replied Deborah, continuing cutting some cucumbers with a smile, as though knowing the reason why Ludwig's voice sounded different this time.

Nonetheless, unconsciously ignoring the answer, Ludwig approached his mother and stood by her side, childishly observing how his mother was preparing the feast. In attempt to hide his heavy breathing, he quickly asked again, "Maybe there is something I could do for you?"

Speechlessly, Deborah took a plastic yellow tray, a knife, and a bowl full of potatoes and gave it all to Ludwig.

"Thank you, my sunshine," she said with a smile, as they both continued cutting vegetables side by side. "How are you feeling today? You are always very excited about Christmas!"

"I am. I just have a lot on my mind lately."

"I know."

"You do?"

"A mother always knows what's on her child's mind."

"I guess, then, you are already aware that I've come here to talk to you about something, Mother," he asked rather carefully, still suffering under the dark cloud of doubt whether it was a right thing to do.

"I had a few suspicions," answered Deborah amiably, ceasing to smile not for a single instant.

"Frankly, I'd like to talk to you about certain changes in my faith and standpoints."

"Yes, I must admit I've noticed a few changes in the way you behave and talk, Ludwig. I'd really like to hear about it if you don't mind."

Afterwards, Ludwig sighed deeply, and, continuing cutting potatoes, said, "About a week ago, when you told me to go to the church and drop the envelope with money in it into the chest, I met some young fellas who invited me to join them in their prayer group. They introduced me to Catholic prayers, their traditions, and Catholic faith in general." At this point, Ludwig heard how his mother started cutting vegetables faster, with more disappointment and tension in it. Ludwig could feel what his mother was thinking, though, since there was no going back right now, he continued telling the entire story which he himself could never believe in if it hadn't happened to him. "We prayed for many people, and it was all wonderful, to tell the truth! They taught me how to pray the rosary, and what heavenly mysteries it hid. Then, a few days later, I once again went to that prayer group, and there I met Father John. When he saw me, he looked quite surprised. He said he had seen my eyes somewhere before, and after several minutes of talking, he remembered me and whose son I was. Do you remember him, Mother?"

"I do," replied Deborah coldly, but still with a smile on her face. "He is a very nice man. Your father loved him as his brother."

"My father knew Father John?"

"Yes. Though their point of views differed a little, they were very close."

"Interesting, I never knew that," said Ludwig cheerfully, trying to imagine his father discussing about God and religious matters with Father John. Indeed, there were a few resemblances between the two as far as Ludwig could remember them at the moment.

"And, John, what did he tell you?"

"He gave me a rosary. It was his gift. Besides, we talked a lot about Christianity and truth in our religion. The way he sees fellowship in God and who we are on this earth is a very interesting and deep matter, Mother. I must admit, I've never dared to even think like he does. Father John told me a lot about Catholicism and the meaning behind its practices and rites. I see no fault in the way they accept and visualize service to the Lord. After going to masses more than twice a week, I've come to know that God is indeed in the hearts of the Catholics, and his love and power reign in their churches and rites. I don't know how to tell you this, Mother, but I seem to have become a very strict Catholic. Hence, I think I want to live my life according to

Catholic traditions and beliefs." He paused and waited for a response, for a sound, for anything he could find hope in. Since silence was all he could get in reply, he said slightly uncomfortably, "All I want, Mother, is your opinion and advice. The fact that I've made some decisions on my own doesn't necessarily mean that I don't need your guidance."

"What you have shared with me is a very serious matter, son," Deborah finally said. "I thank you for your honesty. Frankly, I feel a little bit out of words at the moment, Ludwig. Are you seeking for my approval? I have nothing against Catholicism. I just always considered their way of serving our God a little bit wrong. Their rites and, as you say, traditions never looked godly in my eyes."

"I thought like that too, Mother! But that was until I was explained what they meant!"

"I understand your excitement, but in my eyes, Christianity is not about rites, my son. I was more than sure that you knew this."

"Catholicism combined with what I've learned from you about Christianity is perfection itself. The power of Catholic prayers is beyond our understanding, and the holiness behind fasting is what draws us near to God. I read a lot about this, and I've also been explained that such a way of life, in fasting and prayer, is what path unto God contains of. I'd be glad to tell you more about this, Mother!" said Ludwig with an elated heart and a joyous tone of voice.

"Thank you, my dear." Then she stopped cutting vegetables, turned to her son, and said with a loving smile, "I love you with all my heart, Ludwig. The purpose of my life is not to admire nature or become a well-known scientist. I live to see my both boys standing firm on their roads which lead them straight into the heart of God Almighty. Perhaps I know little about this life or Christianity, but what I do know for certain is that love is more important than life, because the latter cannot be true without love. Whether you're a Catholic or a Lutheran, it doesn't matter as long as you love God with your heart." Then she gently took his hand, and resumed, "If God wants you to be a Catholic believer, then I can only thank him for his decision. I trust God and I know that whatever he does, he does it for a reason greater than our simple minds are able to comprehend. He never makes a mistake, and if what you feel inside is God's call, then I rejoice with you, my son."

"What you say is filling my heart, Mom."

"It should, because it all comes out of mine." After a brief and thoughtful pause, she added, "Live the life God gave you, Ludwig, and never doubt in God's decisions and, most importantly, plans."

"You really think that these changes are mere details of his plan for me?"

"I have no doubts," said Deborah firmly, returning to cutting her vegetables. "By the way, have you told your brother about your secret faith?"

"I thought that to be rather foolish. Knowing his temperament, he may react unpredictably. I think I'll wait for the right occasion."

Later, when all the dishes were ready and two candles were already spreading light on their table, they all stood around it, took each other's hand, and thanked God for all those gifts that he had brought on their table. They afterwards began eating and talking about various joyous things, laughing and enjoying the cheer and peace of the evening, which was also slightly enchanted with a silent jazz music on the radio. The evening was an unforgettable gift which felt more like a blessing of grace from above.

7

Weeks later, Ludwig managed to find enough courage in his heart and resolved to tell his brother about his new faith and reborn spiritual life. At first, Russell seemed to be indifferent, but later, as he revised the entire story, he asked if Ludwig had got involved in a religious sect.

"Are you kidding me? Catholic church is not a sect!" was what Ludwig replied with great dissatisfaction.

"If so, why has it influenced your faith in Jesus and God's Word?" said Russell, as fury was slowly arising in his eyes.

"It hasn't."

"Yet you don't read your Bible, do you? All I see you read is catechism and some books written by monks or priests. You really think those men will save your soul?"

"My soul has already been saved," replied Ludwig firmly.

"I'm glad you haven't forgotten that. But don't worry," he added with a smile, putting his hand on Ludwig's shoulder, "I'm sure your new faith will fix it with time."

"Fix what?"

In reply, Russell only sighed, darted a glance of pity at his brother, and left the room. Regardless of how their conversation had ended, Ludwig was nevertheless happy that a stone had been rolled away from his heart—he was as though released from a struggle with the fear of revealing his newly created heart and soul to his younger brother. He nodded a couple of times, realizing that his faith and what he was feeling inside could never be understood by anyone save Father John and his fellow believers in the church. At some point, he even found himself utterly banished from the world for simply choosing to walk the Catholic path. Ludwig foresaw that, and he had even been warned by other Catholics that the world was not much fond of them. All the scandals and criticism toward Catholicism was the result of hatred and evil powers reigning in the world. This was what he had been told and what he openheartedly believed in. With days turning into weeks, he became aware that living a Catholic life was not that easy. He could find shelter absolutely nowhere save in the church, where he was feeling as if at home—as if standing one step away from the kingdom of God. Prayers and depth of the religion was what often helped him to overcome inner battles and resist the temptations of darkness. The rosary never left his hand, as well as the prayer was always on his mind. Even before night, he always prayed the rosary until he fell asleep, and then, since the rosary was around his wrist during nights too, started praying it first thing in the morning. Besides prayers and numerous Catholic books that he read, he also came to know that without deeds, his religion was nothing but an empty desert, where neither life nor eternity could risk to abide. Utterly forgetting what his mother had taught him about good deeds and truly Christian life, Ludwig started learning the basics anew. He was convinced that Catholic perspective differed from his mother's or brother's or Christianity's in general, which is why he unwillingly decided to ignore them all and start living a life tied to Catholicism only. Therefore, he often took his savings, and sometimes even begged his mother to give him some money, and went on the streets donating the money to the poor he encountered. To some he bought a loaf of bread, to others a bottle of water or juice. He gave money to whomever he wished, without seriously considering consequences or how beneficial it was. Ludwig had become a kind and generous Catholic who attended church twice a day and cared about absolutely nothing but his spiritual path and the light his faith was able to bring to the people and the world. He completely ceased to work in his mother's fields, as well as he stopped thinking about his studies and future. Russell and Deborah were most bothered and annoyed by this; seeing Ludwig living a life of absentmindedness and utmost carelessness was a hurtful pain and something they both knew not how to change or at least slightly adjust. Hearing Ludwig praising the Lord in his locked room in the morning and saying long prayers with his eyes closed and head lowered before meal times was something that was truly complicated to get used to, especially when he openly enjoyed the solitude and exclusivity of it. He often acted as though his annoying behavior was imperceptible, although the obscurity behind the entire matter was more than doubtful and fearsome. Rarely did he join discussions at the table, reckoning that his ideas and worldview would not be understood. What Ludwig had become was a lonely cloud, hanging innocently in the immeasurable and limitless distances of sky. He needed neither the wind nor the sun while his raindrops were slowly but surely penetrating deep into the hearts of those he touched and laid his eyes upon.

Russell was always trying to avoid his brother and see him as seldom as possible. He couldn't stand his, as he called it, hypocritical appearance, which was both hurting Deborah and obscuring the entire atmosphere in their home. Russell even got used to gnashing his teeth at the meal times and biting his lips whenever he wished to say something neither Catholics nor Bible-believing Christians would've found holy. Perhaps this unimaginable hatred had arisen in Russell's heart not because of Ludwig's spirituality, but because it hurt mother. Deborah never regretted having supported Ludwig in his resolution to become a strict

Catholic, although at the same time, she prayed earnestly to God to help her son follow him the way the Almighty wanted. While Ludwig thought there was not a single soul in the world who prayed more than him (for he prayed usually five hours a day including masses), his mother prayed for him even more. Somehow, somewhere deep inside her heart, Deborah knew that both paths of her sons were right and holy in the sight of God. Her heart was calm and her entire soul was utterly devoted to the Heavenly Father's will. Her prayers and trust were usually accompanied by inner peace and the kind of heavenly silence which only saints could feel. If there was anything she suspected to be untrue or unholy, her motherly instincts would always fix the mistakes, enlighten the darkness, and make crooked paths straight again.

One day, when the sun was shining bright and when spring was approaching the destiny of time faster than usually, Ludwig came to Father John's office and knocked at his door.

"Come in, whoever you are!" The priest gladly shouted from the inside. "Ah! Ludwig! So good to see you, my boy! Sit down, please."

"I am sorry, Father, but I'm afraid I don't have much time," said the boy modestly. "Is this urgent?"

"Urgent as nothing else in the world!" exclaimed the priest joyfully, looking for a chair to sit down. "Have I already told you about the monks?"

"What monks?" he asked, frowning.

"You don't know? That's good. You see, there is a wonderful and very powerful monastery about an hour away from here. It is called the Benedictine monastery. Our bothers there heard of a young man whose conversion to Catholicism impressed them a great deal. So they are coming here in no more than"—he looked at his watch—"ten or fifteen minutes."

"And I suppose I am the Catholic they wish to meet."

"Yes!" exclaimed Father John again. "It is an honor, Ludwig. Those brothers are very holy men, and I can't wait to introduce you to them. You may learn a great deal from their experience and knowledge," he said barely in a whisper. "They are very wise, Ludwig. Were I you, I'd listen carefully to what they say and what advices they give. Well, of course, it was I who brought them here."

"Thank you, Father John. I feel much obliged to you."

"You should. They are very interested in you."

"What exactly did you tell them about me, Father?"

"I told them how you found Catholicism, and how you became the most dedicated Catholic believer I've ever known. Believe me, they were astonished!"

"But I don't know what to tell them," muttered the boy rather frightened.

"You don't tell them anything, my son. Just open your heart and try to distinguish the voice of God in what they'll tell you."

"I'm afraid I don't have much time, Father. My mother is expecting me in less than twenty minutes."

"Would you like me to call 'er and tell that you won't come?" he asked indifferently, what somewhat offended Ludwig's feelings.

"No, I'm afraid I'll have to go, Father John. Please do forgive me, but it is really urgent."

"What can be more important than your soul, my child?" asked the priest amiably and with a smile.

"My mother is getting ready a very big dinner, for this evening is very important to us."

"Is it your mother's birthday?" asked the old man. Ludwig shook his head. "Your brother's?"

"It's nobody's birthday, Father. We just gather together once in a while to have some family time. We talk about different topics, enjoy our food, laugh, and do various crazy stuff. It's like our family's tradition—to spend as much time together as possible."

"That's a wonderful tradition, my child, but those men who are coming here right now are, I think, of greater importance than laughter or food. I don't think you should let this chance slip through your fingers. Family time is a sacred matter, Ludwig, but your soul and wisdom you may obtain are priceless. It will not take long, but surely you can leave right now if you want to. It's your right."

Ludwig decided to stay. He called his mother and told her he would be late. Deep inside his heart, he was sincerely sorry for disappointing his mother (not to mention angering his brother once again), but he eagerly wanted to meet those brothers, whom he imagined to be full of wisdom, understanding and holiness. Ludwig reckoned they would be like angels, all dressed in white, with rosaries in their hands, and paradisiacal light in their eyes. He wasn't aware of how many brothers would come, but he hoped this would change his life for the better.

Meanwhile, Deborah and Russell were sitting at their dinner table in hope that Ludwig would change his mind and come back home. She kept looking at the clock on the wall, counting minutes and praying to God to lead her son back to the warmth of her embrace.

"I don't think he's coming, Mother," said Russell sadly, keeping the fury and hatred outside his mother's sight. "Let's just start eating."

"Maybe five more minutes," she said, looking at the clock. "Let's wait a little more, darling."

Russell sighed, and they both kept waiting in silence. Radio wasn't on that evening, and not even a single dish was touched at all. Only a lonely candle was burning slowly and in peace on their dinner table. The clock was ticking, and the hope was dying out. Holding his mother by the hand, Russell was sitting beside her for more than three hours until Ludwig came back. What he found, however, was a sight he would never be able to forget—mother's head was gently put on Russell's shoulder, and they both were asleep at the table. There was dead silence in the room—only Ludwig's heart was beating fast, as though running back to the moment when he called his mother and firmly told her he would be late.

He wished he didn't have to wake them up; in fact, he was feeling so ashamed that he didn't wish to show his face. When he approached his mother (wishing with all his heart that Russell would remain asleep) and was about to touch her hand, she woke up before he was even able to move his finger and smiled, seeing her Ludwig before her loving eyes.

8

Back to when Ludwig was waiting in the Father John's office for some monks to arrive, they also had a long a discussion about a monastic life and what great purpose it served. During the conversation, Ludwig put all his efforts and imagination into creating an idea of how the monks would look like. As far as he could remember, he had never even seen one. He imagined them to be old, with long grey beards reaching to their knees, easily breakable and cheap glasses on their faces, and with long white robes touching the ground, covering even their tiny feet. He imagined their bodies to be flabby and skinny. In general, Ludwig saw them as angels of wisdom descending with glory and promises of eternity. Much more could be said about how he pictured the yet unseen mysterious monks, but the most important fact was that he waited for them with eagerness and inner trembling, as if convincing himself that his entire future depended on it.

Before the Benedictine brothers came, Father John told the boy a lot about the monastery and their life. The profound mystery which the story contained immediately drew Ludwig's interest and curiosity—not only did he wish to be told more, but also to experience everything himself. The latter feeling was queer even to the boy, though he couldn't help it either. Considering the monks to be true saints of this world, he earnestly wished to touch them, to listen to their advices, and to receive their wisdom into his heart. Everything he needed now was to lay his eyes upon them—to see if his high expectations really matched the truth.

"Here they come," Father John suddenly said, looking at the monks through a tiny window coming in the distance. He stood up and went to meet them. Ludwig followed, trembling with curiosity and magical wonder.

They both stood at the doorstep, observing three figures slowly approaching them at the other end of the road. The three shades of something unearthly were dressed in black robes, and they were entirely contrary to Ludwig's creative youthful mind. To say the boy was surprised by what he saw would be a great understatement—he was shocked to see three good-looking and well-built men in their early forties, holding their old Bibles in their hands. Peculiar though sacred smiles were on their faces, and there was nothing more to tell about them save a mere mention of the unbelievable simplicity in their eyes.

As they finally arrived, one of them, gently shaking Ludwig's hand, said, "Good afternoon. I'm brother Andrew, and this is brother Victor"—he pointed at the man standing on his right—"and brother Lucas," he added, pointing at the monk standing on his left. Both brothers who had been introduced shook Ludwig's hand and bowed their heads as a gesture of holy meekness.

"Nice meeting you, sir," replied the boy. "My name is Ludwig Preston."

"So you are the boy?" brother Lucas asked friendly.

"I suppose," said Ludwig, giving up the modesty through his voice. "Depends on who you're looking for."

"Clever boy!" exclaimed brother Victor, who looked like the wisest of them all.

"Please come inside, my dear brothers!" said Father John eventually.

They all went in, and, making themselves at home, sat down at the table for some coffee and tea. Ludwig observed them all with childish curiosity and questions passing through his mind. Being a shy person, he tried to avoid any eye contact possible, while at the same time he couldn't help but stare at every single movement the brothers were making. He was breathing slowly, allowing himself to listen to the monks' minds and heartbeat. Everything about them was interesting and of great importance to the boy. He could sense and even smell the holiness all around them. Hardly explainable factors concerning the monks were as real as nothing else in the world for the newly reborn Catholic believer.

"So, Ludwig," said brother Lucas, "I've heard a great deal about you. From a simple villager into the strongest Catholic Father John has ever seen. That sounds pretty impressive. When I first heard it, I thought—no offense—that our dear Father John has reached the point of honorable madness which usually comes along with wisdom and age." The priest only laughed at it and continued picking the type of black tea he wanted to taste the most from a big wooden box where dozens of tastes were abiding. "And even now, when I see you sitting in front of me, I still find it hard to believe. May I ask you to open my eyes, brother?"

"Brother?" echoed Ludwig. He misunderstood the way he was addressed in.

"Yes," brother Lucas calmly nodded. "We all here are brothers, Ludwig. Does that surprise you?"

"Not at all! I'm sorry, I must've thought something else."

"Your story fascinated me, too, Ludwig," said brother Andrew. "The grace of God is certainly upon you, brother. He has clearly blessed you immeasurably."

"Besides," brother Lucas said again, "do you mind if I ask you about your family? Are they Catholics too?"

"I'm afraid there is not much to tell in the first place," Ludwig humbly confessed, glancing at each monk with astonishment and honor. "I am just a simple Catholic, who attends masses perhaps too often than is required. That's my whole secret, brothers. My mother and brother are simple Christians, who have nothing against my beliefs and perspective—my mother even supports me on my decisions and opinion. In fact, I don't know what else to tell you."

"Sometimes, one simple gaze can tell you much more than long and vain repetitions, brother," said brother Victor. "The very instant I saw you I knew that God's spirit abides in those blue eyes of yours. Now, when I hear you talk, I am convinced that you are no ordinary believer, Ludwig. Did anything special happen to you lately, or do you feel something extraordinary inside you?"

"I am not sure," said Ludwig, feeling like in a doctor's office. "I think the most magical thing that has happened to me and that reigns in my heart is that deep willingness to pray and serve. Sometimes I think there is nothing I want more. I want to learn to see things beyond the sight of my faith and turn my love into a rhyme, which could encompass people's hearts, filling them with holiness and inspiration. To be completely frank, I want to run away from this world and to enter a place where I could wait upon the Lord in peace. I don't want to study history or physics—I see no interest and purpose in that. I wish only to serve and keep believing without stumbling or doubts. However, I don't know if you'll agree with me, but I somehow feel I don't belong to this sinful world. I see no beauty in today's system and rush. I guess my service is in need of calmness and holiness, which I cannot find anywhere."

"How old are you, Ludwig?" asked brother Victor, as everyone else was listening with marvel, being touched by such an unusual confession.

"I'm twenty-three."

"Impressive," muttered the brother. "And all of this just comes out of your heart? I mean, have read some religions literature or have you been instructed by some religions groups outside your church?"

Not utterly understanding what brother Victor was talking about, Ludwig replied, "I guess not. What I read daily is my catechism and certain autobiography books, but I don't think my opinion has been influenced by them."

"Certainly not," agreed brother Victor. "Please forgive me my habit of suspecting certain things to be influenced by the evil darker than we can imagine." After a while, sipping his hot coffee, he asked, "Tell me, Ludwig, have you thought about your future?"

"Frankly, no. I try to think of future as little as possible, since I reckon that only fools make their plans for the following day."

"Indeed. So, as far as I've understood, you don't think of entering a university or pursuing something what in the eyes of this world is great and meaningful. Am I correct?"

"More or less. I'm still looking for my purpose in this world, thanks to God, I've become a Catholic, and I consider that to be a great honor and a gift. I've learned much, though there is no limit to wisdom, is it? I want to grow as a believer, seeking peace for the world and fighting for justice. When I see a beggar on a street, my soul is touched and my heart is moved. I instantly forget education and my future, for all I care about is helping those who had been rejected by the world and driven into poverty and hunger. I cannot help this holy instinct which as though has been inscribed on the palm of my nature. I could starve to death, but I would never pass by a poor and homeless person, whose life depends on the mercy of people who just got luckier in this mad world of vanity."

"You sound like you've been studying theology for quite some time now," remarked brother Lucas, at which Father John nodded with a smile.

"You're right, my brother," said the priest, silently sitting under the evening shadow next to a cupboard and observing everything from afar. "Ludwig has indeed been studying a lot. Not without my help, of course. He doesn't have a degree in Theology studies, but I can assure you he is a very wise Catholic, who knows the difference between a lie and the truth."

"I don't think that's difficult to spot." Brother Andrew chuckled. "The difference between a lie and the truth is clear even to those who know little about Catholicism, Father John. Do you have any stronger arguments than this?"

"Easy to spot, you say? Interesting, but if it's so, why almost the entire world is drawing in the lying tongue of Satan? If people knew what a lie and the truth are, the world wouldn't serve the evil powers of violence and lies. I think that few are able to see the difference, and Ludwig's certainly one of them."

Andrew glanced at the modest-looking boy, and then turned to the old man again.

"I agree with you, Father John, but we must not forget about the light which is also fighting for survival. Our prayers, service, and consecrated dedication to Jesus Christ is what prevents that barely noticeable light from dying out completely and forever. This life is not only about us, but also about future generations and those who have never even heard about Jesus Christ. Selfishly, fearlessly, and encouraging one another, we must keep on believing and praying so that others, who now are far from what we find holy and true, may have hope which would show them the path into the promised land. We know well enough that this life is not about how much money you make, how healthy you eat, or how eternally you think you're going to live on this earth. We must pray unceasingly for all, regardless of how blind they are, because apart from us, I think no one else will do it."

"What you say is pure wisdom and words of love, brother," said the priest. "This, I believe, is also a very good introduction to your marvelous monastery, which is surrounded by holiness of your daily prayers."

"I'm glad you heard it this way," said brother Andrew with a smile.

Later, they discussed Judaism, its roots and greatness, and then moved on to talking about the history of Catholic Church. Meanwhile, Ludwig, being more silent than a mouse, listened to every single word that was spoken, bringing each one into his heart, where he would later reconsider every wise opinion more than thirty times. He observed the entire scene with awe, imagining himself being that prudent and faithful one day.

After some more time, the monks departed, leaving Ludwig in an odd philosophical state which he had never been in before. Unwillingly enough, he started thinking deeper, seeing farther, and even found himself eager to reach higher than ever. The vanity, which he always liked to accuse the world of, didn't disturb his inner stillness at the moment—troubles and hellishness surrounding the lies of evil were not on his mind at the moment. His to-do list was clear, and all he could thoroughly reckon was holiness— something only those three monks were able to utterly reveal to him. Until then, it had been nothing but a secret, which was dwelling in every living being on the planet. Now, Ludwig's eyes were full of happiness, in which the reflections of the three angels in black robes were still alive.

"Well, what do you think?" asked Father John, minutes later after the brothers left.

"Impossible to put it into words, Father," replied Ludwig absentmindedly, obviously allowing his mind to wander in way farther lands than the present moment. "So many thoughts passing through…"

"Good. The more you think, the clearer you'll see this world and everything both in and around it. Thinking is incredibly beneficial, especially after meeting such people as those monks."

"This was the first time I ever saw a monk, to be honest."

"Hopefully not the last," said the priest, looking for something beneath the table and all around the floor.

"Are you looking for something?"

"Yeah, my cat."

"I didn't know you had a cat."

"Neither did I, my boy. He slipped here through an open door last night, and I kind of liked him so I reckoned to keep him. However, now I cannot find him anywhere."

"Have you named him?"

"I did, but I doubt he would answer if called. I called him Crazy, but he is not used to this name."

"Crazy?" Ludwig chuckled, looking for the cat all around the place.

"Yeah! He's nothing more than a crazy creature! Who else could enter a priest's office at night? Besides, I still suspect he wanted to steal a bottle of milk of one of my rats."

"I don't think you have rats here, Father." Ludwig laughed. "It's very clean, and I've never seen a rat in here."

"He'd find one, believe me. He's a crazy bandit! That's what he does."

While searching for a missing cat, Ludwig didn't notice how another twenty minutes had passed. When he looked at his watch, he reckoned it was too late to get back the precious minutes which now were lost. Though the poor cat had still not been found, he politely excused himself and said he had to go back home as quickly as possible.

"Well, go if you need to, my son," said the priest with a rather unhappy face. Whether it was because he couldn't find his cat or because Ludwig had to leave, the boy had neither time nor willingness to stay and find out. "Will I see you tomorrow?"

"Sure you will! Good night, Father."

"Yes, good," he muttered, losing the thought inside his deep interest in searching for the lost cat, which could've been anywhere in the village by then.

9

As a tree of words growing out of an opened book of wisdom, so was Ludwig's Catholic convictions getting bigger and stronger each day. His spirit was constantly encouraged by Father John and other spiritually strong men like the Benedictine brothers from the monastery that Ludwig was already acquainted with. The boy, forgetting his family life and perspectives for the future, spent a huge amount of time with those who in his eyes were pure saints—innocent, holy, and as wise as prophets of the Bible. They all daily united in rosary and many other prayers, also without abandoning the Holy Scriptures which they read and discussed during meals and tea times. Ludwig attended holy masses twice a day, and soon he became quite a renowned believer in their little village, where it was impossible to pass unnoticed or without being gossiped about. Catholics who attended holy masses each Sunday began to see Ludwig in the first rows rather often, and it was a perfect reason for everyone to start talking and lift up their voices in the streets once again. Rumors about a possible new priest in their church had reached Deborah's ears in no time, and it was then when Ludwig was seriously asked to share what exactly was going on in his life lately. For the boy, it was an unpleasant thing to do, for keeping his life and beliefs in secret was what he found to be a bliss and something he had come to be unable to live without. His life was his personal matter, and no one could stick their noses into what he considered sacredly private. This was his opinion, carefully cherished and valued, though his mother's commands were nevertheless exceeding his will or temptation to disobey.

One day, after an unpleasant and hurting conversation with a neighbor at a local market, Deborah came back home disappointed and willing to make herself believe that rumors which had touched her that morning were nothing but lies, created to sting someone living a happy life and hurt them as much as possible. This was a common thing among the villagers, which is why Deborah would not have been surprised if all the gossips had turned out to be false.

She saw her son rarely, for he spent most of the time either in the church or helping the poor in other towns. It even often occurred that he didn't spend nights at home, which also made his mother's nights sleepless and without a sign of rest. Nevertheless, being blessed by simple luck, Deborah was able to catch Ludwig on his way to the church. He was bound for the evening service, and although he seemed to be in a rush, he couldn't reject to sit with his mother and talk. Seeing sparks of unhappiness in his mother's eyes, Ludwig's heart was troubled, knowing that there must've been a very good reason for his mother, which was usually happy and satisfied, to be upset.

He sat down on a sofa in their cozy sitting room and carefully listened to what she had to say. Surely, his eyes were darting glances at the clock on the wall every now and then, but what bothered him the most at the time was his mother's worried soul.

"A rumor has reached my ears, Ludwig," began Deborah, standing in front of him and leaning back against the wall. "I remember when you told me that you had become a Catholic, and as far as I recall, I supported you on this. It was not easy for me to know that my dear son has converted from a good Christian into a strict Catholic. There is a difference, you know. But despite all the philosophy and suspicions, I trusted God's will and received the news gladly, believing it to be God's guiding hand behind it all. Since then, however, we've never ate at one table, and we talked one minute a week at most. I don't see how you let yourself be manipulated by your new faith, but most of all, I can't understand why it stops you from being a part of this family. I do not like what I see, Ludwig, and I can't promise you that I'll tolerate this. You refuse to work with me, that's fine. But throwing your life into a trash can is something I will not allow you to do."

"I'm not throwing my life into a trash can, Mother."

"Your actions prove you wrong, darling. You live as if you don't have a family or life whatsoever. I'm not against your Catholic convictions. I am fully against what you've become. For instance, what have you done to your room and clothes? Why have you thrown your books and CDs away?"

"Because they were unholy, Mother," answered Ludwig guiltily.

"Do explain," she said strictly, frowning a little.

"Posters of different music bands and movie stars on my walls were like idols to me. I couldn't let that take the place of God. I realized that what were hanging on the walls in my room were my idols, and I unconsciously worshipped them. It is a sin, Mother. Also, over the last two months, I've learned a lot about satanic symbolism and how demons take control of those who lay their eyes upon it. When my eyes were opened, I saw those symbols everywhere—on the streets, on clothes, in shops, and basically everywhere whatever I dared to look at. It is real and true. Evil powers come to us through certain satanic hand signs and demonic images. It is like a curse which is cast upon us, and thus our minds become corrupted. Certain figures or emblems may seem innocent, but there is a subliminal message behind them all! That's why I threw away my music and movie CDs because demonic messages were there as well! Books which I had were unholy and most of them said not a word about our God. I got rid of everything what I found to be evil at least a little bit. My clothes, also. Forgive me, Mother, but on some of my T-shirts, there were playing cards portrayed, which symbolize greed and sinful addictions. I cannot let myself touch or be a part of anything unholy and anti-Christian. My wish is to live a holy life, because that's what God wants me to do." After a brief pause, he continued, "I don't mean to hurt you, Mother. You are my dearest angel, and I love you more than myself! I beseech you to understand me, for without your support, I won't be able to become the saint I strive with all my heart and soul to be."

"And you think to become a saint means to detach yourself from your life and those who surround you? Sainthood is not about separation, it's about unification, my boy. Abandoning evil will not help you completely emancipate yourself from it. God and love is what you need to become a saint, for hating evil will just draw you closer to it."

"I completely understand what's your point, but—"

"You don't," interrupted Deborah, shaking her head sadly. "You've gone astray a very long distance, Ludwig. Don't you think this life is much simpler than you and your Father John can imagine?"

Ludwig disrespectfully shook his head as well, and again raising his eyes to his mother, said, "Let's stay away from philosophizing about what life is, Mother. Rarely do such discussions lead to something more than another dispute and antagonism between two different opinions."

"What do you plan to do with your tomorrow, Ludwig?" she asked as strictly she could this time. "If you plan to work, I want to know where. If, on the other hand, your intention is to study, I also want to be enlightened by your idea."

"Actually, Mom, I've been thinking about something what might shock you a little." Then he paused, glanced at her somewhat weary eyes, and proceeded, "For the last two months or so, I've been guided and spiritually strengthened by certain monks from a Benedictine monastery not far from here. After numerous hours of talking to them about various matters concerning both this sinful world and a beautiful life which awaits us, I've come to a decision to live a life God's given me to live. This may sound a little odd, but this is what brings me happiness and lightens up the sky above me. I am not doing this because I am afraid of the unknown in the doubtful tomorrow or because hard work or studies scare me. Quite the contrary, the path I've chosen offers me both studies and hard work." At this point, Deborah's face expression changed, and her eyes started seeing much more than they were meant to. "My wish is to become a monk, Mom. Actually, I've been invited to look around in there next week. It's just for a couple of nights, and then I'll be able to make my final decision."

"Haven't you already?" she asked calmly.

"I have, but it is a necessary procedure to help me better picture the life of a monk," he replied enthusiastically, believing his mother was genuinely interested in the

BROTHERS AND SAINTS

monastery or the life within it. He was looking at her, waiting for her to ask him some more questions about what was immeasurably valuable and spiritually important to him. Deborah, on the contrary, was speechless. She was staring deep into her son's eyes and slightly nodding her head as though convincing herself that the present instant was real indeed.

Somewhat distracted by his mother's mute reaction, Ludwig smiled, and said again, "I reckoned that I ought to think of the life to come and of the lives of others, instead of taking care for myself and trying to earn a living so that I could have a nice refrigerator or a microwave oven. Moreover, I don't want to spend my life working ten hours a day so that I could pay for gas, which I use to get to my work. Doesn't this sound like vanity to you, Mother? This world is more than recalling and foreseeing. We must reject ourselves and live for others simply because we were not created to go to shops and take care of our bodies."

"Is that what the monks told you?"

"They told me a lot, Mother. I honestly doubt if their wisdom could ever be measured or at least comprehended. My wish is to learn from them and seek perfection in sainthood. However, I don't think I will ever be able to find sainthood in this world."

"Is that the reason why you're running away into the monastery? You hope not to be touched by this world and safely in prayer wait upon either the coming of our Lord

Jesus Christ or the hour when you shall be called by the voice greater than any. Am I wrong? You hope to eat, drink, sleep, and pray unceasingly, and thus try to attain what you call sainthood and spiritual perfection, don't you? You think God will buy this? Crumbs and modest apparel cannot buy God's kingdom, my dear. Your heart overfilled with love is what makes God smile. Joy and bliss of a family is more precious than numerous hours of devoted prayers. I am not against it, don't get me wrong. All I'm saying is that God gave this life for you to share it with others in love and not to run away from it and hide in a cave, where nothing but a dreadful voice of loneliness abides. Being lonely is not what God intended for you, or any one of us, sweetheart. We, Christians, are one big family, and we must stick together if we want to know what warmth and bliss of it all feels like. It's like a music and a rhyme of a song of grace and mercy."

"Your words are inspiring and beautiful, but my conviction tells me other things," said Ludwig indifferently. "Allow me to become a saint, Mother. I promise you'll be proud of me."

"I already am. You don't have to prove anything. Both God and myself love you as you are."

"Sure, I know," he muttered, grinning a little. "Your blessing would mean everything to me," he continued as if proudly begging. "All I want is to live for the glory of God, and do it as best as I can."

"Go to the church," said Deborah unexpectedly. "You're gonna be late."

94

"Can I get your answer, Mother?" insisted Ludwig.

"You're gonna be late. Go now. This conversation is most certainly not over."

With a happy heart full of questions, the boy was off, running to the church with a Liturgy Prayer Book in his hand. He knew he was already late, but that didn't seem to matter at the moment. He was running fast and thinking of his future—for the first time in many months. Trying to imagine himself in a monk's robes, which he never tried to do before, he was smiling widely, hoping that once that day would come. He was whispering to himself that he would pray more than any monk in the world and become a true saint, even at such a young age.

His perspectives were running before him, and he was as though trying to catch them all and never let go; the boy was happy and bound for glory of perfection. Though the mother's answer had not yet been given, Ludwig was already feeling as monk with an experience of many decades. That's what he wished for—to become an idol of a monk which he had created some time ago.

Meanwhile, Deborah was kneeling in the same place where she had been standing during the dispute with Ludwig and praying to God for guidance and enlightenment.

"If only I could do something," was what she muttered, with her head lowered and her tears modestly rolling down her soft cheeks. "Lord, you are the greatest and wisest. Please, do as you wish. May your will, and not mine, be done! You see farther than I, and I am sure you're admiring the entire plan you have for both of my sons right now. Therefore, may your holy will be done, my Lord and Savior. If you want Ludwig to become a monk, please, give me a sign. Show me something so that I may do what is right."

Thus, in deep prayer and contemplation, an hour had passed. She was now in her room, reading a few psalms and trying to calm herself a little. Some time later, Russell came back from the work in his mother's fields. This was a temporary job for him until he made up his mind what to do about his future. As soon as Deborah heard that someone had returned home, she quickly went downstairs.

"Russell!" she said, approaching her son and embracing him tightly. "How was your work?"

"Not bad," replied the boy. "A little bit tired though. You'll never guess what happened to me today!"

"Tell me that in the kitchen," she said, turning around. "You need to eat now."

"While in the fields," the boy began, "I took our old wooden cart, and as usual, put all the tulips in it and waited for the car to arrive. Edwin was probably too busy because I waited for an hour or so! And I'm sure I would've been waiting for him even until now if it wasn't for some monks who helped me out."

"Monks?" asked Deborah, utterly stopping moving and breathing.

"Yeah. I took the cart and approached the road. There are not too many cars passing by as you know, but I reckoned this was still better than waiting in vain in the middle of the tulip field."

"So how did you meet those monks?"

"They were passing by on foot—more than five of them. On seeing me, they quickly approached and asked me if I needed any help. It was ten miles away from our village, and I prayed to God they would have a mobile phone or something like that. Well, they were monks, and everything I saw in their hands were some kind of bracelets. It seemed like they had gone for a walk without any particular purpose. I told them I was waiting for a car which probably would not arrive, so one of them took out a mobile phone from his black robe's pocket and called his friend, also a monk as I found out later. I was standing there with them for a while, feeling quite uncomfortable to be honest, until a blue minivan arrived. That's pretty much everything. They drove me to our base, and from there brought me here. Frankly, they were not so bad."

"Did you talk?"

"Little. You know me, Mother. I don't even bother thinking about Catholicism or those who practice it. I don't like them. I never liked them. Their hypocritical appearances are nothing but shameful examples of sin."

"You shouldn't talk like that. Your brother's a Catholic. Besides, those monks did help you, didn't they? Where's your sense of gratitude?"

"I'm grateful to God, not to hypocrites in ridiculous robes. Ludwig? Yes, he's Catholic all right. Sometimes, when I can't avoid looking at him, I close my eyes in order to prevent my tongue say everything I think about him. I will one day, you know. I can't stand his mask of 'Mr. Kind and Holy'. He's a hypocrite, Mother. Can't you see that? Why do you tolerate this disgraceful act of his? He thinks he lives a Christian life? Sure, I'd be happy to open his eyes if you let me."

"God's plan for him is not something we ought to judge. I'll be very happy if I don't hear such words coming out of your mouth again. He is your brother, and you mustn't talk about him with such wrath in your voice."

"Loving people like him is a difficult thing to do, Mother. Even his smile looks hypocritical to me. He's acting holy, but I know him from inside. I know real Ludwig, and when he acts as some saint, it irritates me to such a hatred that words cannot convey."

To pause the unpleasant conversation at least for a minute, Deborah put a plate of fish and fried potatoes before him on the table and told him to eat and talk little, since enjoying fish was not for distracted minds.

"Your brother is leaving soon, Russell."

"Good riddance," he said, taking little bones from his mouth. "For how many centuries?"

"Perhaps forever," replied Deborah sadly and that immediately drew Russell's attention. This time, he had no willingness to joke, for he had distinguished a few notes of truth in his mother's voice. Moreover, when he looked at her eyes, he was sure he wasn't mistaken.

"What do you mean? He found a girl?"

"That would've been great," she said, tittering a little, being tortured by the melancholy of the fact.

"Is he sick?" asked Russell slowly, fearing to hear the answer.

"No, God forbid. He is leaving us to become a monk."

"He's going to a monastery?" shouted Ludwig, relieved from the tension of obscurity. Deborah nodded sadly. "Well, at least now I have a pretty good reason to dig a grave for him in our backyard."

"Stop talking nonsense!" exclaimed Deborah, somewhat terrified by what she heard.

"But look at what he's doing, Mom! He's not only destroying his own life, but he's also dragging ours down into an abyss along with his! Allow me to punch him in the face! Just one time? Maybe then he'll wake up."

"You will not touch your brother, Russell. If it is God's will, we must not gainsay it."

"God's will? What's happened to you, Mom? Ludwig is just doing this to show off and be a saint in everyone's eyes. Entire village is already admiring him, don't you know? He is a pompous and arrogant idiot, who wishes just to prove that he's better than I or others. It's obvious."

"Eat your fish, dear. Enough of vain disputes."

"Will you let him become a monk?"

"If it is what God wants, then sure I will."

"How do you know he wants it?"

"I reckon he does," said she thoughtfully, staring at the fish in her son's plate.

Later that evening, when Ludwig came back home with hope sparkling all around him, he immediately went to his mother who was in a sitting room, eating some grapes and enjoying the view of the fire in their fireplace. As a matter of fact, she was deeply immersed into prayer, thinking of what was right, wrong, and the difference in between. When she saw Ludwig coming in, she asked him to sit next to her, for they needed to talk. Meanwhile, Russell was in his room, reading a horror book in complete unawareness that his brother had come back home. Perhaps if he had heard the door slam, that evening would've gained different colors and atmosphere in the air.

"I thought a great deal about your dream and purpose, Ludwig," began Deborah, putting a bowl full of grapes aside, as they were surrounded by complete silence of the night. There were no sounds other than those coming out of their fireplace—those warm and cozy whispers of a lively fire. "Is it really something you feel in your heart, or is it just an eagerness to strive for perfection? Can you find an answer to this question?"

"I want to become a monk, Mom, because holiness is the only path into eternal kingdom of God."

"I always thought that love was."

"It is, but love cannot exist without absolute and genuine holiness in a believer's heart. Monastery is a place where I can find what I seek."

With a deep sigh of desperation, Deborah put her hand on Ludwig's shoulder and said rather unwillingly, "I give you my blessing, Ludwig. May God's will be glorified in you."

"Mom!" exclaimed Ludwig, jumping off his seat and into his mother's embrace. "Thank you, dear mother! Thank you! I will not disappoint you. I'll seek to become a saint you always wanted me to be."

"I love you, my son, and God does too. Follow his will and guiding hand, and then you'll never be lost."

"I will," said the boy, literally glowing with happiness all around him. "I'll go call Father John to cheer him up. Oh, this is literally the best day of my life!" Once again, he hugged his mother, who was smiling as well, and went away to make a phone call.

Deborah was sincerely happy for her boy, and now there were no signs of either guilt or regret in her heart. She was glad to see her son walking on a holy path, and she could see no fault in that. The woman observed how Ludwig called Father John and told him the good news, how cheerfully he was speaking, and how elated he looked. At the moment, she could do nothing but thank the Lord from the bottom of her pious heart, and that was greater and more than the longest litanies or prayer ropes in the world. Features of sadness were struggling for survival in her eyes as happiness was trying to take its place. She was now a mother who was letting her firstborn son go into the cruel world on his own. Her heart was trembling with worry, but her soul, somewhere deep inside where not even she was able to reach, rejoiced. That was a spiritual state she could live with, knowing that her beloved boy was safely abiding in the hands of the Almighty, whose ways were not always comprehensible or, moreover, predictable.

10

Two week later, after Ludwig had gone to see the monastery from inside, the day had come for him to leave his home and depart. Throughout those fourteen days, Russell never said a word to his brother, though keeping his tongue under control was an unexplainable torture. Although Ludwig did attempt to create some sort of discussions, Russell ignored him each time, unwilling even to lay his eyes upon the future monk.

Eventually, the moment to say good-bye to Ludwig had come, even though only Deborah was there to hug her son. It was still an early morning, but Russell had already gone off to work. He was well aware that his elder brother was leaving, yet he had no willingness to wish him good luck whatsoever.

"It is all for the sake of the Lord," said Ludwig, standing at the doorstep with a bag hanging on his shoulder. He was ready as he had never been before, eager to become a saint and enter through the gates of heaven being dressed in a robe as white as snow.

"I know," said Deborah, crying. She also had spoken with senior monks about letting her son go to the monastery, and with time, her heart had been consoled. She was not afraid or worried anymore. "Please come back whenever you have a day off," she added naively. "Know that these doors are always open to you."

"I know, Mother," said Ludwig, smiling. "Unless of course if Russell is not standing behind them." They both chuckled, understanding the irony behind the innocent joke.

"He loves you as much as I, and he wishes only the best for you, my dear," she said, looking at her son's blue eyes with grateful and nostalgic heart. "Do you want me to come with you? I can accompany you to the very doors of your monastery."

"That's not necessary, Mother," said Ludwig, smiling with affability and touching his mother's warm and a little bit grey hair. He embraced her one more time and, putting his chin on her shoulder, said, "I am now leaving the worst behind, and there is nothing but truth waiting for me ahead. The most beautiful thing about it is that I invite you to join me, Mother. I will always be praying for you in my lonely cell, and I ask you to pray for me in return. Thus we will be together forevermore. Each morning and evening and throughout a day, I ask you to be with me in thoughts and prayers so that not even the darkest of the demons could ever separate us. This will help us sleep well and know that this life is nothing but a glimpse, after which we once again shall meet."

"You speak consolingly, my dear," said Deborah in return. Her teardrops were falling down on her son's shoulder, and her happiness at the instant could never be measured. "If you ever are in need of help or if struggles or temptations dare to arise, I ask and beg you to return and run back home as fast as God will let you. This shoulder your chin is touching will always be here for you to lean upon and find comfort and your mother's warmth on. Do not ever be afraid, my son; yet, if you are, remember my eyes and my smile, my face features and my hands, then you will know that your mother will always protect you no matter what." After they let each other go, Deborah looked in his eyes and continued, "Although you leave me now to become a saint, a monk and a faithful follower of Jesus, I nevertheless am happy because I see God's love in your eyes, my child. Serve the Lord with holiness and love, Ludwig. Do God's will and follow his footsteps without any doubts. The train to God's kingdom leaves very soon. Help the unfaithful and open the eyes of the blind, Ludwig. Try to get as many people on that train as possible, for it will neither stop nor return—it goes straight into the eternal kingdom of light, where it shall remain forever. Be a saint, Ludwig, and selflessly help those who cannot hear or feel. Speak, preach, touch, and embrace tightly those who need warmth and love more than silver or gold." Then she stepped closer to him and hugged him tightly again. "I love you, my saint. You are my angel, and both I and your father are proud of you."

Enough was said, although they could talk like that until forever came. Without saying another word, Ludwig kissed his mother on her warm cheek and departed.

He got into a bus, and was eventually off. Until the moment when the bus eternally disappeared in the distance, Deborah couldn't make herself believe it was indeed happening. Afterwards, when she went into the house and shut the door, she momentarily felt the silence and solitude in the air. She looked around as far as her eyes could reach and saw no one and nothing save hope that it was all for a brief minute and that soon the house would once again be filled with music, laughter, and feasting.

Though the monastery's opened doors and hospitality were already expecting Ludwig to come, the boy was far from it both physically and mentally. He neither thought of it nor was on the right bus at all. His destination at the moment was other than his destiny or monk's eternity.

He got off somewhere where not even roads were clothed with concrete. Immeasurable fields of green and yellow were all around him, and this was the first time his heart felt a relief that day. With his bag around his shoulder and slight features of dread in his soul, he took off his shoes, and, holding them in his hand, started slowly walking on a beautiful and heavenly green grass, which minutes later transformed itself into the fields of yellow tulips. There was no tree or bush whatsoever. The boundless fields of yellow tulips were disturbed not even by an animal or wind. The only thing worthy to touch the beauty of the instant was the sun, covering the entire picture in gold, developing an atmosphere which was completely immersed into yellow color both from above and beneath. As he reached the line where the fields of tulips began, he stopped, bent down until his nose touched one tulip, and breathed in deeply. His eyes were closed and his mind was utterly overtaken by the freshness and lively smell of heaven. He exhaled through his mouth, and then inhaled once again even deeper. For Ludwig, the smell of flowers, especially tulips, was the best medicine and proof of God there could ever be found on the planet earth. The aroma of those yellow tulips instantly made him think of heaven and eternal beauty of God's everlasting kingdom of love. He was standing like that for a minute or so, until a familiar voice disturbed his euphoria and magic of paradisiacal scent.

"I thought you would be in monastery by now," said Russell, standing behind his brother. He was standing from afar, having no willingness to come any closer whatsoever.

Having heard Russell's voice, Ludwig turned around and said, "My brother is still of more importance than my own destiny."

"Your destiny is with your other brothers now," he said, stepping forward to be able to hear Ludwig better.

"You judge me for choosing to become a monk?" he asked, also moving closer a little.

"I have way better things to do than to think about your destiny and dreams."

"Yet your judgment is overfilled with anger and grudge."

"It's because that unlike you I'm genuinely worried for my mother."

"You think I care only for myself?"

"Aren't you?"

"It's amazing how blinded you are by your sinful wrath," said Ludwig thoughtfully.

"What do you want here?" continued Russell angrily. "What have you forgotten in this place? You left both me and mother so that you could be called a saint by those who look at you. You care neither for this family nor for what God has given you."

"He has given me understanding and willingness to become something more than just a simple Christian!"

"He has given you this family!" shouted Russell in fury. "A mother who loves you more than anything in this stupid world, and a brother who would give his life so that you never lacked a loaf of bread! God has given you much more, but you are just too blinded by your brothers, monks, to see it!"

"God's calling is greater than my own desires or will. I would stay if I could, but I hear his voice calling me to go this path. I cannot refuse to follow him."

"It is not God's voice speaking to you, you fool. It is your arrogance and pride. I could also call you greedy because you're never satisfied with what the Lord gives you."

"In the same way you judge others, you will be judged."

"I do not judge, Ludwig. No. I brotherly want to open your eyes, because people were created not to care only for themselves."

"Look at what you've become, Russell. You used to be a pious Christian, firmly standing on the rock of the Gospel. Why are saying such hurtful words to me? Do you wish to sting me deep inside my heart? Your eyes are overfilled with wrath, and hatred is what comes out of your mouth along with those evil words. You think I've hurt mother by resolving to follow God's voice. It is merely your opinion, and nothing more than that. It is not true, and both you and I know it. The grudge you're holding has absolutely nothing to do with my decision, has it? Share it, Russell. Don't be so afraid! Why are you as if ready to do the unthinkable to make my soul suffer? You're against Catholic Church. That's fine with me. But why are you against your brother who loves you? Aren't you happy that at least one of us is striving to be a saint?"

Russell, after Ludwig finished his glorious speech, approached him slowly until merely ten feet were separating them and said in calm but firm voice tone, "I don't care about you or about your monks. I don't care about your destiny or eagerness to become a saint. My mother is my only concern, and I will never be able to call a man, who is leaving his mother to escape from responsibilities and duties, my brother. Admit it, Ludwig. You're simply running away so you don't have to take care of mother and give her the warmth she deserves. You're blaming the world for being cruel and evil, while you yourself are leaving your family in it and departing in search of sainthood and a spiritual shelter. Instead of being a part of this family, you've decided to join some foolish monks under the pretext of finding this world evil and full of sin. You know, now I think that perhaps this world is what you say it is, merely because men like you refuse to be warriors God has made them to be; and instead, they run away from their duties and spend their lives either in the shelter of alcohol or, as in your case, spirituality. Christianity is not in prayers, it's in everything you touch, speak to, and share your love with. Only I think you are too perfect and wise to take these words in. You hope to safely abide in your lonely cell without anyone to hug or comfort you, and you expect God to award you with the crown of nobility and virtue for that?" After a short pause, he continued in a brotherly voice, "I've nothing to say to you, Ludwig. Go, run, hide. Do whatever you think will please God and soften his judgment. Frankly, I don't care."

"I'll pray that God opens your eyes, brother. I hope one day God will enlighten you the way he enlightened me. He has a path for each one of us, and all I'm asking is not to judge me for doing what the Creator has given me to do through grace and love of Jesus Christ."

"There is one more thing I know," he said with an arrogant smile. "We can talk and debate about God and his plans for twenty-four hours a day, but if we don't love our neighbor and give a helping hand to those in need, our words are nothing but vanity which offends God a great deal. Go, Ludwig. Your monastery is waiting for you. I hope you'll find what you seek, although you've already missed all the gifts you've been given. Path that God has for each one of us, you say? I think you're right at this point, except for the fact that believers tend to create their own paths, which they think are from God. Good luck to you. I sincerely hope that tomorrow you'll come back, but if you don't, I'd appreciate if you didn't forget that you have a brother closer than your monks."

"You will forever remain my brother, Russell. No matter what."

"Sure," muttered Russell, and turning around added, "Excuse me, but I have work to do now."

"Good luck to you, too, brother. I'll be praying for you."

"Don't," said Russell, stopping. "Pray for yourself instead. I think you're more in need of that than anyone else."

"Won't you hug me before I leave?" he asked desperately.

"And you? Will you hug me before leaving?" asked Russell, staring at his brother with eyes full of questions and discontentment.

"If you let me," answer Ludwig.

"God bless you, Ludwig. I sincerely hope you'll be happy in the path you've chosen." Then he turned around and went back to his work.

With sadness penetrating into his soul, Ludwig left the fields of yellow and gold minutes later. He said not another word to his brother. He only glanced at him and sighed out of sadness. Soon he got into a bus again and was eventually off.

11

It was now the middle of spring, and the time was as though begging for a reason and a cause to celebrate and feast until the dawn broke in. Sunny days were replaced by even sunnier ones, and smiles on the villagers' faces were transformed into sounds of joy and gladness. Without waiting for a permission or a command, the trees all around were slowly, even slightly modestly, turning into green, thus enchanting not only the village but also the entire world with love and kindness, which often was a greatly uncommon thing in a place like that. Notes of that bountiful time of the year were uniting into one chord and melody, which often was as a signature of every single spring since the beginning of the world.

A week after Ludwig had joined the brotherhood of those whose sainthood had many explanations, Russell and Deborah decided to have something what had been absent from their home for a very long time. They turned on Deborah's favorite Elvis Presley's music, opened the windows in their sitting room to let the fresh spring air in, and made their usual Saturday evening feast. Again as usual, fried potatoes, delicious salmon, vegetables, souses, and dozens of spices were on the table—that was enough for Russell and his mom to call it a feast.

As they sat at the table, they took each other's hand, lowered their heads, and Deborah said, "Lord, we thank you for what you've given us this day. You are good, kind, merciful and gracious. There are no words to describe your greatness which is unimaginable and boundless. We thank you for this food, for our health, and also for financial support." After a sigh which foretold what she was about to say, Deborah continued, "We also ask you, our Lord Jesus Christ, to help my son, Ludwig, in the life he's chosen. Be with him, strengthen him, and never let him doubt your guiding hand. Allow him to reach whatever you want him to reach, to be whoever you want him to be, and to go wherever you want him to go. May your holy will, our dear God, be done both in his life and in ours.

"We also pray for Russell and his decisions. Bless him, Lord, and may you be glorified through his life and deeds. May your holy face and will shine through Russell's acts and words. This is my deepest request, my Lord. My both boys are in your hands, and I want you to abide in their hearts, decisions, and lives. They need you, Jesus, even when they don't know that. You are the Lord. You know everything, and you see much more than the sometimes blind eyes of our faith. Thank you, our eternal Lord, for your patience, kindness, and gentleness. Forgive us, God. Please, do forgive us our sins. Amen," she added and opened her eyes, letting Russell's hand go.

"Amen," said Russell. "That was a beautiful prayer, Mother."

"Thank you," she replied with a warm smile. "Please, dig in!"

They began eating their blessed food and sharing the glory of the moment. It was a family time which could be compared to nothing else in the universe.

"It is very important for a family to always be together, Russell," Deborah said after a while. "Not only literally, but also in thoughts and hearts." She was looking straight at her son, conveying the importance of what she was saying through her eyes. "I cannot tell how great is the gift of having a family—someone to hug you, to hold you by your hand, to wish you good night, to smile at you, and someone to share the food on your table with."

"But if one has a family to take care for, what about God and a life devoted to him? I don't think a man is able to serve two things at the same time."

"Interesting though horrible thought, my dear," said Deborah, filling two glasses with a soft drink. "You see, a man without a family is like a man who does not believe in God with all his heart. One day, when you meet a girl whom God will send you, you'll understand my words. Then you'll know that family is like the church of Christ where nothing but love, unity, and everlasting happiness abide. No one is meant to be alone, Russell. That would be like a church with a pastor in it, but no other people sitting there whatsoever. Family is the best place in the world where God's face can be seen as clearly as nowhere else. Besides, service to God does not mean we have to pray five hours a day and fast thrice a week to please our Lord. Personally, I don't think the Creator's that naive," she tittered. "The way we help others, the way we love our family, and how we take care for little ones is what tells how strong our faith and love for God really are. We can shout to the whole world saying that we love God, and we can even make a tattoo on our foreheads stating the same thing, but if we don't clothe the poor, comfort those who cry, and share the life in happiness with our family, then we are nothing but hypocrites, spending our lifetime in abyss of lies and doubts, which are more painful than the sharpest knives that can be found."

"What about Ludwig, then? He has abandoned us, and I really doubt he will find a girlfriend there in the monastery."

"The Lord works in mysterious ways," she said thoughtfully. "I don't know what is God's plan for him, but I think we shouldn't question his will. Ludwig is also a part of a family now, Russell."

"Monastery?"

"I assume spiritual brotherhood and families are also important."

"But not as important as a real family, right?"

In reply, Deborah grinned, allowing her son to find the answer in her reaction himself.

"Why did you allow him to leave us, Mom?" inquired Russell, some time later. "You know Catholicism is not exactly the right path, especially an isolated life in a monastery."

"I prayed to God to show me if it was his will, darling. I prayed earnestly and all I wanted was to be sure whether it was God's voice calling him or not. Looking Ludwig in the eyes, I saw that it was neither his pride nor that fanaticism the Catholicism had taught him. There were signs of truth in what he said, and I had no reason whatsoever not to obey God's will."

"Were I you, I could've never done that, Mom," said Russell, shaking his head.

"Be more humble, my dear. God's love is stronger than any mother's in the world. If our Heavenly Father wanted Ludwig to become a monk, there was nothing I could do against it."

Then Russell gently put his hand on his mother's and said barely in a whisper, "I love you, Mother, and I will never leave you."

Suddenly, Deborah frowned and strictly replied, "Don't you dare to say that again to me, Russell! What do you mean you'll never leave me?"

"I mean I will take care of you as long as I live. You are all I have in this big and dumb world."

"Russell Preston, I want you to promise me to never say these words again!"

"Have I offended you, Mom?" asked the boy, a little scared.

"No, but you did surprise me! I don't want you to spend the best years of your life taking care of me! I can take care of myself, you know. You are a man, and you must live like one. Find a girl, get married, and make me the happiest person on earth by giving me an honor to become a grandmother! Did you really mean what you said? I hope you didn't. Life is not about taking care for your parents, it's exclusively for moving forward and enjoying the life God gave you. I am not ill, and even if I were, I would never allow you to sit beside my bed!" she said, what to Russell sounded more like a strange kind of humor. "Are you laughing? I am not joking, my dear! Of course, education is also important."

"I would like to work with you and help you run our flower business," he said, unaware how to comprehend the entire discussion which was beyond oddity.

"Good for you, but a degree will never do you any harm, you know. Anyway, we'll talk about this later." Then she sipped some soft drink from her glass and said, "I don't want you to worry about me, my dear. I am never lonely, because I have God. Besides, marriage does not necessarily mean that you'll leave me forever, does it?"

"I will always be near you, Mom," he said, kissing her warm motherly hand, which smelled better than boundless fields of tulips. Her hand was as though keeping all the memories and nostalgic moments of the past, while at the same time it was spreading the indescribable scent of love. Were it Russell's will, he would've never let that hand go, for in it was much more than mere eternal security. It was like a heavenly candle which could revive and warm up any indifferent and frozen heart. Her soft skin was overflowing with God's heart's beating; Deborah's motherly and protective hand was eternal, and no armies of demons could ever come near to those who would hold on to it. This was what Russell experienced when his lips touched the hand, and that was the moment which always made him feel a little eternal as well. He was as though already in heaven, where there was nothing to be afraid of anymore and where nothing but light was reigning in the limitless time, which, in fact, wasn't there at all.

Minutes later, while they were friendly talking about the horror of loneliness and deaf silence in a solitary man's heart, someone knocked at their door. Though the Elvis Presley music was playing loud enough, the knock was heard clearly. That immediately gave away the fact that it was a man's hand knocking.

"Speaking of loneliness," said Russell in a tone of humor when his mother approached the door with a warm smile on her face. On opening the door, she saw Alexander standing with a bucket of tulips in his hand. The man was also smiling widely, and the hope which was easy to discern was all over his face; it was as if his own personal aura, covering him entirely and making him shine bright.

"Good evening," said Alexander courteously, as a true gentleman. The gentleman was dressed in blue jeans, white sneakers, and carefully ironed white shirt. There was still an odor of a strong aftershave lotion spreading all around the man, establishing sort of a protective shield from any weaker scents. Even the red tulips seemed to smell like their holder's thoroughly shaved face.

"Good evening, Alexander," said Deborah in reply, standing in front of him. "How are you?" she added, not realizing what to say to the man.

"The evening is beautiful as well as you are," he said anxiously and a little timidly. "I am very well, thank you, Debby. Can I call you like that? Or do you find that offensive?"

"By all means! After all, that's my name, isn't it?" she said with a wide and lovely smile. Indeed, her beauty that evening was overcoming any starry sky or bouquets of flowers.

At that moment, Russell left their dinner table and quickly went upstairs for the boy could hold his laughter no longer. Deborah could feel that, for silent sounds of tittering were reaching even her attentive ears. Russell went to his room, took a pillow, completely covered his face with it, and laughed as loudly as he could until even tears of joy started uncontrollably rolling down his cheeks. He laughed as probably never before, for his own sake not even daring to remember the image of Alexander standing again by their doorstep with a bouquet of flowers and asking those same questions as always.

"This is for you, by the way," said Alexander humbly, giving her the flowers with a somewhat trembling hand. "And how are you, Debby?"

"Fine, thank you so much," she said, smelling the flowers. "My God, these are wonderful tulips! Thank you very much, Alexander."

"I am sorry if I'm interrupting something. It's often difficult to find a proper time to come."

"Indeed, I understand. I was just having dinner with my son."

"Besides, I've heard Ludwig had gone into a monastery. That's great, you know! Many here are proud of him."

"Yes, thank you, Alexander—"

"Please, call me Alex," he interrupted quickly.

"Yes, Alex. I'm proud of him as well."

"And what about Russell? How is he doing?"

"Oh, he's fine. Doing really great," replied Deborah, wishing to end the conversation as soon as possible. "So, thank you again for the flowers, Alex," she said amiably.

"Sure, glad you like them. By the way, I…well…I just thought that maybe if you ever are hungry or have no one to talk to, I…" he stammered and knew not how to continue. "You know, I would just like to…if you don't mind, of course, to…well, ask you sort of out."

"Oh," said Debby, unsuccessfully faking her surprise. "You see, Alex, I'm kind of busy right now…All this work with my flowers and all that stuff, you know! But thank you so much for the invitation. I really appreciate it."

"Of course. If you don't mind, we can have a dinner anytime you're not busy, Debby," insisted Alex, hiding his noticeably shaking hand behind him. His voice was also quivering a little, but that was carefully disguised under occasional coughs.

"Yeah, that'd be great. However, would you mind if I thought a little? Could you give me some time? I'm sure you understand that it's not that easy for me to make quick and reckless decisions as far as relationships are concerned."

"I do understand, of course! Take as much time as you need, Debby!" replied Alex, almost jumping out of happiness. "Maybe I can call you someday? At what time do you usually finish your work?"

"At five o'clock," she said, regretting that she had to say that.

"Wonderful! I'll call then someday!"

"I look forward to that," she said with a forced smile. "Well, have a nice evening, Alex. Thank you once again for the flowers."

"You're welcome! Good evening!" Then he smiled at Deborah, turned around, and was off.

At the some instant when the door was shut, Russell, barely breathing, came downstairs. His eyes were covered in tears, and he was even touching his belly with his hand, for it had even begun to ache a little.

"Dear God, I cannot breathe," he said, slowly approaching the table and sitting down. "I thought I'd die there in my room," he added and burst out laughing again. Deborah joined him at the table, chuckling a little as well. "I literally can't afford to laugh a single second more. I think I'm gonna have a heart attack."

"He's a poor man, Russell. I feel sorry for him. He's a lonely soul which is desperately searching for salvation."

"If I ever see him standing by our doorstep with a bouquet of flowers in his hands again, I think that'll be the last thing I'll ever lay my eyes upon." Then he burst out laughing again as tears continued rolling down his cheeks. His belly was aching indeed, though he couldn't help it. "Please let's not talk about him anymore. I literally can't breathe."

Giving her son a minute to calm down, she stood up, tittering herself, took a vase from their cupboard, and put the flowers in it. As she sat at the table again, she said, "Being lonely is no funny matter, my dear."

"Are you going out with him?" asked Russell, wiping his face with a sleeve.

"Good one, Russell."

"Why not? He seems like a very nice man," he remarked and laughed again.

"Most of the time, I think about the blessed time your father and I shared," she said thoughtfully, mentally going back to those nostalgic times where everything seemed to be everlasting. Russell immediately stopped laughing and looked at his mother with sincere pity and an apology for making fun of the entire situation. "I daily recall when I first saw him, our first kiss, and the first time we danced. Your father is in my heart—how can I let myself even think of dating someone else?"

"I didn't mean to offend you, Mother. I am sorry."

"Everything's fine." Then she as if departed into the land of unknown and resumed, "Yes, I recollect the first time we danced. It was waltz, and I will never forget the rhythm my heart was beating in when I was looking him in the eyes and following his steps and moves. No writer in the world could ever put those feelings into words, even I find them difficult to convey."

"Are you there right now?" asked Russell carefully, not willing to disturb his mother's memories and feelings she was utterly immersed in.

"Yes. I relive that dance every day, thanking the Lord for those unforgettable moments which never let my heart fall into sadness and despair. I dance waltz with him in my most precious and beautiful dreams."

"It's a good thing we live and die in Christ, isn't it? Thus we know we will be united with those we miss for entire eternity once again."

"Those are some true words, my dear."

"Have you ever thought of a possibly of you and Dad dancing together once again in the everlasting kingdom of God? I'm pretty sure the Creator would get ready a very good and nicely polished dancing floor for you two. I can only imagine a square and shiny floor surrounded by castles of gold and trees of life, you and Dad standing before each other, and millions of believers and Christ-lovers would stand around that area and watch you two dancing. The music would also be playing there, and that would be not waltz or tango, but the most beautiful, angelic melody of all. You'd be dressed in white dress like a bride, and my dad would be standing in a funny-looking tuxedo. Of course, I wouldn't laugh at that, unless God allowed me to, which I doubt. Yeah, that would be great."

"God willing, that will be great, my dear," corrected Deborah, being captured by Russell's story and its beauty.

"Ludwig and I would also be there, carefully observing every step with curiosity and thoroughness. Everyone would be watching you without any jealousy, for there isn't any. Love would be in the air, and your dance would be something what would make God smile and rejoice."

"You are a poet, Russell."

"We all are in the hands of God. Frankly, I firmly believe that Christianity and faith in God without romance is a vain and dead ingredient which only ruins the entire dish of salvation. Don't you find that true?" Deborah raised her eyebrows in surprise, for never before had she thought of such a marvelous idea, which immediately drew her attention. "Indeed, romance in the sight of God is nothing but Christianity itself, I believe. Who are we if we don't love Jesus? Who are we if we don't love our family or our neighbors? Love and romance is Christianity, I think."

"You have a strong faith, Russell," remarked Deborah with amazement. "I am very proud of you, my son." Then she, rising up from her seat a little, kissed his forehead and was about to sit back, but someone knocked at their door. "I can't believe this is really happening," she said, standing up with a grin. She sincerely hoped this was not Alexander, for frankly, she had become tired of always trying to find inoffensive excuses or ways to politely get rid of the bothersome admirer. As for Russell, a smile ready to be turned into painful laugher suddenly appeared on his happy face, and he was as though ready to again leave the table with tears rolling down his cheeks.

"Surprise!" was what Deborah heard and was as if impacted by when she opened the door. The cry was so loud that it reminded her of a strong wind blowing right into her pretty face.

There were five women, whose age ranged from fifty to seventy-five, standing in front of her, with different cakes and bags full of exotic vegetables in their hands. Some of them unceremoniously tried to go in without even asking for a permission, but the way Deborah was standing prevented them from doing so. She had opened the door insofar as her body could be seen, for had she let those supposedly kind women in, their family dinner would've come to an end that very instant.

"Hello, my dear neighbors!" said Deborah, trying to make an impression that she was sincerely glad to see those who always reminded her of destructions, catastrophes, and irreversible consequences. Women in their village, as probably in any other, were always considered to be more dangerous than a well-equipped army of trained soldiers. Their tongues could without a doubt do more harm than ten tanks approaching a defenseless city, and their craft of gossiping and creating what has never occurred before was beyond amazement and horror. "Wanda, Sarah, Agatha, Ann, and Martha—girls, it's so nice to see you all here! How are you?"

"We're good…wonderful actually," answer a woman named Sarah, who was standing in front with a very cheap chocolate cake. "Will you invite us in?" she asked plainly. "We brought cakes and fruits, and we're ready to celebrate!"

"I'm sorry, but I don't really understand," confessed Deborah modestly. "Celebrate what?"

"A saint has been born in our blessed town!" cried a fifty-nine-year-old lady named Wanda.

"A saint?"

"Yes! Don't you happen to know him by chance? He is your son!"

"Ludwig?"

"Yes!" replied seventy-year-old Martha—a widow who had been daily eating with her late husband's photo standing on the other side of the table for the last fifteen years. "Our little village has our own saint now, and that surely brings blessings upon us!"

"I think that you, dear girls, misunderstand the entire fact. Ludwig is just a monk, and he has been there for only a week."

"We know, but our Good Lord guides him, and we pray that someday he will return and preach to us!" cried Martha again.

"I am very happy to see you all excited, girls, but I'm afraid I can't celebrate with you right now because I'm a little bit busy, and…Well, I'm really sorry, ladies. I hope you'll be able to forgive me. Besides, I'll invite you to come over some other day if you don't mind. Then we will be able to celebrate for as long as you want," said Deborah guiltily, dreading to see what their reaction would be.

"You are a mother of a saint, Deborah," said one rather unhappily. "We don't want to make you uncomfortable. We thank you and praise you for raising such a wonderful boy!

If you ever need help or anything else, you don't hesitate a second and come to us, okay?"

"I sure will. Thank you so much for coming. I really appreciate the gesture," she said, slowly closing the door, while the women, with all their gifts, turned around and murmuring something, left.

Wearied by playing a role of a kind and hospitable person, Deborah sighed deeply and locked the door. She went back into the sitting room, and as she approached the table, she was momentarily stopped by very familiar notes of a melody which this time was something more than just a memory. As she went into the room, a warm atmosphere of beautiful waltz music had reached her ears and enlightened her heart. She immediately smiled, being relieved from any tension or frightening thoughts. Russell was standing by a CD player, waiting for his mother to come. He had a compact disc of classical music, which included waltz, and before Deborah came in, he had turned on the tune.

On seeing her, Russell approached her like a gentleman, walking steady and straight, and, stretching forth his hand, said, "Care to dance, madam?"

And dance they did.

They were moving like two angels of freedom in the light of two innocent candles on their dinner table. Smiling at each other, they had forgotten everything at all, including darkness and all the evil in the world. The rhythm and the beauty of the music was perfectly accompanied by their steps and movements. Their souls were as if united in one aura of bliss—in a very extraordinary way they were as if taken into that dance floor in the kingdom of God. They were now dancing in that world of golden castles with millions of God-lovers surrounding them and admiring the way they were moved by the music. It was a time of unexplainable glory for both of them—a time they will remain and abide in forevermore.

12

Seven years later.

In a yard full of silence next to which was a lonely and a poor-looking monastery standing in misery and sadness, a young man was shoveling the snow so that an old minivan could get to a town which was fifty miles away. The one shoveling the snow was on a tight schedule, for four monks were anxiously waiting for him to finish as quickly as he could. They couldn't give him a hand at the time, simply because they were ready to leave and couldn't afford to get wet. It was the end of November, but the weather was almost unbearable—it was probably the coldest fall their country had ever seen so far. The young monk shoveling the snow, besides his black monk's apparel, was wearing only a thin jacket, a watch cap, and a long scarf wrapped around his neck. He was also wearing gloves, but it seemed as though he wasn't. When the hard job was done, he went back inside the monastery, where the cold seemed to be highly similar to the one outside.

"Good job, brother," said one monk, approaching him. "Thank you. God bless," he added and left. Other three monks, who had been waiting with anticipation, followed him without saying a word. One of them even glanced at the monk with a shovel in his frozen hand with dissatisfaction.

The monk put the shovel into a small storage room next to the front door and slowly started moving toward his cell, where nothing but silence was waiting for him. He was walking deep in thought, trying to figure out whether it was colder inside or outside the monastery. The tall grey walls of it were cold and fearsome. For a moment, the monk even thought he had better stayed outside, for at least there was sun desperately shining from above. Nevertheless, he went back into his cell and closed the door behind him. Weary as he was, he took off the jacket and the watch cap, keeping the scarf in its place where it belonged. Afterwards, he also took off the gloves and sat at his table. There was only a notebook, a pen, and a few books one of which was the Holy Bible. He took it and began to read some psalms barely in a whisper.

The cell was as lonely and frightening as it could be. There was an uncomfortable bed beneath a small window which opened a view to endless lands covered with snow, a table with an almost broken chair next to it, a small wardrobe, and a wooden cross independently hanging on a wall. All his books were kept in drawers in the table, for there were no bookshelves in the cell. The walls were painted in white, which daily reminded the monk of hospitals and made him feel as a patient in a ward without any hope to get well. Despite all the uncomfortable and unpleasant circumstances, the monk was happy about what he had become, what kind of apparel he was wearing, and who he was at all. He was happy about being wise, faithful to God, and a good brother to his fellow monks. The number of books he had read since the first day he got there could never be known even to him. Countless tons of knowledge were now in his head, daily being put into actions of kindness and love, according to the Lord's biggest command. Because of that, the monk was now wearing modest reading glasses, which in fact unwillingly forced him to feel even cleverer and a more experienced brother.

He was a very thin man, for eating was not his highest priority. Caring for the sick and hungry of towns big and small all over the country was what the monk lived for every day. It was as though his unwritten duty, as if something he had to do in order to make himself sleep at night. Many called him a saint because of his obedience and admirable faith. He was a brother of modest honor, though it all was not without some ingredients of envy from others. Sometimes it was really tough for him to pass through all the tension and evil forces reigning among the thoughts and glances of other brothers; yet he never gave up and was faithful to his daily prayers, fasting, and habit of doing good to those most in need of it.

Half an hour later, someone knocked at the monk's cell door.

"Come in," he said, still reading the book of Psalms.

"A letter for you," said a young monk, who had entered the room. He handed him the envelope and left.

"Thank you," said the modest saint, after the deliverer had gone. He opened the envelope, unfolded the paper and read:

Ludwig,

Mother is dying. Situation is very bad. Hurry and come back; she may leave us any day now.

Russell

The monk was as if stabbed in the heart with the sharpest knife ever. For a few long minutes, he found it hard to breathe, feeling how his holy soul was slowly but surely entering the chamber of despair and hopelessness. It was as if the world had immediately been covered with darkness, and even the sun had lost its rays and light in a matter of an instant. Ludwig, before asking for a permission to leave the monastery, kneeled down, closed his eyes, and said in a hurry, "Dear Lord, I beseech you, do not take my mother! Don't take her. Not now!"

For the last seven years, he had been talking with his mother on the phone almost every single day. Sometimes, they even wrote letters to each other, trying to stay as close as possible. During the last month, however, they had talked merely a few times, and Ludwig was already aware that his mother was ill. Moreover, sadly enough, they had met not a single time since he left his house with a bag hanging around his shoulder seven years ago. It broke poor Deborah's heart, but she never regretted or complained, fully trusting in God's will. Her photograph was always shining brightly as a bookmark in Ludwig's Bible. There were days when he stared at the photo longer than he read his Bible. Mother's eyes and her lovely face was as his icon, his secret idol at which he could look unceasingly, both while saying prayers and at all other times.

With Russell, on the other hand, he had never even talked throughout those long and rather lonely years. Not a single letter, not a single word was exchanged. Silence was their only way of communicating. They did think of each other, but none dared to humble himself and make a phone call. Russell's figure and soul were often in Ludwig's prayers; mostly, he asked God to grant his brother wisdom and freedom from the anger he was a slave of. He was sure Russell still couldn't forgive him for following God's voice; sometimes, he seemed to have let it go, while there were other times when it grieved his heart more than he could bear it. The tensed relationship between the brothers was

Ludwig's cross which he bore on his shoulders every day, along with sadness which now had been lasting for more than seven years; it also brought heaviness and regrets into the young monk's soul and life.

Now, after folding the letter and putting it into his bag, he quickly packed his things, put on his jacket and the watch cap, and left. He went to the office of a senior monk, who was the wisest and oldest of them all in the monastery. Without even knocking at the door, he went in and rushed to explain the entire situation. The senior monk listened carefully, and after Ludwig finished speaking, he said, "I understand. You may go, brother. I give more than a month. I'll be expecting you after the New Year. Meanwhile, brothers and I will be praying for your mother."

With loud words of gratitude, Ludwig was off.

The nearest bus station was a mile away from the monastery. The road leading to it was long and covered not only with snow but thoughtfulness as well. Signs of the minivan which had passed the road earlier that day were showing Ludwig the direction, though the small bus station soon became visible far way in the distance. The cold was running up and down his entire body—his cheeks and nose were red, and sometimes it hurt to move a finger or even blink. His hands were folded warmly as he was walking, though it seemed there was no safe haven to hide from the freezing wind and the air with nothing but cold in it. The cloudless sky from where the sun was eagerly trying to break through into that frosty November morning was making Ludwig feel as the only man left alive on the planet; looking above, he saw nothing but endlessness and silence, while he was utterly surrounded by boundless distance of snow. The monk was walking as a lonely angel, suffering the frost and pain it caused in order to save or at least warmly hug those whom he selfishly loved. He was trying to mutter a few prayers, but his lips were as frozen together. His mind, on the other hand, was crying for God's mercy and reciting every single prayer Ludwig knew. Above all, mentally abandoning his mind which was praying unceasingly, he also managed to recall the last time he saw his mother's eyes and when was the last time he kissed her soft cheek. He was aiming to recollect his mother's hand movement, the way she walked, and, most of all, her open arms welcoming him whenever he came back home. Deep inside him, there was a terrifying voice which told him that those shades of the past would never take place again. He was scared by the thought, although he also knew that life was not without losses and sorrow.

Immersed in his thoughts and fears, he reached the station in no time. He had no watch around his wrist to see when the next bus would come. Looking at the schedule hanging on an information board, he thought of nothing and had no idea whatsoever why he was doing that. His mind was too seriously influenced by the idea of losing his dear mother, and now depression and panic was beginning to overtake his heart, emotions, and feelings.

He sat down on a wooden bench, and, biting his lip, tried to do the best he could in order not to cry. Feeling how cold was capturing and hurting his entire body, he quickly stood up and started jumping in one place. The road was clear—neither a car nor sounds of a bus approaching were there. Though it hurt even more to jump with his legs frozen, he nonetheless found the idea better than sitting in one place until he could move no more. Willingness to cry seemed to have left him, though the sorrow and painful sadness were still making his innocent heart ache.

Thirty minutes later, a bus was finally seen in the distance. All this time, Ludwig had been jumping and doing different movements, although not for a single second did he feel warmed up. When the bus stopped, he got in with nothing but gratitude in his eyes and took out his wallet to pay for the ticket. On coming in, he also noticed that he was the only passenger in the bus, which made him question whether the bus was really bound for the village.

"Do I know you from somewhere?" the driver suddenly asked, who was a very old man, as they slowly moved forward.

"I don't know," he replied sadly, looking for a coin in his wallet. "I doubt it."

"What is your name?" insisted the driver, darting glances both at the monk and at the road.

"Ludwig, why?" he replied, making it clear that he wasn't in the mood to talk.

"Ludwig Preston?"

"Yes," said the boy surprised, giving the money to the driver.

"Oh, I can't take that," said the driver, looking at the money. "Better put those coins back in."

"Is something wrong?"

"Are you kidding me? A saint is coming back to our village!"

"What saint?" asked Ludwig, utterly unaware of what was going on. He frowned and tried to understand what the driver was talking about. He was still holding the money in his hand, though the happy man would not take it. "Listen, I just want to pay for the ticket and get to the village as soon as possible."

"Are you in a hurry?" asked the old man and glimpsed again at the monk.

"I am, to be honest," he said calmly.

"Put those money back in, Ludwig. Our entire village has been waiting for you to come back for many years. Every Sunday, we prayed for you in the church, in hope that one day you would return. You are a saint, and what people in our village are in need of the most these days is someone who will lead them. As you probably know, Father John has passed away a few years ago, and since then, many priests had come and gone. None stayed here for more than five months. We are like sheep without a shepherd. But now, God has heard our prayers," added the old man happily. "I can only imagine what'll happen when they see you!"

"Thank you, I'm flattered," he said sadly, going to the back of the bus and sitting down.

Looking through the window and trying to control his emotions, Ludwig started silently reciting a few prayers, asking God to save him from falling into distress and panic. As tears started dropping down on his scarf, he closed his eyes and stopped praying. He could do nothing at the moment but weep—as silently as he could in order not to attract the driver's attention. He could neither keep staring through the window, for the view of snow reminded him of all the Christmases he spent with his family, nor think of anything at all. Every single detail or sound made him recall everything what made him cry even more sorrowfully. He simply couldn't help it—fear was overcoming his pain, while hurtful memories seemed to be the most excruciating of all, mercilessly piercing his heart and soul as a sword of darkness. This time, Ludwig was not feeling like a saint or some holy monk sent to humankind by God. Now he was a martyr and a slave of his own regrets and torments.

About an hour later, he got off the bus. The driver said not a single word to the monk, seeing his eyes piteously lowered and his face utterly immersed into a state of misery and pain which was coming from within. Minutes later, he was standing as if rooted in front of his house—a place where the best years of his life were now hiding under the dark shadow of nostalgia. Unconsciously ignoring the cold around him, he started slowly walking toward the house, fearing that its door would be locked and there would be no one to open it regardless of how desperately he would knock. He could sacrifice everything and even his soul just to be told that his mother was inside waiting for him with arms opened wide and with warm dinner ready on the table, at which their entire family would gather in just a couple of minutes. He knew that wasn't true—it wasn't even his mind that was giving him such pictures of what was only an illusion; it was merely a voice of sadness, tormenting him by telling about things which would never take place in this life again. He wished he would be taken back to the start— back to where his life began, although regrettably he knew that he would relive his life the same way he had, ending up standing before a closed door which never seemed to him so cruel and dark.

13

L udwig knocked at the door with fear and a trembling heart. His emotions were jumbled inside his mind, although sadness was not a feeling to be easily hidden. The door was opened after a minute. Russell was now standing in front of him speechless.

"Hello, brother," said Ludwig. In reply, Russell turned around and left, leaving the door open. This was a punch after which it was always difficult to get back on feet. Ludwig did expect a meeting like that, but he hoped his brother would at least say a word. He went in, closing the door behind him.

In the house which long ago was overfilled with joyous sounds of laughter and music and dances was now like a place of mourning full of silence and mysteries, telling the frightening stories about connection and difference between this life and the one to come. He passed through the hallway strenuously trying not to look at neither the photos hanging on the walls, nor anything what could suddenly arise the nostalgia which at the time was Ludwig's biggest spiritual foe and slowly approached Russell standing by the stairs.

"Where is she?" asked Ludwig rather unhappily, fighting with the anger in his heart as well.

"Upstairs in her room," replied Russell in a manly voice tone. "All this time, she was as if waiting for you."

"What do you mean?" asked Ludwig naively, frowning a little.

With a sigh that expressed itself much better than any vain words could, Russell went away into the kitchen, trying not to look at Ludwig at all. It was obvious he was dealing with his fury with great exertion, restraining himself from saying or doing anything he would later regret.

Ludwig went upstairs and slowly, counting every step and second which brought him closer to the moment, entered his mother's room. He saw her helplessly lying in her bed with her eyes closed and a Bible in her hand. He silently approached her, thinking that she might be asleep.

"Come closer, whoever it is," said Deborah silently, not opening her eyes. Ludwig, with tears dropping down one after another, stepped closer and smiled widely. That was when Deborah slowly opened her eyes, which were still full of love, compassion, and kindness. On seeing her son, she smiled with great relief, as if now ready to enter the place which was meant for those who loved God with all their hearts. "My son!" she exclaimed. "You've come back!"

"Mother!" cried Ludwig, falling on his knees by the bed. He took her always warm hand and kissed her. "I am so sorry for everything!" He hugged her motionless and lifeless body and kissed her forehead thrice. All Deborah was strong enough to do in return was take Ludwig's frozen hand and warm it up with her love and tenderness.

"You're sorry?" she said quietly, not having enough energy to fully open her eyes. Even her voice sounded weak and tired—it was a melody fading away into eternal silence and peace. "For what, my dear? You've come back. God brought you here, didn't he?" she asked with a smile.

"He did," answer Ludwig, unable to control his teardrops falling down.

"You're crying?" she remarked, looking at him in the eyes with pity and endless love.

"Tears of joy, Mom," he said, wiping his face. "I'm sorry I didn't come earlier. I…I didn't know."

"Everything's okay, my dear. God's will is greater than ours." Then she sighed and resumed, "I am very glad that you're home again."

"This home is nothing without you, Mother."

"Do not be afraid, Ludwig. Both you and I know well that this brief life on this earth is nothing—a drop in the ocean—compared to the eternal life in the kingdom of God our Father. Even though I am leaving you, doesn't mean I'm not gonna be in your hearts and memories full of joyous and unforgettable moments. Do not weep or regret, my dear. Aren't you happy being with me now? Who knows what tomorrow brings. Maybe I'll be able to stand up and hug you as tightly as never before."

"I love you more than anything in this world, Mommy," muttered Ludwig, weeping as a child over his mother's hand.

"I want you to promise me something, Ludwig," she said seriously this time, barely breathing.

"Anything!"

"I want you to make peace with your brother. He loves you more than anyone. I can see that in his eyes. Be reconciled with him, Ludwig. Forgive, and you will be forgiven."

"I'll try," said Ludwig and kissed her weary hand twice.

"I beseech you. This is my only wish before I leave you, boys. God is great and merciful," she continued, looking above. "His love is impossible to even imagine! He is our Father and loves us regardless of how sinful and angry we often are."

"Tell me, Mommy, more about it," said Ludwig, leaning closer to his mother. "I want to continuously hear your voice."

"You know more than I can tell you, my little saint," she replied with an amiable smile. "I look at you and I see a holy man, who is doing what's right in God's sight. Thank you, Ludwig. Don't ever lose that spiritually innocent and holy look in your eyes—lead, preach, and fight the good fight of the faith. People need saints like you, for darkness is already all over the world. People need to hear about God and how to live this life according to his commands."

"May I pray with you, Mother?" asked Ludwig, taking out a rosary from his pocket.

"Of course, my son," replied Deborah and glanced at the wooden rosary in his hands. "Only please without that," she added. "Let's pray what is in our hearts instead."

"As you wish," he answered and put the rosary back into his jacket pocket. Then he once again took his mother's hand, closed his eyes, lowered his head, and commenced to pray. "Dear Lord, allow us to thank you for your compassion, patience, and loving-kindness which is like air to us, your children. Be with my mother, Lord Jesus Christ, and always hold her heart and soul in your hands." Then he opened his eyes and looked at Deborah, who by the time had already fallen asleep. Weariness and absolute absence of energy was probably the cause. Whatever it was, however, it didn't prevent Ludwig from resuming. "She loves you, God. I'm sure you know that. She has sacrificed so much for our sake. She is the kindest and most selfless person I've ever known. I don't want to lose her, Father. If it is your will, please let her stay here a little while longer. Both Russell and myself need her. She is our wings without which we could never fly again. I am sorry, God, for every single time I offended her or said too much. Now she calls me a saint, but in fact, I am just a believer, trying in my humble way to make the world a better place. It's not because I've achieved all this. My mother, now lying helpless on this bed, is a true saint who always supported me, and it's because of her faith in you that I am a monk who loves you more than anything in this world." After a brief pause, he silently added, "Thank you, God. I will thank you till the end of my days for giving me such a blessed mother. Yes, I'll never cease to thank you."

He had been kneeling by her bed for about an hour more, and although everything he wanted to say was still to be put into his words of prayers and pleas, he afterwards let his mother's hand go, and, as quietly as he could, left the room. Going downstairs, he thought of what he would say to his brother and how we would begin the conversation which was as unpredictable as everything concerning God's sense of humor and plans for his children. He was somewhat troubled by the commotion of emotions and doubts in his heart, although he knew that the stage of making peace still had to take place one way or the other. As he went into the kitchen, he saw Russell sitting at the table and thoughtfully drinking some tea.

"I would've been really glad if you told about mother's situation a few months earlier," said Ludwig accusingly, seating himself in front of Russell at the other end of the table.

"It happened faster than you think," said Russell in response. "How do you think, dear saint. Can God heal cancer?"

"He can do anything," answered Ludwig.

"Sure."

"What do you have against God? As far as I remember, you were always a faithful Christian."

"If that's all you can remember, then I pity you, dear monk."

"Too proud to call me your brother?"

"Too ashamed," said Russell, turning his eyes to Ludwig for the first time during the conversation. "I still can't make myself believe that I have a brother who chose some monks and pursuit of sainthood over our family."

"Your fury will kill you, brother."

"The sooner the better," he said and again sipped some tea.

"What did the doctors say?" suddenly said Ludwig, deeply saddened in his heart.

"A few days at most. They said that a week ago." Then he again looked at Ludwig and added, "She was waiting for you, saint."

"At least she did."

"Yes, she never forgot. You were always present in this house. She talked about, prayed for you, and was always worried."

"And what about you? Why haven't you called or wrote to me? Have I offended you?"

"Even if you have, what is the point of talking about it now? I didn't want to know anything about your holy life with other Catholic monks, and I still don't care how long you pray before meal. You left us so you could pursue holiness. Tell me, holy man, did you find what you sought?"

"And you, brother, where are you now? At least I achieved something in this life!"

"What exactly?"

"Inner peace, spiritual strength, doubtless faith, and holiness which I so eagerly was looking for! And you—who are you?"

"Good question, especially from such an ignorant and selfish person like you. Where I am now, you ask? Probably in the same place where you left me seven years ago. I am still that same happy person choosing family and God over my personal ambitions and dreams."

"Good for you, little brother. Only I still don't understand why you hold the grudge."

"Tell me you're not that stupid. I always thought monks were supposed to be wise."

"You'd be surprised," remarked Ludwig, frowning.

"Would I? I doubt it. A person who cares only for himself can never be wise. For your information, I don't hold the grudge. On the contrary, I'm happy because I don't live in loneliness and silence. I don't need to run away from my own shadows, and I don't go to sleep with trepidation. I see angels in my dreams, and I am daily enlightened by faces of those who are dear to me. Can a person who holds the grudge live such a life? I'm grateful to God that he freed me from anger and helped me to let it go."

"I am sincerely happy to hear that, Russell."

"And I'm not," he retorted. "I am still not happy because one way or another, I still do think about you, and I know that being lonely is the worst punishment there is. My daily joy is not full because I feel your heart, even though sometimes I don't want to. I often remember that I have a brother who is lost and is unlikely to come back home anytime soon."

"I thought you didn't care."

"I try not to, but I can't."

"How can we talk now of each other's madness while we must pray for our mother's soul? What are you doing here, Russell? Sipping tea? Don't you think we should be upstairs, praying without ceasing?"

"Yes, you should," he replied, continuing to sip his tea. "I think it is not she who needs prayers, monk. It's you. You're as though seeking redemption in praying for her, aren't you? Looking to justify yourself by kneeling beside her bed and reciting your rosary?"

"You call me selfish? All this time you've been talking about your own feelings and thoughts! We should pray for our mother and be with her each second of every minute, for now is the time when she needs us the most!"

"Is that so?" Afterwards, Russell leaned forward a little and firmly, emphasizing each word, said, "You were needed here while she could still walk and be merry! What is the use of you now? Yes, she is dying and it breaks my heart to see that, but I know she is with Christ, and her soul is the last thing on earth I am worried about. How will your prayers help her if she is already seeing heavens open? Do you expect to receive an award of honor and praise by coming back here as the holiest person alive?"

"I never sought to be praised for choosing to be a monk. I love Mother, and I could do anything to—"

"You're efforts and innocent wishes are of no use anymore, Ludwig!" interrupted Russell loudly. "Save your prayers and better hurry back to your monastery—for that's the place where you thought you'd find happiness and peace! I hope you did, because now that's all you have left."

"Why are you hurting me, Russell? You're as if blaming me for what's happened to Mother."

"I don't blame you," he said, looking his brother in the eyes. "But neither do I understand you."

"I don't expect you to understand me, brother. A person like you will never be able to."

"A person like me?" cried Russell with anger, being as if impacted by surprise. "Who do you think you are?"

Refusing to answer, Ludwig stood up and left the room with velocity, avoiding even looking at his brother. Russell, on the other hand, barely handling the fury and hatred that had suddenly arisen in his heart, left sitting there, contemplating on how could once a happy family like theirs have come to where they were now. He wondered with vast curiosity how disorder, conflicts, and vagueness of dark shades of evil that now abided between him and

Ludwig could turn out to be as real as life after death itself. His mind and contemplations were not without regrets. While Ludwig was in mother's room, kneeling by her bed and reciting the rosary, Russell continued sipping his already cold as ice tea with tears dropping down into his cup. They both prayed, only in different shapes of godliness. They both were saints in their own eyes, wishing that day could turn out to be only a nightmare. Oddly though unsurprisingly, shedding their tears in different rooms and atmospheres of sainthood, they both wished they could return to the time when they were still spiritually clean children, playing basketball in their backyard and waiting to be called for dinner. They both recalled those great days of their blessed past, which now was nothing but a ruin of pleasant memories only.

14

A day after Ludwig came back home, Deborah Preston passed away. It happened in the middle of the following night, which probably was the most silent night ever. Neither a breeze was howling, nor any kind of hopeful sound was alive that night. Ludwig was beside Deborah's bed, unceasingly reciting his wooden rosary and praying God to save his mother from spiritual fear and pain. He didn't intend to sleep or have a rest that night, knowing that his mother was greatly in need of his prayers. Somewhere deep inside him, he was convinced that his pleas and repetitions could heal her. And if it couldn't, he at least hoped his recitations could encourage her soul and ease her fears of passing from this life to another. He was ready to pray without a pause for as long as it would take, although he could've never predicted that the moment of death would come so quickly. He knew the exact time when it happened. He witnessed it with his ears, hearing as she exhaled her last breath. It was a moment when Ludwig stopped praying and raised his head. "Mother! I love you!" he cried, all in tears. "Forgive me, Mother! I beseech you— forgive my sins!" He cried emotionally and loudly, what made even Russell wake up from his uneasy sleep and rush into the room minutes later. The younger brother was quick to realize what had happened, although he didn't believe his suspicions and Ludwig's tears until he approached his mother's lifeless body and gently touched her hand. At the moment, he fell on his knees next to Ludwig and wept. He leaned forward and put his head on her shoulder, asking her to hug him. Afterwards, he felt Ludwig's brotherly hand on his back, and that's when he ignorantly stood up, not saying a word. Both weeping like little boys, they looked each other in the eyes, unable to find proper words to exchange. The moment was speaking for itself—it needed neither consolation nor words of regrets. It was full of much more than thoughts or prayers already. After a few brief minutes, Russell managed to stop crying. He later approached the window behind which there was much more than just a speechless night and looked at the starry sky above. Another instant later, he smiled, closed his eyes, and allowed his heart to say his last good-bye. Then, while Ludwig was still kneeling by the bed with the rosary in his hand, Russell left the room and went to make a phone call.

A day later, the funeral took place. Not many people came to support the boys; besides them, there were three more participants, two of which just came by out of mere curiosity. The third man expressing his compassion was Alexander—a man who never had a chance to go on a date with the woman lying in a light green dress, whose soul was now probably rejoicing in the kingdom of eternal light. Many candles were burning in the viewing room on that extremely cold day, accompanied by a silent organ music coming out from a small room next door. Russell and Ludwig had been standing by the open coffin for many long hours, until the time had come to say their last farewells.

Later that day, when the brothers speechlessly came back home, frozen and cold, they made some hot tea and sat at the kitchen table in front of each other. Everything was in deep quietness, even their souls had nothing to say this time, not a prayer of confession. Not laying their eyes upon each other, they were staring either at their cups full of hot tea or at their minds, which at the moment were fully though slightly vainly immersed into the dim roads of the past that had slowly led them to where they were now. Unwilling to speak or be spoken to, they both contemplated on what happened and what could've taken place instead.

Sitting at the table at which they once used to eat their breakfast before going to school brought a lot of grief and even more memories on it. They couldn't help those memories filling their minds and the air all around them with nostalgic feelings. They all were as if sent by their mother from above to remind them of all the good times they spent together.

"What're you thinking of?" asked Russell finally, when it was already dark outside and nothing but a dim light of a candle on their table was attempting to enlighten the air and warm them up—not only their hands or still red noses, but also their souls, which were desperately in need of mother's embrace and touch.

"Things I never had a chance to tell her," replied Ludwig, absentmindedly, looking at the burning candle in front of him. "And you?"

"Every single time she told me she loved me."

"Can you forgive me?" asked Ludwig all of a sudden.

"For what?" was what Russell said in reply, being surprised by the question not a little bit. He was also looking at the light coming out of the candle with his entire soul imbued with recollections of happy times of long ago.

"I don't know," said the monk with a sigh. "I hoped you could tell me."

"Maybe I can, but will that change things?"

"No, but that's important."

"Is it? Then I do," he said, still staring at the candle as well as his brother. They were speaking calmly and rather silently too, both mentally perambulating around the blessed land of joyous recollections and its lost and broken pieces.

"Do you?" asked Ludwig an instant later.

"You're surprised?"

"Quite the contrary, pleased."

"And you, do you forgive me?"

"No," replied Ludwig. "There's nothing to forgive."

"You're mistaken."

"Enlighten me, then."

"I refuse," said Russell with a sigh. "Perhaps only God knows my sins."

"You're wrong. If our sins are not confused, they torment us from within, not allowing us to sleep well and feel free."

"I forgave you without confession. Does that mean your sin remains?"

"No. I didn't confess because you knew my sins."

"Why then do we have to confess our sins to God, who also knows everything we've done wrong?"

"I don't know."

"You should."

"Yes, I should, but nevertheless I don't."

"Is your soul now freed?"

"After you forgave me? Yes, but now it's tormented by worries for your soul."

"In vain," said Russell, still in the same absentminded mode.

"Just want to forgive you in return."

"Do it, then."

"I can't. There's nothing to forgive," he said again, feeling how the conversation was slowly but surely consoling them both by simply granting them hope.

"There is," said Russell. "I just don't understand why you refuse to free my soul as I did yours."

"Because a sinner cannot forgive a saint."

"But you're not a sinner anymore. I freed you, didn't I?"

"You did, but that doesn't make me a saint."

"How then do my sins make me a saint?"

"You misunderstand, you didn't sin against me."

"But I did."

"Then I forgive you."

"Do you really? After all I've said about you? You're also unaware of what I thought about you."

"I don't need to. Forgiveness can also take place without judgment, you know."

"Does that mean I am free as well?"

"Do you feel free?"

"I do. Thank you."

"For what?"

"For forgiving me, thus breaking the bondage of sin."

"You're forgiven not because I forgave you, brother," said Ludwig thoughtfully.

"I think you are again mistaken," said Russell in reply.

"I am not—certainly not this time. You're freed not because I said I forgave you, but because you first forgave me. You can be freed and forgiven only when you forgive others their sins. If you don't, your sin also remains. You forgave me, and that's why I didn't know what to forgive you for. Your soul had already been cleansed."

"By whom?"

"By the one who sees and hears it all."

"Even this conversation taking place in silence and light of this dimly burning candle?"

"Yes. Don't you believe he's here at this moment?"

"I do. And our mother, can she hear what we're talking about right now?"

"I think you know the answer yourself."

"I certainly do. I just wanted to know your thoughts."

"I assume you know those as well, brother."

"I do. Nonetheless, can you put them into words?"

"She can."

"How?"

"This I do not know."

"You think we will one day?"

"I am sure about that. God willing," he added and smiled at his brother.

"Amen," said Russell, smiling back.

They continued sitting in the peaceful aura of silence for about one hour. They neither ate nor drank, nor talked throughout that hour at all. As though stagnated in their recollections and pictures of Deborah, her eyes, smiles, and hand movements, they were sitting still and staring at the candle on their kitchen table with thoughtfulness and peace, which had come into their hearts after the divine act of forgiveness took place. It was an unforgettable time spent in contemplations and prayers echoing somewhere at the farthest corners of their minds. Though sadness was supposed to be overfilling their hearts with pain and doubts concerning both the past and the future, the brothers looked rather relieved of any kind of darkness or uncertainty, which included fear, sorrow, and even shades of madness. They cried not, nor did they want to anymore; all tears had already been shed, which also signified that now peace was to come into their souls and give them hope—a thing they thought they had lost along with their mother, whose presence never left the boys, even after the agonizing ceremony of the funeral.

"Do you want to sleep?" asked Russell a while later, when the candle was minutes away from fading away along with the light which had been warming up the boys, giving them some time to think, forgive, and be redeemed.

"I do," replied Ludwig with a deep sigh. "Do you?"

"Haven't decided yet."

"We both need to rest. Is my room still in its place?"

"It is," replied Russell with a barely visible grin. "Are you going back?" he asked rather sadly this time, looking at his brother with hope.

"I've been given a month," answered Ludwig. "After that, I will go back to where I belong."

"You don t belong there."

"Let's not go in there, Russell," said Ludwig, sighing. "Let us save this controversial conversation for a more cheerful evening."

"Our mother's entered into the eternal kingdom of God, what kind of sorrow or egoistic sadness can shatter such joy?"

"Thank you," said Ludwig, smiling.

"For what?"

"For telling the truth."

"So what about that sleep?"

"Only after an evening prayer is said."

"Can't you go to sleep otherwise?"

"Not this time. Not when we have a chance to pray together again after so many years."

Russell nodded in agreement, and the candle finally faded away, passing its light to the fire of their evening prayers, which were recited with love, gratitude, and absolute absence of both inner pain and regrets.

15

The following day, early in the morning, Ludwig, dressed in his usual monk's apparel, went outside into their backyard, which was entirely covered in snow. It was as cold as on the day before, but by no means did it stop Ludwig from visiting a place where half of his childhood was spent and engraved upon. There were about five bare apples trees—leafless and fruitless as always at that time of year; nothing but frozen branches were unwillingly hanging in the frosty air, reminding Ludwig of all winters he spent there with his mother and brother, playing with snow and making snowmen look amusing and friendly. Having closed the back door behind him, he stepped into the plenteousness of snow, which reached even up to his knees. Thus, not going any farther and standing as though rooted in that one place, he gazed upon the five apple trees which seemed to have been there for more than a thousand years and were to stay there for twice as more years to come.

Behind those naked and sad-looking trees, there was a sun slowly rising up—a new day, unlike any other in the history of the world, was dawning. It was a spectacular scene full of divine energy and proofs of beauty and eternity—the sun, slowly approaching the unreachable heights of what was above and thus enlightening their little village, was as though proclaiming the entrance and perpetual reign of hope, which at the time didn't seem to be that close. The sun's rays were uselessly attempting to warm up the skies and everything it fell upon, yet all efforts were shattered, unable to reach even what it usually did. The skies were cloudless, not even a shade of those white bubbles of water or their never audible echo was there. The breeze was also silent, making itself believe in the existence of other natural sounds, which were not there at the moment. Everything was in deep quietness and abyss of peace. Ludwig, breathing in to feel the air of that miraculous morning, closed his eyes, and found himself in an extraordinary position of utterly and unconsciously ignoring both shadows of the past and expectations of tomorrow. He was happy about that morning, not wishing to be revealed the events that would take place in an hour or even a month. Raising his arms with palms faced upwards, sideways up to the level of his shoulders, he looked above at the endless and certainly boundless blue sky and silently said, "Bless this morning, Lord, and bless this day that is now dawning in front of my eyes. May this day be a gift of peace and happiness to all, and especially to those who are unable to smile or be merry. Thank you, God, for this sight beyond words. Thank you also for everything you do for us and for all those gifts you'll bestow upon us this day. I know this will happen, my Lord—the fact that we can walk is already a gift of love. And even if some cannot walk, remind them that they have eyes to see and ears to hear. To those who think they have nothing, tell, God our Lord, that they have you. This sunrise also testifies that you are kind and merciful, God. May you be glorified forevermore!"

Then he took his rosary which had been wrapped around his wrist and recited the prayer a few times.

His praying habit was as though innate. He could barely last an hour without muttering or quickly reciting at least the frailest or shortest of prayers. This propensity for talking to God had been written on his heart ever since he became an obedient and strong in his faith monk. Being proud of that in a holy manner, Ludwig quickly found himself eligible to even teach others how and when to pray. This was his strongest side as far as his sainthood was concerned—praying for him was faith itself, although among his long repetitions of prayers and meditations lasting up to three hours at a time, he barely found time to believe in his prayers at all. His mouth was used to saying various Catholic litanies, and sometimes he did that even unwillingly—his heart speaking for himself even when he was unconscious of it. That usually occurred during the first five minutes after waking up or while he contemplated on certain stories and events from the Bible. He often thanked the Lord Jesus for having given him this gift of praying without ceasing, for he never doubted it was the greatest gift that could do much more than just fill some free time with meaningfulness and benefits. Ludwig was strong and stiff-necked in his belief that prayers could heal, raise dead back to life, and change the world of the twenty-first century, in which Russell and himself were trying to survive in different ways of faith, religion, and life itself.

Ludwig prayed standing in front of the rising sun until he could feel his feet no longer. Though the beauty of the nature in front of him was easily overcoming and easing any pain, his feet would nevertheless disobey his eagerness to keep reciting the prayer and go back inside the house. His nose, as well as cheeks, was red, and though he had been wearing gloves, his hands were literally as cold as ice. The rosary in his hand had almost turned into a stupendous piece of ice with little wooden bead inside of it. His entire body was trembling from within, and even though he had started thinking only of hot tea by then, his heart was still willing to continue praying despite the frost and the snow. With his lips still reciting the Hail Mary prayer, he absentmindedly made himself some hot tea and sat at the kitchen table, in one hand holding his rosary and in the other his cup.

After he'd finished praying and had drunk his tea, Ludwig put the rosary on the table and sighed, closing his eyes. He was in his own euphoria of satisfaction, feeling grateful and proud of his inner peace which allowed him to pray as long as he wished. In his own opinion, it was solely his prayers that kept him safe, faithful and healthy all those years. He also prayed for Russell as many as three times a day, perpetually asking God to grant him wisdom, understanding, and a gift of being born-again.

Apart from his family, fellow monks, and simply old friends, Ludwig never ceased to pray for those few lights of holiness that had left in the world. Considering the world to be a wildly evil place full of darkness, sins, and vanity, Ludwig devoted most of his time praying for the world to repent and turn back to the Creator. He never refused to condemn the world in his heart, asking God to be just and rightful in his ways as far as the darkness in the world was concerned. He daily waited eagerly upon the Lord Jesus Christ to come, not being able to stand the sins and hellishness utterly ruling the world. The only thing which happened to be holy in his sight was the power and beauty of nature, which clearly was impossible to understand. Concerning the rest, Ludwig was as judgmental and merciless as human being could be. He tried neither to understand nor justify the darkness of sin, whose the place of abidance was the world. He always judged with temerity whether it was the world or people living according to its regulations and customs. Above all, not once did he admit to himself that he enjoyed such a position; he always felt safe in it, knowing the difference between the right and the wrong.

After an hour or so, Russell, still looking sleepy, came downstairs. "Morning," he muttered, making himself some tea. "Want some?"

"Yes, thank you," replied Ludwig, handing him the empty cup he had been drinking from.

"Got up early?" asked Russell, while his eyes were still struggling with the willingness to have some more rest.

"I did. Couldn't miss the sunrise."

"Never knew you liked it," replied Russell, standing by the kettle and waiting for a click sound.

"Many things changed in my life after I started walking the path of truth."

Unwilling to continue the discussion which clearly promised nothing pleasant, Russell said, "Happy for you, brother."

"And how did you sleep?"

"Queer question, don't you think? Besides, I'd be forever grateful if you didn't pray that loud under my room window anymore."

"You mean my morning prayer?"

"Thank you for telling me what it was. Yes that was what woke me up."

"You speak rightly, brother. Prayers do wake us up. They have the power to heal, to comfort, and to open the eyes of the blind. Your words are full of truth."

Russell, filling the cups with hot water and afterwards coming to join Ludwig at the table, said not a single word more. He could hardly control his unhappiness, hiding it behind an obvious silence of anger. He leaned back in his ample chair and stared at his cup standing in front on the table.

"So what about your life, Russell?" asked Ludwig a while later. "What are your plans? Are you thinking of having a family one day?"

"I do. I have a girlfriend. Her name is Ruth."

"You never told me about her!"

"Well, you never asked!" replied Russell loudly. "After all, it's like third or fourth time we have a discussion after seven years of silence. I reckon we have a lot to discuss, though frankly I don't think we have much in common. Your eyes are always living as if inside your lonely cell, while you say things I don't quite comprehend. You live a life of your own sainthood, brother, and I live a life of my own. Now I see that we are different saints, believing in the same God in hardly comprehensible to each other ways. I'll be unfriendly and possessed by darkness in your eyes, but I nevertheless want to say it. I don't want to know anything about your monastery, or about how holy you are. I care little about your life of purity, chastity, and honesty, and I beg you not to talk to me about how many hours a day you pray."

"Why are you saying such words of evil? It's a very rude way of telling that you don't care about me."

"Save me from your lectures of morality. I neither accept nor try to understand what you're saying, Ludwig. Pray, fast, kneel before images of Jesus, bow down to idols made out of wood and stone, and spend as many mornings talking to the sunrise as you want. My only request is not to involve me. I don't want to hear you, and I don't want to see you praying in our sitting room while I watch my favorite talk show. You are my brother, and I understand your eagerness to attract me to your silly and vain Catholic faith, but I assure you beforehand that I am not on your side, and I will never be. I'm on God's side, wherein I'll stay until I die."

"And you mean to tell me you're always doing what God wants you to do?"

"This matter concerns only me and God, Ludwig. Stay out of it. Better go and pray for my soul if you think that'll help."

"That is why I chose monastery over you, my friends, and these villagers. Regardless of how close one thinks he is to God, he will never be able to approach him completely because of the evil that reigns in this world. I've visited many towns and small villages throughout those seven years, and I've met more people than I can recall at the moment; yet, though most of them were strict Catholics and faithful believers, barely a few could really understand my words. Most of them, finding me holy, thought I was a crazy monk who had spent too much time in his cell. Absolutely no one but my brothers could understand and support me in my opinion and standpoints."

"Your brothers?" repeated Russell, frowning with intimidation.

"Yes," Ludwig coldly replied. "They understand me, and it is with them that I can be myself and speak freely of my beliefs."

"You call yourself a saint, Ludwig, but I don't see why. Have you saved someone? Have you sacrificed something for others? I always thought that only a man who does something sacrificial for his neighbor could hold this title. As far as I assume, all you do all day long is pray, eat, and talk with your brothers about God and religion. How do you help the poor? What use do you bring, and how exactly are you making this world a better place?"

"I don't aim to make this world better. This is not my goal."

"What is it, then?"

"You won't understand even if I tell you."

"I see," said Russell with a grin of surprise. "I believe you're right," he added, nodding.

"I don't mean to insult you, brother. I only tell the truth."

"I don't blame you. Besides, what do you have against this world which God has created? You're as if running away from it, fearing what it might do to you."

"And do your really think this world is just a happy place for everyone to share bread and water in? Why do people cry, then? Why prisons and churches are overfilled with heartbroken and doomed to die men and women?"

"Because they've made mistakes in life for which they have to pay. As for churches, people simply seek redemption and forgiveness. Don't you see beauty in couples standing before the altar and saying vows in children being born, in poor being helped, in strong men praying for their offsprings and their neighbors, in progress of science which makes life easier, in beauty of art and nature, in weak being defended by strong, in God's power manifesting itself in the life of every single man on this planet, in God's purposes for each of us? Why is it that all you see is darkness, vanity, and things controlled by demons and kingdoms of hell? Let me tell you something, brother. Don't judge the world or other people by your own heart and beliefs. If your heart is cold and ignorant and angry with yourself, that doesn't mean that the world is in the same state of godlessness as you. I see this world full of beauty and wonders; even when people die, it doesn't signify that sadness is worth to take place. People just go to the place whence they came—to our eternal home, where we will be with the Lord God forever."

"You call this world a wonderful place and this life a gift? You're mistaken greatly, brother. Tell that to a parentless boy who is on the streets, dying of hunger; tell that to a mother whose son died in a car accident; tell that the world and life are beautiful and full of blessings to a man who has been convicted of a crime which he didn't commit. I'm sure that a penniless beggar who is about to die with no one to hold his hand would agree with you, as well as alcoholics who beat their children and wives. Indeed, this life is nothing but a miracle full of light and happiness. Wars, dying soldiers, and innocent people suffering hellish pain in local hospitals—that is indeed a life of grace and blessings. We should tell that to every doctor who works in an abortion clinic, to every weak teenager who is bullied and beaten every day, to every Christian who is persecuted in Middle East or elsewhere at this very moment, to poor people addicted to drugs, cigarettes, and alcohol, to those who have no arms or legs, to those who cannot speak or hear or see. How often do you watch television, Russell? You're talking about beauty and purpose in life, do you find usefulness and godliness in talk shows or violent movies? All sorts of entertainment nowadays proclaim only lusts, sinfulness, and essence of evil. Have you ever heard of satanic churches? I often hear about them more than about Catholic church or its progress in this unstoppable and repeatable circle of time. It, the satanic cult, has influenced more people on this planet than the life of purity and holiness. Why do you think that is? Is it because life is beautiful? Such path of beauty will lead us all straight to the lake of fire, whence we will never get out. People worship evil more than God, and they forget about their Creator because they enjoy their happy lives." After a brief pause, he carried on, "Life is not meant to be enjoyed—it's not for you to love it, dear brother. It's for you to come to know the value of the gift which God has prepared for you in the life to come. All we must do is wait for the second coming of Christ with patience and prayer—in holiness and love, encouraging and strengthening one another daily. There will be tears and sadness no more; why, then, may I ask you, we so eagerly strive to become immortal in this world of evil while we are given a free gift to eternally live in the place where we will neither hunger nor thirst, where we shall forever enjoy the presence of the Lord our God?"

"So you're saying that we all, believers in Jesus, should never get married, forget our duties, become obedient and pious monks, and, in prayer and fasting, wait for the Lord to come? Is that what you're saying, Ludwig?" asked Russell with an unhappy grimace, though he seemed to have been caught in the trap of interest and curiosity. While his one ear was ignorantly denying all the information which was conveyed by Ludwig with enthusiastic charisma, his other ear was slowly and carefully, as though counting each word with diligence, accepting his brother's opinion and thoroughly placing it into the important archives of his mind.

"Each of us should be a monk, secretly abiding in his own monastery, brother. You putting on monk's apparel and carrying a rosary in your hand, doesn't necessarily mean that you're a soldier of God's army. I firmly believe that monk is a person who prefers God and holiness to this world of demons."

"You speak of holiness, but I still don't quite comprehend your words. Is a holy life in your eyes a life of solitude and deserts? So you refuse to have a job, get married, and have children simply because it doesn't fit your understanding of what a sacred life is, correct? You mean to tell me that days spent with me and Mother long ago were nothing more than aspects of this hellish world belonging to darkness? Are you really happy in your lonely cell with no one to call you a friend, or are you just going through it with severe pain in your heart in attempt to reach that vain goal of what you call a pure and decent life? Holiness is not about chastity or thoughts of light, it's all about how strong and unconditionally you love others and how selflessly you are willing to sacrifice yourself for the sake of your family and neighbors. Holiness is not a term by which you wish to entitle your poor life, Ludwig. It's life itself, boundlessly enjoyed by those who love God with all their hearts. I understand you are a man of theology, and you do not agree with my words. Frankly, I don't care. But my whole life, I've been reading and studying my Bible, and I know pretty well what life is about. Do you know who taught me this? My mother's life and her love for me told me everything I needed to know about the purpose and essence of a godly life. You can speak of theology and history of Catholic Church for twenty-four hours a day, and you can pray even more than that, but I can assure you, all God wants is your heart and soul filled with love and compassion. The fact that you see this world as a place of evil forces reigning all over it only explains why your eyes are so unhappy and miserable. The way you judge others is the same way you see yourself."

"This is a highly complex topic, which is not for uneducated minds to discuss," commented Ludwig, shaking his head.

"I am well aware that my knowledge does not even come close to yours. I've never studied in a college, and I never got a degree in religious studies. I perfectly understand and acknowledge that you are wiser and, without a doubt, holier person at this point," he said with a grin which implied his deep and sorrowful dissatisfaction and kind of hatred which could even be called innocent. He inquisitively looked at his brother and pointed at the rosary pompously lying on the table. "You really think that piece of wood can save your soul? Who is your God, Ludwig? I don't seem to know him. He is so unlike my God and Savior Jesus Christ. By looking at you, I see rigid convictions of inanity— putting your trust in idols and customs of your religion will make you as lifeless and breathless as they are. God didn't intend you to be alone. You are more than your religion, and you were not created to pray continuously and discuss the matters of Catholicism! Wake up, brother. Life is not as evil as you think." Here Ludwig looked at his brother with eyes expressing weakness and doubts, and said not a word, allowing him to resume. "There is beauty in a smile of a baby, in a mother's warm embrace, and in a father's wise advice. Families that have dinner together and laugh and talk in one echo are greater than all the philosophy of ancient times combined! Wisdom does not lie in erudition or the number of books you read at one time. Since the very beginning, it was all about love!"

"Love?" repeated Ludwig calmly, raising his eyebrows. "What is love, Russell? How do you understand love? Is it something you do for others so that others may see how godly life you live?"

"This is your way of expressing love, I'm sure. I don't want to be seen. Mother and I used to bring home beggars and poor children from the streets and feed them and give them a warm bed as well as new clothes. We never sought fame or attention. We always did that in secret, for good deeds cannot be seen by others."

"And this is how you understand love? By bringing home poor people you encounter on the streets?"

"Well, if you think that love is when you sit in your lonely cell and read catechism all day long, then I don't judge you for not understanding my words."

"You understand not a thing about my life, which is why your judgment is blind and wrong."

"Of course, I am wrong, Ludwig! You are the only one perfect in this world. Your life is full of prayers and devotedness to God and chastity. A saint like you could never understand a sinner like me. I'm even surprised you let yourself sit at one table with me—a man who is dark and lives in a world of evil."

"Step out of it, then. Why are you proud of what is leading you to destruction and condemnation? You think this is a joke, Russell? Christ is coming soon, and all you do is enjoy your life! Why do you refuse to open your eyes?"

"And do what?"

"Pray!" yelled Ludwig, losing his control. "Repent, fast, and pray. There is no other way into sainthood, which is the only way into God's eternal kingdom!"

"Jesus is my way. Not your prayers and certainly not some bracelet made out of wood!" replied Russell in anger. "Besides, tell me, blessed saint. Is your only goal to enter the kingdom of heaven?"

"My goal is to live a godly life."

"So that you could attain heaven, correct?" Seeing that Ludwig had nothing to say in response, Russell continued, "I see that you care little about God or his love for your… all you want is to enter paradise, the everlasting kingdom of life and peace, and you're using this path of holiness in order to bribe God, and be accounted worthy of a room in that castle of light. Am I right, brother?" he asked with a cheeky smile, looking at Ludwig at some transparent glass, which at the time was empty and dry.

"After what you've just said, I indeed see that those who abide in this world and enjoy its fruits are as full of darkness as everything else in this vain and temporal life." Then he leaned forward and said, "Daily work, entertainment, and satanic cult, which is almost everywhere these days, are the things which we enjoy if we allow this world to take us. God has become only a shade which we remember every Sunday out of pure routine, and what we enjoy more after that is music, dances, movies, and sin. This is not how a godly life should be lived. We need purity more than violence, and people need Jesus more than money. Yet, they chose to be educated by people who understand not a thing about this life instead! Jesus is no more regarded as God. He's become more of a cult and a reason for sects to earn some money. This world was never beautiful, Russell," he resumed in a calm and friendly voice tone. "Sin was always present here, and demons constantly wait for us to slip or disobey our Creator. Countless number of people are being killed, women are being raped, and children are being abandoned every single day. This surely doesn't come from a blessed life of happiness, brother. The world we live in belongs to the enemy, and we are but strangers in this land of sin. We must face the truth and try to stay in that profound state of purity and innocence as much as possible. We are not alone, however—Holy Spirit is here to help and strengthen us. We will never be left alone in this battle, and we will not lose if we stay on God's side till the end. This world of happiness, as you call it, is coming to an end, brother. There will be no more cinemas, football games, or bars in every second corner of a town. We have to prepare our hearts and souls for the kingdom which is to come, for this is where we're bound for."

"If people concentrated only on what you say, there would be no happy families, Ludwig."

"On the contrary, I believe that people divorce because they don't know God."

"I agree, but maybe they are afraid to come to know him because they hear and listen to people like you talking about evil, darkness, etc. Don't you think your theories and beliefs draw people away from God, because they are frightened and displeased with such perspective on life?"

"So you'd prefer to tell them only what they want to hear? I find that rather hypocritical."

"I'd prefer not to speak at all! We are here not to preach in words, but in deeds of love. Just like people believed Jesus not on account of his words only, but also of his deeds."

"Are you saying Jesus should not be preached?" cried Ludwig with a laugh, being astonished as he'd never been before.

Russell opened his mouth to reply, but he was immediately stopped by a knock at their door. This signified the end of their ardent and indefinite discussion, although both men were secretly glad about it. On standing up, Russell wanted to add something, but he went to open the door instead.

16

Opening the door, Russell saw a man and a woman of about thirty years old, standing in front of him with wide smiles on their shining faces. At first, Russell had a feeling that he'd seen those people somewhere before, and his doubts were scattered once the woman, who looked like she had just won a lottery, said, "Good morning, Russell. My name is Monica, and this is my friend Martin. I hope we do not cause any inconvenience to you."

Russell momentarily recalled where he had seen the girl and her friend before. They were Ludwig's fellow believers who had come to their house many times before Ludwig had gone into the monastery. Conveying his discontentment through his eyes, Russell answered, "No inconvenience. May I be of any assistance to you this day?"

"Yes, brother," said Martin amiably, almost jumping out of happiness. "We heard that brother Ludwig has come back. We thought that he might be here."

At the time, Ludwig, still calmly sitting at the kitchen table, was carefully listening to every single word. He was smiling, for his elation knew no end. He wanted to stand up and reveal himself, but, possessed by curiosity, he decided to wait until called instead.

"I see. And I thought you came to express your compassion after we lost our mother. But this is my bad. I'm sorry for being so selfish."

"We—" Monica began saying.

"Ludwig!" interrupted Russell, unwilling to hear anything more. Not saying another word, he turned around and departed, leaving the door half open. He went upstairs to save himself from they joy that was to take place at any moment.

Approaching the open door, Ludwig opened it fully and raised his arms sideways. "My beloved!" he cried with a wide smile enlightening his face. Both Monica and Martin approached the monk and embraced him tightly. He was more than a brother to them. He was even more than a saint sent by God. For his fellow believers, Ludwig was a light inside the gloomy world they lived in. He was looked at as an angel ready to guide, advise, love, and forgive.

"Please come inside, my friends! It's freezing outside," he said, letting the believers in and closing the door behind them. For the time being, he suggested they stayed in their coats until he lighted up the fireplace. He invited them into the sitting room and said, "Make yourself at home!"

"We are at home. You have come back to us!" cried Monica, observing Ludwig with wonder and mystery.

While the modest monk took matches and commenced to light the fireplace, Martin, shivering with cold, said, "I can't believe you are with us once again, brother!"

"Relax, brother, I'm but a simple believer just like you," he humbly replied.

"When did you return, Ludwig?" inquired Monica, rubbing her hands that were as frozen as the atmosphere inside the room.

"A day before my mother passed away."

"We are very sorry about that," said Martin.

"Thank you. It wasn't easy to be right beside her at that final moment when she—"

"We are with you now, brother," said Monica, approaching Ludwig and hugging him. "Your mother is with God now. Our community has prayed for her soul and you. Sometimes, it's not those we lose that need our prayers, but those who stay here in pain and distress. You were always in our prayers and hearts."

"I am grateful to you, my brothers and sisters!" he said, hugging Monica as his most beloved sister. "You were always in my prayers as well! I cannot even express how much I missed you."

"You can always trust us as your family, Ludwig," said Martin, admiring Monica's and Ludwig's warm hug.

"I know. It's so good to be back."

A while later, Monica and Martin took off their coats and made themselves comfortable on the sofa in front of the fireplace, whence warmth and coziness were being spread as light of Jesus's love. Ludwig made some hot chocolate for his friends and sat down on a stool right next to the fireplace to make himself warm. On a small table in the middle of the room, he put a plate of candies and a small bowl of walnuts. It was a warm atmosphere in the room, which reminded them all of typical images of a Christmas morning.

"So how have you been, brother?" asked Martin with genuine attentiveness and excitement. "How is a monk's life to you? Haven't you grown tired of it a little?"

"No, I wouldn't say so," replied Ludwig, shrugging. "Once I first entered the monastery and when those tall and slightly intimidating doors were loudly closed behind me, I was sure that this life was meant for me to live. I like the beauty and the essence of it—solitude, silence, plenty of time for both prayer and contemplations. I loved all of it. I've seen a few monks who couldn't stand such routine anymore, but as for me, I was probably the only monk there who sincerely enjoyed that kind of life. Even though I am home now, I still don't feel as comfortable and safe as I used to many years ago. My mother's now with God, and I have no reason to want to stay here whatsoever. I look forward to going back, although I don't mind staying here awhile."

"Please don't dare to run away soon!" exclaimed Monica cheerfully. "We missed you! We want to hear what you've learned, and what you have to say to us. You are a saint in this village. Everyone knows that. You are as if our own icon—our own monk who can guide and instruct us!"

"Those who think so are wrong, sister," replied Ludwig humbly. "I am just a pious believer, who lives a modest life of a monk. I don't have much, and I don't want it. This world is not a place where I belong and where I want to stay. Don't look upon me as a saint." Then he looked up at the stairs leading up to the second floor and said, "I can assure you, not everyone is fond of seeing me back. After all, why should people rejoice? I believe soldiers who come back alive after battles are worth more praise than monks who are forced to come back home, even though there is no one waiting for them there."

Seeing sadness passing through their brother's eyes, Martin and Monica glanced at each other worriedly, and the girl said, "We are here to support you, Ludwig. Do not let sorrow overwhelm your sacred heart. Life is but a glimpse. It passes faster than we can notice, but, as you said, we don't belong to this life. We are all bound for the life which is yet to come."

"Thank you for encouraging and strengthening me, sister," said Ludwig with a tiny smile. "I see that being a part of a community and having your brothers and sisters near you is one of the greatest gifts of all. Having someone who can understand, support, and pray for you is truly a grace. I am grateful to God that I have you, my friends."

"On the contrary, brother," said Monica enthusiastically and energetically as always. "We are happy to have you with us. You can't even imagine how much you mean to us. You are our brother, and we truly love you more than ourselves."

"Honestly," said Ludwig, looking at the mug of hot chocolate in his hand, "I've never even knew that a brotherhood besides Russell can essentially be real. Until I've come to know you, guys, I always thought that the only brother I had was Russell, and that all other people were just my friends, neighbors, and merely someone I accidentally encounter on my life's mountainous journey. Now, however, I am sure that those with whom you share bread, with whom you pray, and who you love are your true brothers and sisters in Jesus. My fellow monks are also my brothers, and among them, I never feel like a stranger. They are indeed as a family to me. You, Monica and Martin, are also my family, and I devout much more than just my time when I pray for you and your souls. This is no silly matter and not to be accepted as something temporal. Having a family like this is a bliss, which each of us enjoy in his or her own life of sainthood. We cannot be the same. We are all created by God for different purposes, although our goal is what unites us. By the Almighty's grace, we are one in our love for Jesus, and that's how our family is born."

"Listening to you is like hearing the choirs of angels singing songs of praise," said Monica in astonishment. "Many want to see you and hear you preach, Ludwig. We'd be more than happy to help you in any way we can. Many villagers are already talking about you, and you are expected in our old little church. Do you remember it?"

"How can I forget a place where I first met you, my sister," said Ludwig in reply, smiling amiably.

"Indeed, many want to meet you, brother," said Martin, sipping his hot chocolate. "When do you plan to come to our community?"

"How is your community doing, by the way?"

"Oh, it's doing great," replied Monica joyfully. "We have more than twenty members now, and we gather in our church or sometimes in each other's houses more than three times a week! People who come to pray are wonderful believers—strong in their faith and so pious that you could simply mistake them for angels. We are very proud of our brothers and sisters there!"

"God be glorified!" said Ludwig. "You know very well that I'd be more than happy to come, but I don't think now is the best time. I'm still struggling with the shock, and my heart, despite of how desperately I try to console myself, is grieved by the loss of my mother. She was everything to me, and without her, I feel as a dried lake—empty, useless, and purposeless. I find it complicated to put my sorrow feelings into words, for they are vain and can do nothing but hurt me even more. I'm not exaggerating and neither do I seek to be comforted. I just miss my mother, and I feel I could do anything just to touch her hair or hand once more. Therefore, I must apologize and say that I don't think I will come to visit you anytime soon. It's complicated, and I need some time alone."

"But I thought that we could help you overcome this hard time, Ludwig," said Monica with a worried face expression. "That's why we're here—to be with you at this difficult time of your life. If brother and sisters were with each other only in happiness and prosperity, then there would be no such things as community, brotherhood, or friendship. Therefore, we cannot, and we will not, leave you alone, Ludwig. We love you, and we insist that you come to pray with us before long." Then Monica turned to Martin, who had been eating walnuts which were on the table for a few minutes now, and said barely in a whisper, "Stop chewing when I talk, Martin. It's very disrespectful."

"I promise I'll come, only I can't say when," said Ludwig thoughtfully.

"Would you mind if we prayed together now?" suggested Monica, stretching her arm toward Ludwig. The latter gently took it with a nod and came closer on his knees to reach also Martin. After they were holding each other by the hand, Monica said, "Lord, we thank you for bringing back Ludwig. We missed him very much, and now our joy is full for our dear brother is with us again. God Almighty, you know what great and agonizing pain is now in Ludwig's heart. His mother is with you now, we believe. But our brother is in need of mother's warmth and care. Virgin Mary, our dear mother, come to Ludwig and comfort him as his spiritual mother. We trust your love and guidance, and we know you shall not abandon us in the time of need. Come to Ludwig's heart and abide in there, always whispering in his ear that you are near. Mary, mother of Jesus, we pray for your protection and motherly guidance. All saints and martyrs in heaven, pray for us!" Then she stopped, turned to Ludwig, and said, "Could you, brother, say a few words?"

He nodded, and they all closed their eyes and bowed their heads.

"Dear Lord, Jesus Christ," Ludwig began, "we pray for your mercy and forgiveness. We acknowledge that we have sinned. We are weak, dear Lord, but you are strong. Therefore, we put our trust in you and pray to never let us fall. And if we do, we beseech you, Lord, to help us stand up on our feet again and continue walking, holding your guiding hand with trust and devotion.

"Thank you for reminding me, dear God Almighty, that I have brothers and sisters who love me and care for me. I'll be forever grateful for what you've given me. Allow me to help my brothers and sisters as well as I can and teach them your ways. May my short staying in this village bring use and warmth into the hearts of those whom I shall teach and preach to. Help us all, Jesus, turn to holiness and abandon evil of this world. This, of course, is impossible without you, and therefore we pray to never leave us and help us all live holy lives so that you may be glorified."

"Amen!" said Monica and Martin at the same time.

"I also want to pray for my brother," continued Ludwig, not opening his eyes. Feeling highly uncomfortable, Martin and Monica quickly closed their eyes again and bowed down their heads. "Russell is in need of you, God," continued Ludwig after a brief pause. "I know he is with you, but let him know the truth and turn away from this dark and evil world. I love him, God, and I know that you love him even more. We pray for his soul and his future. Mary, mother of God, pray for Russell and all my brothers and sisters. We are in your hands, dear Mother. Please, pray for us."

Once another pause took place, Martin and Monica glanced at each other with doubts in their faces whether the prayer was finished or not. Then Ludwig opened his eyes, looked at them, and said, "Amen."

"Amen," they said again in one voice.

"I feel a little bit relieved right now," said Ludwig. "Thank you for praying with me."

In discussing various topics and lives of others, another hour had passed unnoticed. After that, they prayed again. Only this time, they recited the holy rosary, which was a beautiful sight to see—three keen and hearty Catholics reciting the rosary prayer in one sound and echo was something filled with divinity and sense of eternity. They recited the prayer with such a love and tenderness that even Russell, who at the time was in his room reading some best-selling horror book, found the faint echo of the prayer which had hardly reached his ears heavenly attractive and sublime. For a moment, he stopped reading the book and just humbly listened to what he couldn't understand. The curiosity grew stronger as his profound state of ignorance had finally approached its dawn. Russell got up and opened the door of his room to be able to hear the prayer better. Though he disliked that prayer and the entire fact of Catholicism, Russell nevertheless found that rosary prayer and the way it was recited miraculous and strangely powerful. He liked what he heard although he did not know what exactly it was. He heard some voice as if answering to Ludwig's prayers, some intentions being said, and some parts of Jesus's life being gloriously announced, after what the prayer would continue.

After about twenty minutes, the prayer had ended. Russell, again silently, closed his door and couldn't make himself believe that he in fact listened to a Catholic prayer and, at some point, even dared to admire it. He again opened his book, but his mind was too distracted and troubled to concentrate on reading in calmness. Not knowing what to do next, he just sat at his computer, put on headphones, and turned on some music that was supposed to relax him.

A few more hours had passed until the time had come for Monica and Martin to leave. They were sorry they couldn't stay any longer, although they were slightly comforted by hope that they would see Ludwig soon again. Before leaving, however, Monica said, "So will you come tomorrow? We really need you there, brother."

"I will," said Ludwig firmly, and afterwards bid her and Martin good-bye.

Having closed the door and returned to the sitting room where they were praying and talking minutes ago, Ludwig immediately sensed how the entire place was imbued with holiness and aura which usually reigned either in church or in the hearts of saints. It was warm in there, not even cold could disturb such atmosphere of peace in the room. Unwilling to lose that sacred moment, Ludwig calmly sat down on the sofa, took his rosary again, and started reciting the prayer in his heart one more time, thinking not only of the mysteries of the life of Jesus which he was supposed to meditate on while praying, but also of Russell and his spiritual life. Being brotherly worried for him, he even stopped reciting the rosary somewhere in the middle of it, for thoughts of his brother and his late mother were never leaving him, not for a single instant. All he could do to console and free himself from those anxious and rather hurtful thoughts was pray, but now, unable to do even that, he laid the rosary aside and muttered, "I cannot pray anymore, God. My heart is aching too much. Forgive me, God. I admit that I was wrong."

17

Later that day, Ludwig went to the church for evening masses. It was a thrilling feeling which even caused him to worry a little; he hadn't stepped a foot in that church for nearly seven years, and it was exciting to enter a place where his truthful spiritual life began. It was in that church when Ludwig put the envelope with a considerable amount of money into the "Good Deeds" chest. It was then when he met Monica for the first time, who led him to her prayer group, which is when the birth of a new believer took place. As always, he came to the church one hour earlier, willing to spend some time in inner contemplations and thoughts of no great purpose. There, as he kneeled before the altar and by everything he laid his tired eyes upon, he was reminded of Father John and masses he used to hold; he recollected his eyes, voice tone, and that unforgettable and amusing moment when the father was looking for his lost cat without a name. Father John was the man Ludwig desperately missed; now he would go to him for an advice or a simple opinion. Though he was an educated monk himself, knowing much more than was required, he seemed to be out of strength and confidence at the moment. What bothered and troubled him the most was Russell and the hardly destructible walls they both had built up between them. In addition, his mother's loss was like a sword, slowly and constantly piercing his heart and cutting his soul into tiny pieces, which afterwards were mercilessly scattered all around the world which Ludwig so eagerly wanted to run away from.

He had been kneeling in front of the altar for more than thirty minutes. After that, he sat down on a pew somewhere in the back of the church, where he was most likely not to be noticed.

The mass began on time, though the priest who held it didn't seem to be familiar to Ludwig. He was a young man of about thirty years old, who had probably just been out of the seminary. The way he held masses was laudable, though half of the praise could be given for his efforts and obvious fears to make at least slightest of mistakes. The only thing which Ludwig found rather amusing and silly was the priest's sermon, although, considering the audience which mostly consisted of old, God-fearing ladies and indifferent men who had most likely been forced to come by their pious wives, it wasn't as bad as some might think.

During the mass, Ludwig diligently surveyed the believers who had come to unite in prayer and daily celebration of the Eucharist gift. Finding the sermon utterly dull, the monk spent that time looking at the people modestly listening to the priest's highly questionable teachings. It was as though written in their eyes that they doubtlessly believed in every word which was coming out of the young priest's mouth. Taking the sermon deep into their open hearts, the Catholics who had gathered there that evening were sitting calmly, filling the aura of the mass with obedience and silence, thus allowing only the priest's voice to be heard and echoed. Ludwig admired such attitude during holy masses—that was the aspect he was most fond of as far as attending church was concerned.

Before the sermon was over, Ludwig managed to notice a few ladies whispering something to each other, while one of them was looking at Ludwig at some ghost of the most horrifying cemetery in the world. Ludwig didn't need much time to come to know what all the hustle and bustle which took place a moment later was about. People, completely forgetting and mentally abandoning the sermon which they had been genuinely interested in minutes ago, started turning around and darting glances at Ludwig sitting in the back, under the shadow of a tall pillar, which was expected to hide him from what he could avoid no more. He started leaning toward the pillar in vain hope to be hidden as if inside of it, yet there was no place to hide from the eyes of those villagers, who recognized him and were as though ready to end the mass themselves before even receiving the holy Eucharist.

"It's Debby's son!" he heard one lady saying. "It's the monk! He's come back," said some other lady in a whisper that sounded more like a silent yelling.

The priest, finding the situation awkward and rather uncomfortable, coughed a few times to attract some attention, but his efforts were to no avail. He was neither listened to nor look upon anymore. The mass was as though over, and that greatly displeased the priest who was still unaware what was the cause of the disturbance.

"I would like to ask you to keep silence and order, my children," said the priest, confused a little himself. People seemed to have calmed down, but that only lasted a minute until the hustle rose again. This time, the angry priest continued the mass without anymore warnings, skipping a few trivial parts of the rites, seeing that no one seemed to care.

After the mass was over, Ludwig commenced to think how to depart from the church without attracting any additional attention. However, since every eye was observing him with great exertion, Ludwig forced himself to accept the fact that there was no way out from what was bound to happen. Still, optimistically holding on to the hope that he wouldn't be noticed and simply passed by, he kept sitting under the same shadow of the pillar, trying to avoid any eye contacts or making any unnecessary and sudden moves. Yet, his naive mind and silly expectations happened to be nothing but a mirage of hope, which was but an unreal fragment of his imagination.

All the believers that were in the church suddenly approached him like a huge crowd of music band fans. Some of them were trying to say something, while others were literally yelling with excitement. Poor Ludwig found himself as afraid as never before; unaware of what to expect or how to behave, he barely managed to keep on breathing at all. Seeing people's eyes as they were hastily approaching him, he felt as someone who could heal, save, redeem, and comfort them all. The admiration in the believer's eyes was what encouraged him to be fond of the situation and made him somewhat enjoy it.

"Ludwig!" cried one woman, who was the first to take Ludwig's shaking hand. She was of about eighty years old, but now she seemed to be as full of life as never. "You're back my dear! Don't you remember me? Oh, no worries, my child. Come," she said, leading him after her as all other believers followed them. "Now you'll tell us everything, my dear!"

Speechlessly, he allowed himself to be led into a large room which at first reminded Ludwig of the priest's office, although it wasn't. It was a room right next to it, where usually gatherings of prayer groups and different other communities took place. All believers, which were about twenty in number, were talking something, each of his own intention and struggles of life. Ludwig could barely hear his own inner voice among such chaos, which was like a combination of dozens of different songs playing at the same time. There was no real possibility to discern at least a rhyme or a word. At some point, the modest monk reckoned this was nothing more than a dream, which was to come to an end before long.

The woman, who had been leading him by the hand, now hugged him tightly and said into his ear, "We are very sorry for what happened to your mother, dear. She was our dearest sister, and her soul is always in our prayers." Then the strangely happy woman let the boy go and added, "We are very happy that you've come back."

"I'm sorry, but I don't quite understand what is happening right now," he said, looking at all the faces in front of him. The room was entirely overfilled with faithful Catholic believers, what eventually turned out to be a beneficial thing, for at least they didn't have to worry about the cold which was reigning outside without a pause.

After the same old woman raised her arm as a signature for everyone to stop talking and making any kinds of sounds whatsoever, she looked at the boy with an amiable smile on her face and said, "Ludwig, we're grateful to God that he sent you back to us. This is where you belong, and we missed you very much."

"I do not mean to be rude," said the monk humbly, "but I don't think I deserve such praise. I've done nothing worth honoring me for."

"We honor you now for your deeds, but simply because you are with us," replied the woman, whose role was still an enigma to Ludwig. "We know that every Catholic monk in this world is like a secret light which constantly and selflessly prays for others. We, however, have been given a gift to have our own monk with whom we used to pray and share the gift of Eucharist long ago. You've returned, Ludwig, and we want to hear everything you have to reveal to us. We know we are blind, but you are the light which can show us the way, correct?"

"We want to hear you preach, brother!" said some man about forty years of age.

"We don't have our own priest here, Ludwig," continued the woman as if trying to convince the monk of something only he was aware of. "Many come and go, and we are like sheep without a shepherd. We want sermons, instructions, and to be enlightened by those anointed by God Almighty himself."

"I'm not a saint," confessed Ludwig, what even surprised himself. "I'd be glad to help you, but have in mind that I'm merely a simple believer who has devoted his life to God. I am seeking to be who you think I already am, but there is still a long and mountainous journey lying ahead of me."

"What journey? Are you leaving us again?" asked some woman doubtfully.

"No, I meant…never mind. I think I'll stay here for some time."

"We all want you to pray for us, darling," said the old woman again. "Ann here"—she took some young woman by the hand and brought her to Ludwig—"has lost her four-year-old daughter a few months ago. Can you pray for her, Ludwig?"

He looked at the hopeless-looking woman and suddenly felt how compassion overwhelmed both his heart and soul. He looked at her with regret, as if blaming himself for the tragedy. Ludwig afterwards, with tears filling his eyes, put his hand on the woman's shoulder, lowered his head, and prayed for the woman in a lightly trembling voice, for somehow he was so touched by what he had been told that it was difficult for him to control his emotions. He prayed with words of unheard compassion and comfort, while utter silence was all around them. All other believers were also standing with their heads bent down, praying in their minds along with Ludwig.

"Thank you, brother Ludwig," said the woman modestly after he finished praying. It was as if the pages of the Holy Bible were brought to life in simple words of Ludwig's rather short though powerful prayer. The woman raised her eyes and looked at him as an angel of light, who was there to protect and console her. The woman, for the first time after her little daughter passed away, managed to grin, seeing a saint standing in front of her and praying for both her and her daughter's souls. "I sense something divine in you and your words," said the woman again as tears commenced to drop down. She was looking at him not even blinking, satisfying that angels and God himself were present in his eyes at that very moment. "You are a saint, brother Ludwig. I thank you from the bottom of my heart."

"There is no need to thank me, sister," said Ludwig, hugging the woman tightly. "God is the one to be thanked and glorified! He is the one behind gifts of blessings. Cry if you want to, my dear sister, but know that all your tears will one day be wiped away by the hand of the Almighty God himself." Then he felt how the woman's crying turned into bitter and loud weeping. She immersed her face into his chest and wept as a child, seeking to be comforted and taken away from that world which had hurt her so greatly. Others standing around them were possessed by bitterness as well. The old woman, so proudly and confidently standing behind the weeping mother, was now modestly shedding tears herself, after what she would wipe them away with a beautiful white handkerchief so that no one would notice how weak and tender she could be. "This world is not our home," resumed Ludwig, still hugging the woman. "We do not belong to this evil place where darkness constantly abides. As true followers of Jesus, we must never let ourselves forget that this world is nothing more than a bridge which leads us back to whence we came, back to our home, where God is waiting for us with a warm pie on a windowsill, and our family and friends already sitting at the table. Those whom we have lost on our journey on that bridge will also be sitting at that old wooden table, waiting for us to come back home." Noticing that everyone was listening with their breaths held with excitement, Ludwig continued, "Our home at the other end of the bridge will be like a cozy wooden hut surrounded by tall and powerful trees. There will be a heavenly smell of something delicious being cooked, coming out through the open windows, and its entire outward appearance will be simple, modest, and even slightly poor, I'd say. Smokes will be coming out of the chimney, and the lockless door will be open, inviting us to enter. Once we walk inside, w-w-we'll see," he stammered and knew not how to finish.

"What, brother Ludwig?" asked one man, standing practically next to the monk. "What will we see?"

"God cooking delicious dinner," he continued with a smile, as if seeing the image before his very eyes. "Also our dear ones and friends sitting at an old table in the kitchen, talking about joyous memories, telling anecdotes, and singing in one rhythm and sound. They would be singing melodies yet unknown to this world—melodies that we have never heard before. Those would be unearthly and utterly divine symphonies of angels. No one will know where the sound is coming from. It will just be there, filling every heart with joy unspeakable and peace unexplainable. Electricity won't exist in the place like that—the prodigious light of God's love will be everywhere, enlightening every tiniest corner in the house. There will be laughter and cheerful noises and music and sense of eternity. Most of all, everyone will feel at home, surrounded by a family who loves you."

"I always thought heaven was like an endless land with golden streets and God sitting on his throne above all," remarked some man with fascination.

In absolute silence and stillness in the air, Ludwig glanced at the believers standing in front of him, and, still holding the woman, who was hugging him in return, in his embrace, said, "None of us knows what it's like, brother. The only thing we know for sure is that God will be there, holding us all in his fatherly hands. Nonetheless, this image which I described to you is most likely to fit the truth, because every time I meditate on it, it brings peace into my heart and consoles my sometimes troubled soul. It's as if my idol upon which I pray and fast, asking God to lead me to that little hut and allow me to walk in."

"Pray for us, Ludwig," said a young woman of about twenty-five years old, standing somewhere in the back of the room. "You are a true saint. Pray for us all, because your words are holy and God listens to you."

"I'd prefer to pray with you instead," replied Ludwig, looking at his brothers and sisters with eyes of compassion and kindness. "Thank you for accepting me as brother. Oh, what nice and blessed people you are!"

"Could you pray with us, Ludwig?" asked again the old lady who had led him here. "Are you in a hurry now? Could you stay awhile and pray for us all?"

"Sure I can," answered the saint, letting go the woman and taking his rosary, which, as usual, was wrapped around his wrist. The woman seemed to be as if resurrected, as if born-again—her eyes were shining, and her liveliness was conveyed through a tiny smile on her face. Though a few tears were left in her eyes, she had no more willingness to cry. Blessed and grateful, she unexpectedly kneeled down before Ludwig's feet and kissed them.

"Sister! Get up this very instant!" said Ludwig, being shocked by what the woman did. He took her arm and helped her get up.

"You are a saint, brother Ludwig," said the woman silently, looking him deep in the eyes. "God bless you!" In reply, Ludwig hugged her one more time and brotherly kissed her forehead.

18

An hour later, after the community, being now under the spiritual protection of the lonely monk, finished praying, which included many long litanies, some of which were said even more than thrice, rosary and different chaplet prayers to angels and Jesus Christ, Ludwig was left sitting in the same room with the old lady who was brimful of excitement and joy to see young Ludwig, Deborah's son, sitting next to her. All other people had gone home, and the room, despite the thick air of warmth and different smells, was practically empty. The old lady and the monk were calmly, not rushing anywhere, discussing the prospects regarding Ludwig's future, and all possible options how he could make his temporal stay in the village as useful as possible.

"People need someone to pray for them, Ludwig," said the old woman, whose name was still an enigma to the young monk. "Sheep without a shepherd will be lost in not time, for there are many ravening wolves out there. There are many sick, hungry, and spiritually lost people who need help. For a village like this, to have a saint like you, is a gift impossible to delineate. It is a blessing that you've come back, for, I believe, now is the time when people need you the most."

"But I don't see where all this admiration have come from," remarked Ludwig, shrugging. "I was not a well-known person in here before I went to the monastery, and I had come to know the community only months prior to leaving. I wouldn't be surprised if those people who had just been here had seen me for the first time. What I'm saying is that the villagers don't even know who they worship. I'm only a monk, and if you asked my brother, he'd tell you many interesting facts about me. After that, you wouldn't even look at me."

"Would those facts be true?"

"Neither true nor false. Those facts are merely his own opinion based on his blindness and ire."

"Why is your brother present here at this moment?" asked the woman inquisitively.

"Is he?"

"Well, you are talking about him, aren't you?"

"I am because I can't help worrying for him."

"Why would you, my son? If he refuses to join us, let him be and better take care for those who need you more." Ludwig said not a word in response. Then the old lady put her light hand on his shoulder and said, "We thank God for having you with us, Ludwig. We've been praying every Sunday for you and your family. There are many children of God who need guidance, spiritual safety, and consolation. And here you are—an angel unexpectedly sent by God Almighty." After a brief moment, she smiled and continued, "Many will come here tomorrow to see you and hear you preach. Many shall come seeking to be healed, given hope, and comforted. Some have lost their dear ones, some have gone astray in their spiritual paths, and others just pray to be healed. This village is not a land of blessings, but that was before you came here. Your prayers are holy, and whoever you touch becomes enlightened by the Holy Spirit."

"I beseech you. Do not exaggerate the whole matter. I am just a monk who likes to pray."

"Yet you believe that your prayers can heal and redeem?"

"I do," said Ludwig confidently.

"Why, then, are you saying that I'm exaggerating? I am just telling the truth." After a while, she sighed and said with a wide smile and attractive charm, "I see you don't really understand who you are talking to, my son. My name is Martha, and we've met before in the church before you left for the monastery." On hearing this, Ludwig suddenly recalled the woman's familiar face and grinned, allowing her to know that too. "After you departed, we met with your mother many times. She missed you a great deal, my son."

"I know," muttered Ludwig.

"Anyway," continued Martha, looking for something in her delicate and expensive-looking purse, "I just asked you to stay, Ludwig, because I needed to give you something very important." Then she took out her big purple wallet, and, handing Ludwig one hundred euros, said, "Take it, darling."

"I beg your pardon?" said Ludwig, incomprehensibly looking at the old woman.

"Take it!" said the woman in a tone like she was giving him a couple of coins. "We, Catholics, should take care for each other, don't you think?"

"Please, ma'am, I cannot possibly accept that," said Ludwig, almost jumping aghast.

"Sure you can!" insisted the woman, pressingly giving him the money.

"Ma'am, I will not take the money, please put them back in your wallet. I can assure you're more in need of them than I."

"Look at yourself, my son. You're all thin and weak! You clearly need to eat more. Here, take these money and don't make me angry," she said, placing the money into Ludwig's hand by force.

"This is really not necessary, ma'am," said Ludwig, not knowing what to do with the money. "I will help the people as much as I can, and I don't need to be paid for that."

"Do you really think I'm giving you this considerable amount of money so you don't refuse to help people in need? Shame on you, silly!"

"Forgive me," he said humbly.

"Take care for yourself, Ludwig, and eat well, because we all need you very much. We need you healthy and strong, because there's a lot of work waiting for you."

"I look forward to that."

"By the way, speaking of your brother, I don't think you should stay with him, Ludwig. He is not as good as you think he is. I would strongly recommend you to move somewhere else. If you want to, I can find you a wonderful place to stay at. You could even live here! We could bring you a bed, and it's really warm enough in here."

"I think I had better stay where I am now," replied the monk. "After all, that is my home."

"It's not easy living with Russell, isn't it?" Receiving only his sigh and saddened eyes in reply, Martha said, "I see. While you were gone, he became quite popular in our village—always rude and unfriendly, he was easily recognized on the streets."

"My brother is not always like that."

"Yet you agree that he's unlike any of us, who piously believe in God and treat others like brothers and sisters?"

"No, he does believe in God, although he has a very peculiar and specific way of accepting and seeing him—the way understandable only to him."

"He wouldn't if he came to church more often and was part of our community, would he?"

"I don't reckon Russell will come to this community. He's not that kind of believer. His position stands against almost everything we find to be sacred. It's intricate. Let us not talk about him."

"I didn't mean to offend you or Russell, Ludwig. I apologize if I did. I just wanted to help you avoid people who have the ability to unconsciously influence others in a very ghastly and fiendish way. You can't deny the fact that Russell is not a person filled with love for God."

"Even if he's not, how would we know that?" asked Ludwig, turning to the woman.

"Deeds are the best testifiers in the world, darling. We can speak about God for numerous hours, but how we live and the way we treat others tell it all about our heart and soul and wherein they lie."

"Perhaps you're right, but we can never know how deep a relationship between a person and God may be. Sometimes others' deeds depend entirely on the way we look at them."

"Well, let's not argue over the matter which does not concern us. I promise I'll say a few prayers for your brother's lost soul," she added proudly.

"I appreciate that. Russell is truly in need of it."

Later, Ludwig went back home, as elated as ever, having been so warmly welcomed by the community of his home town. Continually thinking of Russell, he commenced to rewind the entire conversation with the old lady named Martha. *Perhaps she was right*, thought Ludwig. Russell is indeed a lost soul who ignorantly refuses to be shown the way. He couldn't stop but thinking of how right and profound was Martha's perspective on his brother. He was indeed unlike them and their most cherished beliefs. At some point, Ludwig got irritated and rather angry with Russell's ignorance and obstinateness; on the other hand, his entire soul and mind were extremely sorry for him, without knowing any possible option how to ameliorate the situation.

He returned home, all cold and in a meditative state and stopped, closing the door behind him. He heard that the television was on, but he had no intention to walk into the sitting room whatsoever. For a second or two, he thought about what he would say to his brother and what words of support he could use to make him realize that he was on his side. However, he sighed with disappointment, unable to find even willingness to speak with Russell at all.

Taking off his shoes, he walked into the sitting room with summoned-up courage in his eyes and saw a picture which made him only gasp with relief. His brother was lying asleep on the couch, while on TV, there were some old cartoon being shown. On the table, Ludwig saw a few bottles of soft drink and a half-empty bottle of light beer. Ludwig quickly reckoned that was for the better, although after he turned the TV off, Russell woke up with an unhappy look in his eyes.

"I thought you died," said Russell, again closing his eyes and turning around on his other side.

"Nice to hear that, especially after we suffered the loss of our mother. At least I've been praying for her with other believers!" said Ludwig in a rather loud voice tone.

"Believers?" asked Russell calmly. "You mean those people we used to laugh at and sometimes even mock when we were kids? Have you forgotten how we used to watch them go to church in the evenings and laugh at their hypocritical humbleness? As far as I recall, you were the one by my side, laughing even louder than I."

"I admit that I was wrong," said Ludwig, uncomfortably standing before Russell's back. "But now everything's changed."

"Has it?"

"You also need to change, Russell. You can't live like you do. The way you understand God is wrong, and I have a feeling that you are well aware of that too, only your pride doesn't allow you to admit that."

This time, Russell stood up with velocity and angrily looked at his brother. "So you mean to tell me that mother's way of believing in God was wrong?"

"I did not say that. But look at you, I cannot see God anywhere. Neither in your eyes nor in your actions nor in your words. I am genuinely worried for you, Russell. Please, help me help you."

211

"Of course, surely I'm not like you," he said calmly with a suspicious smile. "My brother is holy, pure, full of light, and heavenly joy." Russell spoke as a poet reciting his poem in front of the mirror, attempting to make an impression before the man in it. "There is no fault in him, only a soul of prayer and an aura of innocence, leading him into God's eternal kingdom!" Then he as if stopped being a poet, and there was no smile on his face anymore. In a normal and full of ire voice, he continued, "Who are you trying to fool, Ludwig? God? Me? Say it! Speak out loud!" he yelled. "You're ridiculing both yourself and me, perambulating with this apparel of shame and playing the role a saint! You are not a saint, and you'll never be one, regardless of how earnestly you try. Stop imagining yourself to be who you're not! I know the real you, Ludwig. You are a good Christian in your heart, and your soul is full of love, but all this"—he pointed at Ludwig from top to bottom—"is nothing but an act, which you perform horribly! While others manage to spot a saint in you, I see only a simple brother of mine, who out of his love for God and others could sacrifice much more than his life. I wish that brother would come back some day, then I'd at least had someone to talk to and tell about this fool standing now in front of me. Believe me, this brother I'm now speaking of would understand and support me, because being a brother to one person for him is more important that being a saint to the whole world. You've probably traveled across the country over these seven years, and you've probably helped numerous people seeking to know God, right? That's admirable and fascinating; only while you, along with your sainthood and imaginary goals for life, were saving those souls, you've lost your only family who sincerely loved you."

"And you suppose Christianity is about drinking beer and watching silly cartoons which do not promote God?"

"It's a light beer," corrected Russell.

"You think this is how Christians should live their lives?"

Sitting back on the couch and giving the air a moment of rest from their interminable debates, Russell sipped some beer, and, raising his eyes again to his brother, said, "If you think that Christianity is about praying without ceasing in attempt to prove to God that you love him, then I pity you, my dear monk."

"Who told you such nonsense?" exclaimed Ludwig, sitting on a stool in front of his brother.

"My sense," he coldly retorted. "Besides, by looking at you, I could say much more nonsense, but I'm afraid you may misunderstand them," he added, giggling. "Okay," said Ludwig with a sigh, seeing that the discussion was leading them to nowhere. "Would you like me to turn your cartoons back on?" he asked a while later, irritated greatly. "Maybe I could bring you another bottle of beer? And don't worry for your soul, brother, for I'll go now to my room and pray for it all night long. Meanwhile, you can just rest here and laugh at what you see on the TV screen."

"Yes, please turn my cartoons back on," said Russell, lying back on the couch again.

Upset and angered, Ludwig turned around, and went upstairs into his room. Meanwhile, Russell didn't turn on the TV either. He just kept lying, staring at the ceiling and deeply contemplating on the memories in which his mother and himself were laughing and having a better time than him at the moment.

19

Two days later, Russell left the house soon after the sunrise when his brother was probably still asleep. It was a cold and sunny morning, although feelings of love and joy in Russell's heart were warming up his entire body, protecting him from any kind of frost. It was a very special day for him because after nearly three weeks of being in different parts of the world, Russell's fiancée was about to come back home. He was now bound for the train station, which, with heart trembling with anticipation, he reached in less than twenty minutes. The station was as desolated as a city after the day of judgment, and for a moment, Russell even had doubts whether the train was coming at all. His soul was bouncing with cheerfulness and nothing seemed to be of greater importance than the moment which was to come to pass any minute. He neither thought nor dreamed of anything at the moment. He was only looking at the endless distance, waiting for the train to finally arrive.

Fifteen minutes later, a slight movement with dim sounds coming out of it was noticed. That's when Russell's heart started beating even faster, for he knew that he was about to embrace the girl he loved with all his heart. When the frozen train stopped and the door was opened, out walked an angel in a fur coat and a blue winter hat on her head. She was a tiny girl of about twenty-five years old, whose stunningly beautiful blue eyes were like entrances into paradise full of flowers, sunshine, and light. Her white hair were tied behind her back, and her angelic smile could never be put into words. Looking each other in the eyes, they said not a word—they only jumped into each other's embrace and intended to stay there forever. They could live without a loaf of bread, a glass of water, or anything what life could offer them—even if it was all the kingdoms and riches of the world. Hugging each other tightly, they were even daunted by the idea of breathing; neither aspects of future nor glimpses of the past were brave enough to bother them. With his eyes closed, Russell smelled the girl's white hair, immersing himself into the land of beauty which the scent contained. After a while, barely believing in his happiness and how much he was blessed, Russell let go his fiancée and kissed her.

"I can't believe it has been three weeks!" she said, still willing to hug him.

"Nineteen days, to be precise," said Russell, taking his fiancée by the hand as they slowly began to walk.

"Russell, how are you, darling?" said the girl and stopped to kiss him on the cheek one more time. Her eyes looked worried, and Russell knew well what she meant. "I've been praying for you all this time!"

"It's been tough," said he, shaking his head. "Let's go have some coffee now. It's cold here."

They quickly went to a nearest cafe, where they were the only customers, and sat at a table next to the fireplace to make themselves warm. After they ordered some coffee and two slices of apple pie, Ruth—that was the girl's name—looked at Russell piteously, took his cold hand and said, "I am very sorry for what happened, darling. I find no words how I can comfort you. I…"

"Please, Ruth, do not shed your tears," said Russell, seeing how a few tears on the girl's face dropped down. He gently wiped her face and was slowly but surely taken by pity and sadness himself. "Do not cry, because there is no reason. My mother is now with God. We should be rejoicing instead."

"She was a woman full of holy wisdom and love. I remember, when you first introduced me to her, she, when you weren't around, said that I was the most beautiful girl she had ever seen in her life. And then she added, 'My boy is way luckier than I thought.' I will never be able to forget her eyes and voice tone—so loving, friendly, and encouraging to believe in something bigger and more beautiful than this world."

"I also remember her reaction when I told her I was going to propose to you," said Russell with a nostalgic smile. "The first thing she did was put her warm hand on my shoulder and bless me, thanking God for such a son. Then she said, 'Since you'll be doing it once, do it unforgettably so that both you and your wife would remember it even when you both enter God's kingdom.' Then she, wiping her tears of joy, gave me a couple ideas how do it properly."

"And when we came to her afterwards, she took our hands and blessed us, calling me her daughter," said Ruth, also smiling. "We can be grateful for those moments, Russell. Her blessing is still upon us."

"Yes," said Russell, nodding. "She was the most selfless person I knew. Her entire time was devoted only to me and my brother, and, after our father passed away, she never dated anyone, as far as I know. She raised us with love and care, and she was always around when we needed her. I don't recall a single time when she was furious or overwhelmed by sadness or nostalgia."

"And how is your brother? Has he come back?"

Momentarily, the smile on Russell's face disappeared. Lowering his eyes, he said, "How is he? I cannot tell for I have no clue whatsoever. Yes, he's back, but he's leaving soon again. I haven't seen him for seven years, but I realize that it would've been better if he hadn't returned at all.

Monastery and the religion he chose to follow has literally killed my brother from inside—that person that's now inside my house is not Ludwig Preston. He's just a monk whom I don't know and wish not to."

"Why do you say such words, sweetheart? Has he offended you?" asked Ruth, taking Russell's hand.

"No, but he's offended everything we've been through and all that we've had. He left me and Mom seven years ago to become a monk and seek sainthood in this life, which, in his eyes, is evil and fiendish. Now, he's returned as a saint whom our entire village adores. No one cares that he's a selfish and ignorant human being dressed in monk's apparel. Everyone sees him as a saint, just because he supposedly prays and fasts more than others. How can people be so blind?" At the moment, their pie and coffee had arrived. "Anyway, let's not talk about him."

"Somehow I feel that we have to," remarked Ruth, thoughtfully and piteously looking at her future husband.

"When he was in his monastery reading spiritual books and endlessly praying with his fellow monks, I was at home taking care of my mother, paying bills, and earning money to afford her medicine," Russell continued rather angrily. "Pursuit of sainthood for him was more important than his own family! He came back like an angel, but who paid for mother's funeral, and who was beside her when she wanted to talk or ask for a glass of water?"

"I don't find your judgment right and holy, Russell," said Ruth, deeply staring at him. "You shouldn't condemn your brother for choosing to live this life on his own. It was his decisions, and sooner or later, he still would've left you."

"The fact that he's a monk is not what bother's me, Ruth. What I can't stand is him trying to be someone he's not. My brother is a true hypocrite, although in everyone's eyes he is a saint sent from heaven!"

"You don't believe in his conversion to Catholicism? My mother is a Catholic, and though I am not, I don't see any fault in that way of believing in God."

"It's difficult to comprehend my words, I know," carried on Russell, calmly and steadfastly. "When I look at him, I see lies, vanity, and hypocrisy. He is everything but a saint, and it so appears that I'm the only person in the world who knows it." After sipping his coffee, he looked at her and said, "Moreover, during wars, people hungered and would've given their lives for a loaf of bread or a glass of water; now, however, when God has given us everything in abundance to enjoy, believers like my brother decide to fast, not to eat meat, refuse to eat sweets, etc."

"No matter what kind of life your brother's living, or how he decided to follow God, you shouldn't judge or condemn him for it, Russell. I agree with what you say, but you mustn't allow anger to take over you heart."

"I'm not mad at him. Quite the contrary, I feel sorry for the monk. Being alone is not a punishment. It's condemnation itself, I think. I don't want this for him. I want him to understand that life is for enjoyment and worshipping God for everything he gives."

"Maybe God has a different purpose for your brother," said Ruth questionably. "Maybe he has a different relationship with him—the kind of relationship which is not for us to understand."

"No, Ruth," retorted Russell firmly. "I know my brother. He's not what he thinks he is. Being a monk for him is like the easiest way to be praised and considered to be a saint. When I tell him that mother and I used to bring home beggars and help them, he just frowns as though not understanding the language I'm speaking in. He does not know what Christianity is all about, which is why he's unaware of what and whom he follows, believing that his modest eating and long prayers will save his soul. He doesn't admit the fact that his soul has already been saved! Why did Jesus, then, die on the cross? So that we would try to attain heaven by living in lonely cells and reciting some wooden bracelets? I doubt it. We are here to love, worship, and enjoy. This is the best thing about being a Christian because that's when all these aspects start making sense."

"Is this what your mother believed in also?" asked Ruth.

"Yes. This is what she taught us."

"How come he decided to become a monk, then?"

"He got involved in some Catholic prayer group, as far as I know," he replied with a sigh. "Frankly, I don't care."

"But I think you do, darling. You love him, and it hurts you to see him leading a life which in your eyes is wrong, correct? Maybe Ludwig is not the problem. Maybe it's your attitude toward him."

"Of course, I'm not calling myself a saint. I'm far from that. I do not pray often, nor do I fast at all. All that I have is my humble love for God."

"Don't you agree that's all you need to live a good Christian life?"

"I do," answered Russell. "But more than that, I want my brother to admit that as well. Sainthood is not about how you live, but about how much you love."

"I agree, Russell, but you cannot force your brother to believe in something he cannot."

"He cannot?" echoed Russell, frowning.

"I assume he's a strict Catholic, which means that your Christian perspective is outlandish to him."

"What do you suggest?" he asked humbly.

"Someone has said that the best way of preaching is through your daily life and deeds of kindness. Words cannot convert and change people into something they're not. Why don't you concentrate more on your life than that of your brother's who is clearly not in need of it?"

"You're right," he said, sipping his coffee.

After a while, when there were no more slices of pie on their plates and when they had finished drinking their coffee, the aura of their discussion had turned into a more cheerful and pleasant one. Ludwig seemed to have been forgotten for a while, as well as everything evil and irrevocably intricate and ghastly. The smiles were on their faces as they were looking at each other with eyes brimful of love and beauty of sympathy. After they ordered some more coffee and a few more slices of that delicious apple pie, Russell looked at his fiancée and said, "Tell me now about your trip, Ruth. I've been praying for you all this time."

"It was great. India was unlike anything I've ever imagined. Our group was helping poor kids there, and I must say we did a really great job. I saw so many faces full of sadness and fear, so many children living in poverty and hopelessness. We visited a few small villages like this one, where people are more in need of food than philosophies about life, you know. Children there need warmth, care, and peace. We didn't talk to them about purposes of life or the meaning of destiny in each of our journeys. All we did there was feed and take a good care of them at least for a little while. Seeing kids not having a T-shirt or a pair of socks made me think a great deal about my life and what I use my money for.

"There was one time," she continued, "when a little boy ran up to me and said something I couldn't understand. Then he pointed at a bottle of water that I was holding in my hand, and I don't quite recall what happened next, but I do recollect what I felt. I don't know whether it was the boy's eyes what touched my soul, or whether it was the fact that I looked like a pompous girl walking around with a bottle of water in my hand while others were dying out of thirst. It's difficult to say right now. Of course, I gave the boy my water, but the image of him standing in front of me and looking at my bottle stayed with me for a very long time. Things I saw there—the way people live, the way they believe, and how they attempt to survive every day—truly changed my attitude toward life and the poor."

"I cannot tell how happy I am to hear that, my dear," said Russell, smiling at his fiancée with love and sensitiveness.

"That's how I felt when you told me about your brother, Russell. Sometimes it's very easy and comfortable for us to create an attitude basing our judgment on what we think we see and hear. The whole different matter, however, is when we try to step in one's shoes and try to see the world through their eyes."

"Do not try to justify him, Ruth. If you saw what I see when I look at him, you'd be horrified, my love."

"Maybe I would, by no means do I try to justify him. I believe you, and I sure understand your position. However, I'm also not saying that I justify you. You see, what I've learned from this trip is that even when we think our judgment is right and deserving praise and acknowledgments, we should still withhold ourselves from condemning others because we can be judged likewise anytime. Even if you're right, do not judge, for with what judgment you judge, you shall be judged. Remember?"

"You misunderstand, Ruth," said Russell, sighing with disappointment. "I do not judge. I just sincerely want to help him! He is a lost soul. What kind of heartless person possessed by darkness should I be to condemn a soul which is utterly lost between this world and the one to come?"

"I know," she said amiably. "I just know for sure that if we are right in judging others, God will also be right in judging us, yet if we are merciful to others, God will also be merciful unto us."

"Strong words, my love."

"The words of truth, my dear," replied the girl, and that signified the end of their philosophical conversation. They both again smiled with relief, unwilling to carry on acting wise.

After about fifteen minutes of joyous discussion about the most amusing happenings that had occurred to them during the past nineteen days, Russell looked at his fiancée with eyes of hope, and, seeing the most precious and most beautiful flower of all sitting in front of him, he asked, "Do you remember our plans for near future, my love?"

"How could I forget," she replied, poetically emphasizing each word.

"I've been thinking about it a great deal, and now, after my mother has entered God's eternal city of perpetual beauty of love and incomputable glory, I reckon we shouldn't wait any longer."

"What do you propose?"

"Grow wings and fly away toward the land where sin and darkness are not meant to exist," answered Russell. "What would you say?"

"I'd say we could do it right now. We are bound by nothing. Why would we refuse to live being taken away by our wings to the land of perpetual and unconditional love."

"Those angelic wings would take us to a little village in Spain, where we would have a small hut and an orange farm. There we would not be disturbed by evil, or cold winters. We would live there happily, growing and selling oranges for a living."

"Sounds drastic, though, I must admit, rather romantic," she said, clearly dreaming of a picture Russell had put before their eyes.

"Is it too much to ask for? I don't seek millions or fame. All I want is a happy family life in a place where there is always sunny, cloudless sky above, and nothing but peace untouched by human hand in the air. What a wonderful life that would be."

"Starry sky at night and sun shining bright all day long," said Ruth as though continuing Russell's tale. "No fences, no neighbors discussing our lives, no troubles with listening music too loud, no boundaries withholding us from living a life we want—who would refuse to seek for such a small fragment of happiness."

"We've been dreaming about that small house in the depths of Spain for a few years now, Ruth," said Russell, slowly returning from his dreams.

"Indeed, we have. You really think now is the time we made it real?"

"As for me, I don't think I will be able to continue Mother's flower business anymore. Surely, it brings a lot of money, and we could run away and live somewhere without working for many years. Yet I think the time has come I started my own business. Besides, working there would constantly remind me of the days past, and I cannot say I want that. My mother is always in my heart, but living in nostalgia and sadness is not right."

"I'd be more than happy to join you in your dreams and goals, Russell. I am just a simple librarian, who sometimes helps the poor in other countries. I'm pretty sure I could be useful in Spain too."

"What do you say if we leave before Christmas?" Russell asked suddenly, bringing out an aura of intrigue and enthusiasm.

"This Christmas?" exclaimed Ruth in surprise. "I don't think this is a very good and circumspect idea, my love. There is a lot to be taken care of before we depart."

"We have money and willingness to do that. What is it that can stop us from being happy?"

"One small detail, we're not even married, Russell. We planned to marry here, but if we move to Spain. On the second thought, there seems to be nothing wrong with that, but it's just happening so fast."

"That's my fault. I am sorry," replied Russell, calming the high tides of his emotions. "If you want, we can get married here and then move to Spain. We have time, darling. I am sorry."

"I understand everything, Russell," she said, gently taking his hand. "We will buy that little house we've dreamed of for so long, and we will have an orange farm and live there happily ever after. I don't want you to worry or be daunted by anything! Both God and I are with you, and we shall stay by your side forevermore. Nothing will ever separate us."

"Not even death?" he asked suddenly in a serious voice tone, what slightly frightened and unpleasantly surprised the girl.

"Death?" she echoed barely with a laughter, which sound was mingled with fear. "Is that the worst that can happen? Isn't death just a door which leads us into a more beautiful and better life? Why should we be intimidated by it…because of how horribly the word sounds? My life, do not be so foolish!"

"You think I'm scared of death because I want to?"

"Why do you fear it, then?"

"I'm afraid of losing you," he replied, looking at her stunningly beautiful blue eyes. "I love you, Ruth, and what I wish the most is to be with you forever. And I don't mean until we turn 110 years old, but I want to be with you in God's kingdom as well, worshipping the Lord and holding you by the hand."

"Maybe I don't know much about this life, darling, but what I know for sure is that death will never be able to separate us or any other couple who are tied by love and God's blessing. Neither death nor kingdoms of hell are that strong to break the vows of love. I love you more than anything in this world, and what I want is to hold this hand of yours until the Lord calls us both by names and says it's time."

"I thank God each day for having you, for without your eyes and your soul abiding in my heart, life would be as meaningless as chasing after the wind."

In reply, she smiled at him and they kissed.

A couple of hours were spent chatting in the cafe and enjoying some very good coffee. They continued talking about anything whatever brought them joy and hope. Happy as they were in being together, they soon left into the cold air outside, having decided to go and visit Russell's parents. After buying two white candles and some matches, they went into the cemetery that was fifteen minutes away in the forest outside their little village. Both a little intimidated and tensed up by an uncomfortable feeling, they took each other by the hand and slowly, contemplating on what they would find and whether this was happening at all, approached the two graves of Deborah and Michael Prestons. Afterwards, they were left speechless. In silence, memories and gratitude for all those wonderful and vastly blessed days spent together with Mom and Dad, whose legacy was now engraved inside their names on the cold yet somewhat lively tombstones, and whose shades of light seemed to still be with them. Indeed it was so, both in their hearts and in God's kingdom.

20

The Christmas day was drawing nigh along with which the cheerfulness on the streets and in the little church of the village was increasing and enlightening the entire atmosphere and the air. It was a time full of blisses, grace, and anticipation of something glorious yet powerfully mysterious on that holy Christmas night. People were walking with smiles on their faces, everyone was greeting each other as brother and sister, and even the custom of continuous gossiping didn't seem so cruel and evil at that time of year. Surely, people were talking. There was a lot to discuss beginning with how others' houses were decorated and ending up with how big Christmas trees the villagers were buying. As always, the eyes which never slept or dared to blink were all over the village. They witnessed everything, and they talked of much more than that. It was a typical preparation for Christmas—every December was immersed into such atmosphere which, in its own way, was rather charming and appealing to everyone, even those who, by mere misfortune, were talked of the most. Moreover, louder than any vain, unending rumors, heavenly organ music and loud singing of choirs were often heard coming out of the church, reaching every single house and filling it with warmth and Christmas cheer.

The cold never left the village. It was probably the coldest winter ever. Cars and other vehicles often failed to start, and soon people even abandoned the idea of essaying. Though the village was rather small, it was a rare scene to see people walking. Every family had a car, except for a few old lonely men to whom walking was the best medicine prescribed by the pain in their backs or irritable mood. Now, as all cars were indefinitely parked in their usual places, all people, with red noses and cold running up and down their bodies, were on the streets, walking and collecting news about others on the way. Everyone was in search of presents, ideas for dishes, and products which were not to be found in a village like that. Therefore, many traveled to bigger cities and towns, looking for something to later boast about before neighbors and friends. Every woman wanted her Christmas table to be the biggest one, and every man wished to be the most generous as far as gifts were concerned. In such pace of challenges and friendly rivalry, the villagers were getting ready to celebrate Christmas with music and unity and joy. Perhaps as sad as it may sound to those having faith in something bigger, it was nevertheless the beauty of that time of the year. When everyone is in a hurry with big smiles on their faces, when believers are singing on the streets, when snowflakes are falling as leafs from an old tree, and when the holiness and silence of a sacred melody of glory is floating in the air, in the church, and in each house, as a boat of freedom, bringing good news to all—both old and big, both young and small.

The huge Christmas tree was already standing in the center of the village, although merely three weeks were left until the holy night. Balls of red and green were on the Christmas tree as well as the golden star on top of it. Daily, many came to admire it—children, believers, skeptics. They were all as if unconsciously united by the tree, standing around it in awe and fascination. Neither personal convictions nor deeds done in the fragile past seemed to make a difference between all those who came to stand and unnoticeably talk to the mysterious Christmas tree, whose legacy and inner voice were likely to be the composer behind each Christmas melody ever written.

Smokes were usually coming out of each chimney in the village as starry sky was wisely leading all God's children into the joy of celebration and the very glory of that holy night. Slowly but surely, people were feeling how the glorious and miraculous night was approaching—not by day, but already by hour. Among the silence and anticipation, notes and melodies of honor and magnificence were ringing inside the walls of the church each day. For many, even less faithful believers included, it was as a core of that bountiful in blessings and merriness time of the years. Church bells and choirs singing were in many eyes the very essence of why Christmas was so important. That aura which was unlike any other in the world was scattering away doubts, envy, anger, and even disbelief. For some, it was a time of salvation, while for others, simply a gift of inner peace.

One day, three weeks before Christmas, Russell came to his brother who was getting ready to go somewhere and said, "When will you come back?"

"I don't know, brother," replied Ludwig absently, putting on his jacket. "I'll be visiting many sick people today, and afterwards our entire prayer group is coming to the church. We'll pray there," he said quickly, tying a scarf around his neck. "Frankly, I've no idea when I will return. Why?"

"I just reckoned it would be nice if we had dinner together," answered Russell humbly. "Besides, we haven't played chess in years. We couldn't live without it as kids, remember?" he asked, smiling childishly as though begging his brother to play with him.

"I can't believe my ears, Russell!" Ludwig suddenly exclaimed, frowning with unhappiness. "What are you talking about? Do you know how many sick people out there need to be healed and how many millions in the world need to be saved? How can we even think of playing chess when people hunger and die in poverty without anyone to help them! The world needs to be saved, and we, as Christians of different sorts, cannot waste our time playing chess!" He laughed angrily.

"As far as I remember, we always used to play chess during cold winter evenings when we were kids. Mugs with hot cocoa would be in our hands, and our minds utterly immersed into the game. Have you forgotten those blessed days?"

"Which are over," he retorted coldly. "That was before I found Jesus, Russell. Once you're a Christian, everything changes, and things like playing chess become as meaningless and useless as dust on that cupboard over there," he said, pointing at the cupboard. "Now we—Catholics and Christians alike—are on a mission, and we're expected to convert, heal, and let everyone know about Jesus. Personally, I have a lot of work to do, and, as a matter of fact, I'd be grateful if you helped me at least a little bit," added Ludwig in a judgmental tone.

"Help you? Is one crazy fanatic in this house not enough?"

"And why am I a fanatic in your eyes? Is it because I selflessly help others without shame?"

"Oh, I apologize, holy one from heaven!" said Russell sarcastically, bowing down a little. "I forgot that you were a saint! How can I—a mere sinner and an evil tenant in this world of darkness—dare to question your duty and purpose. Shame on me!" he exclaimed gloriously.

"Enough of this silly act!" said Ludwig strictly.

"Oh, I wish it was an act," replied Russell, as if returning to his real self. After a brief pause, during which emotions were calmed and taken under control, he said, "After not seeing my brother for seven years, I'd be more than happy to spend some time with him."

"Then come with me and join our prayer group. Your prayers are more useful than your ability to play chess, brother."

"I do not acknowledge such a way of following Jesus, and I never will. Love for God is my religion, and not prayers or community where everyone listens to testimonies how each believer has found God. Okay, go now," he said with a grin. "I believe the world is waiting for you."

And the monk left, firmly shutting the door behind him.

Unaware of how to behave or in what subliminal way disguise his anger, Russell immediately decided to go to his parents for an advice. He somehow reckoned that speaking to his memories instilled on the tombstones of Deborah and Michael would be more beneficial than discussing religious matters with his brother whom, deep inside his heart, he truly loved. On his way to the cemetery, he bought a bottle of beer and put it into his coat pocket in order not to be seen carrying it in his hand. Had he been spotted drinking or at least holding the bottle as he walked, all the tongues and the entire village would've immediately livened up by suspicions and creative rumors about a lonely alcoholic, who was one of the most tragically mysterious people in their village, for he had neither friends nor family, nor was he even a part of their church community. Some would even add that all he had was booze. For gossips and lies to be created, not much, if any, information was required. Seeing a man with a bottle of beer in his hand would be more than enough for others to create even the unimaginable in order to be amused and entertained by the pleasure of sharing lies and falsehood with each other. It was their life—the life in a village, which Russell hoped to abandon soon.

His plans to leave the country and move to a little town in Spain with his fiancée were the only possible and real sources of light and hope, preventing him from stumbling and falling into despair. The vision of him and Ruth perambulating in an orange farm under a clear and sunny sky was continuously with him—in his dreams, hopes, and on his mind—as he was now slowly going to the cemetery. Living a happy life away from tongues and lies and sin was their only purpose and dream. All they wanted was to peacefully abide in a place which innately was outside of this world.

As he now entered the cold and ghostly cemetery, he found himself willing to shriek with pain, but all he did was take out his bottle of beer instead and opened it with a bottle opener that he also happened to have in his coat pocket. Sipping the beer, he, feeling the rhythm of his heartbeat, approached the tombstones of his parents and sat down on the snow, unable to feel any kind of cold at the moment. The picture of the tombstones with names and dates engraved on them was overcoming any kind of frost, fear, or horror whatsoever. Tears of longing were dropping down as he couldn't make himself mutter at least a word. It was more than complicated and much more than impossible. Memories passing through his mind were merciless and cruel, reminding him of what would never be returned. Being aware that his mother and father were together, enjoying the beauty and eternity in God's eternal kingdom, didn't make him feel better, though it did instill a sense of peace in his tumultuous heart. After the bottle was empty, he put it aside, kneeled before the tombstones and said, "If only you knew how much I miss you. If only you could feel how much my heart is hurting. I could die at this very moment just to embrace you and rest my head on your shoulders. Mother, you know that family for me is the most important and valuable thing in the world. I don't need education or riches of this world. I refuse to be wise or deeply religious. All I want is to have something I apparently do not have—a family. Ruth is my fiancée, and I have a feeling that we will live a very beautiful life together, but what I am speaking of is this present moment. I am alone in my house with nothing but memories and photographs, reminding me of how happy I once was. The only place where I meet you is my dreams, but even those are limited; I wake up and wonder which of the worlds is more real.

"I wish you gave an advice how to put up with Ludwig and his fanaticism. I am sure you can see what's happening in our lives and how we communicate. I know it doesn't bring you honor or happiness, but there is little I can do! He is completely possessed by his religion and foolish convictions which lead him to absolute spiritual destruction. You taught me, Mother, that this life is a gift, and we must enjoy and be thankful for every second of it. Why, then, doesn't he understand and admit that? You taught both of us, and we were guided by the same hand and protected under the same wing, weren't we? What's happening to him, Mother? Why did you let him go to the monastery and abandon us? I apologize," he quickly added, bowing his head. "I do not blame you! I know you are very kind, Mother, and you wanted only the best for us. I just don't understand why all of this is happening to me. I thank God for my brother, but sometimes I feel like I don't have one." After a brief pause, he continued, "Anyway, Christmas is drawing nigh, Mother. This will be the first Christmas when you are not with me." He burst into tears and said in a bitter voice, "I just want you to be with me, Mother! I don't want Christmas if you're not with me. I'd rather die and join you in God's kingdom than be here and suffer all this irrevocable pain which has no delineation. Take me with you, Mother. I can't stand this torment in my heart any longer." Afterwards, Russell sighed hopelessly and thought of his reasons to be strong and alive. Ruth was the only figure to appear in his mind, and that was enough for him to wipe his tears and say, "That's all I have. Ruth is the love of my life, and all I wish is to be with her and enjoy this life the way you taught me, Mother. I will not be defeated by sadness because there is none. I'm not sad. Quite the contrary, I am happy because I know you are eternally saved and are now probably standing next to God and looking at me from above. These tears of mine are just the consequence of how much my heart is hurting at the moment. I want you to know that I love you both, and that I will never forget you."

Then Russell stood up, kissed both tombstones, and left, taking the empty bottle with him.

21

Leaving the cemetery, Russell threw the empty bottle of beer into a large pile of snow and stopped for a minute, wishing nothing and having not a thought in his lonesome mind. He was standing right in front of a solitary road called Twenty-five, whose title was as queer as its destinations to either side. Whence the road had got the name, only those forever abiding in the cemetery behind Russell could tell for sure. What now mattered more than history or time was that the road Twenty-five could lead Russell back home, and that's where he wanted to be— inside the coziness and warmth of his own home, where aura of the past was ever present, not allowing him to forget things he never wished to recall again.

As he turned to the right and was about to finally leave, he noticed something he didn't notice a second ago while passing by it. There was a picture which managed to draw his attention without producing a sound or a sign of a desperate plea. Along with sudden attention, the picture also brought out a sense of mercy and compassion inside poor Russell's heart. He was ready to cry and do anything he could for the sake of a beggar without a scarf which was the main character in the picture he saw. There was a middle-aged man sitting on a snow with a paper cup next to his legs, mutely asking visitors to donate at least a coin. It was freezing that day, and seeing a beggar sitting on the snow with a poor-looking jacket and some cotton pants on him was indeed a painful sight to see. The hopeless man looked as if any kind of light in the world had been distinguished, as though there was no hope to guide the people of the earth. His eyes were sad and his humbleness encouraged Russell to forget his dreams of a warm country and an orange farm somewhere where not a shade of darkness could reach him.

Slowly, in order not to scare the defenseless man, Russell approached him, and, surprisingly even to the beggar, sat beside him on the cold snow, feeling how his entire body was being enveloped in unimaginable and certainly unholy frost, which was as far away from heaven and light as any sin originating from envy. Nevertheless, forgetting his pride and abandoning his ego, Russell joined the beggar, independently sitting next to him, with not a care in the world troubling his free soul. The poor man knew not how to properly react; all he did was glance at the stranger once. Tossed between thoughts of fear and doubts of unknown, the beggar resolved to keep sitting in the same silence and peace, hoping that the man would leave soon. Not once was he frightened and oppressed by local vandals and irresponsible teenagers, who were always greatly amused and pleased with the fact that a hopeless person on a street was being ridiculed and mocked. After such fiendish moments, the poor man started to distrust anyone at all— all he wished was just a glimpse of mercy disguised in an act of a coin being thrown into his paper cup. That was everything he needed from the world which was nothing but cruel and cold as that unusual December day in the eyes of the poor man, who now was not as lonely as usual.

"Do you believe in brotherhood, my friend," Russell asked suddenly, looking at the road with a rather odd name. "Please, tell me."

Surprised, to say the least, the beggar turned to Russell, looked at him ghastly and said, "I do."

"Why?" Russell asked quickly again.

"Because I think it exists," replied the beggar with a silent voice that was brimful of pain and scars left on his soul by the hand of the past.

"Good for you, dear saint," said Russell calmly with a sigh, raising his eyes up to the sky. "I have a brother who is a monk. He has a lot of spiritual brothers, and I am the last one on his list of the most beloved ones. I love him more than I love myself. Why don't I get the same in return? Why do hypocrites likes his fellow monks are more dear to him than I?" After a pause, he turned to the beggar and, with a smile of sorrow, said, "You probably have no idea what I am talking about, do you? I understand. Would you like me to give you some money?"

Slightly frightened, the poor man nodded.

"Okay," continued Russell enthusiastically. "I will give you some money, but first I need you to do me a favor. I want you to come with me now. Are you free at the moment?"

"I am, sir," replied the beggar. "But where are we going?"

"Nowhere if you continue calling me sir," retorted Russell. "My name is Russell Preston."

"I'm Ivan," said the man, shaking Russell's hand.

"Are you Russian?"

"I was born in Russia, but I lived here my entire life."

"I see. Fine, then let's move on for the weather is hellishly cold today!"

They did move on, as fast as they could in order to run away from the stingy frost which was as if tearing their faces and entire bodies apart. When they came to Russell's house, the beggar was told to make himself at home and feel no discomfort whatsoever.

"I want you to take a shower, Ivan, and then I will give you some nice warm clothes. I hope you don't mind me telling you what to do," he added, smiling with shyness.

"Why are you helping me, good man?" asked Ivan humbly, standing by the closed front door and fearing to step any farther.

"Because I have no one to share my dinner with, brother," said Russell, and afterwards told his guest to waste no time and have a shower. He showed him the bathroom and gave some shampoo, shower gel, toothpaste along with a toothbrush, and many other hygiene products such as ear cleaners and little scissors for his nail. Acting like a real brother, the stranger's thoughtfulness and kindness were as incomprehensible and hardly believable as the entire fact itself. One minute, the beggar was dying out of cold next to the cemetery, and the other, he was taking a shower in a very nice house, where already hot dinner was waiting for him in the kitchen. Russell had brought him a couple of warm sweaters, brand-new jeans, a couple of T-shirts, and a pair of warm and very expensive boots.

Since this wasn't the first time Russell helped a man on the street, he didn't feel any discomfort or doubts about what he was doing or whether it was safe. Rather, he was happy and joyous, for helping his brothers and sisters lost in poverty was nothing but a gift itself for him. At the moment, he was sitting in the kitchen with warm pasta dish heated in a microwave oven on the table and waiting for Ivan to come and join him. The beggar, dressed in new clothes that fitted him perfectly came about ten minutes later. That was when Russell found himself forced to heat the dish one more time, but it seemed to cause no inconvenience to him whatsoever.

Ivan's long hair were still a little wet and his face had been shaved. In fact, not once, for the last five years, had he felt so clean, and at the moment, he couldn't find proper words to thank Russell for his strange and utterly unusual and unseen generosity. He humbly went into the kitchen and knew not how to behave. He was treated like a brother, although he was but a stranger in that house.

"Ivan! Come in!" exclaimed Russell, approaching his microwave oven to heat up the pasta dish one more time. "How was the shower?"

"I doubt if I have ever been so clean," said Ivan, overfilled with euphoria and gratitude. "I thank you, good man, for your kindness. If only I could ever repay you somehow!"

"You keep talking like that and I shall ask you to leave at once!"

"My apologies, sir. I didn't mean to offend you," said Ivan, slightly intimidated. Standing as if rooted at the doorstep, he was afraid to move or go any farther.

"You didn't, brother. Come in and sit down! Make yourself at home!" said Russell cheerfully, turning on the radio. "I love listening to good music while making dinner. What kind of music do you prefer, Ivan?" he asked, searching for the right station.

"I always liked country music," Ivan modestly replied, slowly sitting on a chair at the table.

"You have good taste, brother. I like it too. Oh, here it is," he suddenly said, having found the right station. It played country music and that immediately brought a lot of positiveness into the air.

After a couple of brief minutes, Russell took the dish out of the microwave oven and brought it onto the table. "Please enjoy, dear fellow. Here are various spices and souses," he said, pointing at various bottles on the table. Then he brought also two bottles of soft drinks and five different juices on the table. "Please feel free to eat as much as you want!" he added and joined the poor man at the table.

Not being scared anymore, the man humbly took a knife and a fork, looked at Russell, and said, "Thank you, brother. I've never met a saint like you."

"Nonsense! Firstly, I'm not a saint, and secondly, dig in while it's hot!"

Both immeasurably hungry, they ate not saying a word, being surrounded by nothing but warmth and country music melodies, which were as wings of angels blessing the dinnertime and their new friendship. After they finished eating, Russell brought onto the table various donuts and chocolate, all of which was gone in just five minutes or less. They ate for about an hour until Ivan finally said, "I'm afraid I am full, brother. I cannot tell how grateful I am."

"Please don't be," said Russell, taking the dirty dishes from off the table. Then he made some coffee and brought two packs of marshmallows. "Let's just warm ourselves with some hot coffee, shall we?"

"I don't mind," said Ivan in reply, feeling happy and grateful. When coffee was ready and they were again sitting at the table in silence, enjoying both the food and the music, Ivan asked, "Do you live alone, Russell?"

"Both yes and no. My brother, the monk I told you about, is staying here with me for a while. I used to live here with my mother, but she passed away."

"I'm sorry." After a thoughtful pause, he said, "Are you married?"

"Not yet. My fiancée and I are still not sure whether it's a good idea to get married here, surrounded by every eye in the village. If you lived here, you must know that whatever happens in secret here is known to all in a matter of an hour. Now, the least what I want is attention. I've attracted enough of it already. My brother, who has come back home because of mother, is probably telling everyone about how evil and sinful I am. My private life is a public advertisement for everyone, thanks to his holy purposes. He left for the monastery seven years ago, and the only place where I could meet him were my dreams. Tell me, what kind of brother would abandon and forget his family in order to pursue religious satisfaction and imaginative peace? Moreover, now, when he's returned and can be with his only brother in this difficult time after our mother's death, he prefers to spend his time with his religious community and devout his entire time to prayers and helping others. Would you do that to your brother?"

"I don't think I would. Besides, I have five of them," replied the man coldly.

"Excuse me? You have five brothers? That's amazing!" exclaimed Russell cheerfully. "You must be a happy man, Ivan."

"Indeed. I once was a happy person. That was thirty years ago when I was nine. Back then, our huge family lacked nothing but eternity, and it sometimes occurred to me that we even had that. We were rich and we lived in a very big house which is no more. Our parents took very good care of us, and we were raised as one brotherly army, always ready to defend the weak and sacrifice ourselves for the sake of each other. We were as one fist able to break any concrete wall. I am not well educated, so I cannot find any more words to describe how strong we were together. My apologies, sir.

"However, a year later, when I turned ten—besides, I must note that I was the youngest child in our family—our parents died. Whether it was a murder or a simple accident, I cannot tell. I felt like I had been struck by a lightning. I was still breathing, but life and happiness were not in my heart anymore. It was beating, but without a rhythm. After that, my brothers started taking care of me. They paid for my school and later they found me a job. I was happy about it, although I didn't live the life I always wanted. I never wanted to be taken care of, and I never asked for help. For as long as I can recall, I always wanted to achieve things myself, not being supported by others."

"So how did you end up sitting next to the cemetery on a cold winter afternoon?" said Russell impatiently.

"I never drank alcohol and I never did drugs if that's what you imply, good man," answered Ivan with a smile. "My brothers told me that I could earn a living myself now, while they left the country and started studying and working abroad. I was left alone here with nothing but hope in my young mind. For many years, I worked honestly until one beautiful August day, I was fired. I never got married, and I do not have kids. All I had until that cruel moment was my work. Working twelve hours a day was the best salvation I could have. I was happy living such a life, and it seemed I didn't need anything else. Unable to find a job, I started sitting next to the church on Sundays and by the cemetery on weekdays, asking people to give me some money. I've been living like that for over six years now, and I don't regret it. I've had a lot of opportunities to work, but I always refused, preferring to rely on strangers' kindness only. I find such a way of life attractive, although I don't deny that I don't wait for the hour of my death."

"Why didn't you go and study like your brothers?"

"I didn't have any money."

"But you were young. You could work hard and pay for your studies."

"What for? So that I could achieve something temporal? I'm not saying I didn't work at all. Sometimes, I shoveled the snow, and during summers, I washed cars. I was satisfied with my miserable life, and I cannot tell I sought something more. I live in a small room where I sleep with cockroaches and rats, but I don't regret it. That's fine with me. I don't regret not having earned millions or not having bought a nice house out of town. Probably the only thing I regret is that I am left alone. I am to blame of course, but the fact greatly saddens my heart. Yet, as far as brotherhood is concerned, I'd like to give you an advice. Do not seek for brotherhood in others, build your own life, and forget about things which do not exist. Being a brother to others is more important than having thousands of brothers and sisters, who can turn their back on you any minute, especially when you least expect it. Surely, my brothers always write letters to me, asking how I am. They'd call me each day, I am sure, but I don't have a telephone. They occasionally ask if I need any help or money, to which I always answer that I am wealthy, healthy, and happy. Brotherhood is important, Russell, but I'm afraid it's a fading matter."

"I don't think you are right, Ivan. It's not yet fading away in this world, although is as frail as Christianity nowadays."

"Maybe," nodded Ivan. "You helped me not knowing who I was or what I believed in. Your kindness does not depend on others, which I find sacred and incredibly rare. That is what I call brotherhood—when love for people does not depend on them." After a short pause, Ivan looked at Russell and said, "By the way, I think I've heard of your brother. Is his name Ludwig?"

"Yes."

"I see. Many people that I know talk about him. They say he's a saint."

"To them, he is."

"And to you?"

"Sometimes, I can hardly call him my brother. Maybe he is a saint. He prays and fasts a lot. If these aspects is what forms an idol of a saint, then my brother is what the villagers think he is. For me, he is nothing but a hypocrite which is ready to sell even his own soul to be glorified and treated like a chosen one, like a redeemer. I cannot stand people like him because such hypocrisy is what draws people away from true Christianity."

"I assume you are a Christian."

"I am. And do you believe in God?"

"I don't know. Would that change something?"

"If you believe, then it would."

"I will try, then. Is Christianity what made you help me, Russell?"

"Not Christianity, but Jesus Christ. Christianity is just a word which tells that one follows Jesus and loves the way he did."

"Thank you, brother, for helping me. Thank you for your honesty and this time," said Ivan and looked at his empty cup where only dark marks of coffee were left. "I think I better go now. Is there anything I could do to somehow repay you?"

"I asked you to follow me not to receive anything in return. Stop even thinking of it." After a moment, he added rather humbly, "I'd be really happy if you stayed a little more. Do you play chess?"

"I do!" answered Ivan joyfully. "My brothers taught me when I was little."

"I have no one to play chess with, Ivan. Would you be so kind and take the place of my opponent?" asked Russell modestly as if beseeching Ivan to stay.

"I'd be more than happy to, brother," said Ivan in reply.

"Wonderful! Then I'll make some more coffee and then we'll start."

After a while, the fireplace was full of light and warmth, and hot coffee was on the table next to a huge wooden chess board. As both players sat down to play, Ivan, before making his first move, looked at Russell and said, "You know, our entire village is calling your brother a saint, but I think a real saint is sitting in front of me. Don't ever doubt it, brother."

"I'm not a saint, Ivan. I am far from holiness. Full of sins and anger, I kneel before Jesus's feet every day and ask for forgiveness. I am nothing but a sinner, seeking to be redeemed."

"Look what you have done for me, isn't this enough? I am dressed in new clothes, I'm not hungry or thirsty anymore, and I've been shown that kindness is still wandering in this world. If you are not a saint, then I don't think this moment is real."

"I don't want to be a saint. I helped you not because I sought to prove my faith in God, but because you are my brother."

"Am I? Are you not mistaken?"

"My brother in God, and that is enough for me to help you."

"I thank you, brother. I don't think I deserve such generosity, but I am nevertheless grateful from the bottom of my heart. Never before have I met someone like you. In fact, I've never even heard of such believers in God. I know what I'm talking about. I sit next to the church door every Sunday, and, believe me, I'm not shown much kindness there. Sometimes, a couple of cents make me feel lucky. You are different kind of believer, aren't you? Besides, I don't think I've ever seen you in our church."

"You probably haven't. I don't go there."

"How then do you believe in God?"

"There is faith and love outside those walls," replied Russell, smiling. "Make your move, brother, and I will tell you all about my faith and love for God."

"A saint who doesn't go to church…that's interesting." Ivan giggled with vast curiosity shining in his eyes, pleading to be told more. Then he made his first move with a pawn and felt relaxed for the first time in many years. He was feeling as though at home, as happy and grateful as ever.

Slowly making their moves, talking and laughing, they finished the game in two hours. After that, they played one more time, drinking coffee, and eating some sweets. The brotherhood which had so suddenly and miraculously appeared between the two men with different beliefs and perspective on life was something both of them could sense in their hearts while sitting in front of each other. Unwillingly checking the opponent's king, Ivan, as their second game was approaching its end, glanced at Russell, who seemed to be utterly relaxed and immersed into the game, and said, "You know, I'm still thinking of what you told me about your brother. If you don't mind, Russell, I'd like to tell you that you should never feel alone. If you have no one to talk to or play chess with, you can always remember me, you know. Maybe I am not rich or well educated, but if you ever need help or anything, just know that you do have a brother."

"Yeah, I know, Ivan," said Russell, nodding.

Another hour later, when there was no one sitting at the chessboard anymore, Russell took a backpack and put there various clothes, food, drinks, and most importantly, money. The exact amount of it was unknown even to Russell, although he was sure that it would be enough for Ivan to stay satisfied and full at least for a couple of months. The poor man who was about to leave knew not how to thank, or whether to kiss Russell's feet or not. Surprisingly, this pure and true feeling of gratitude was not caused by what Russell put into the backpack, for he didn't see it. Ivan was simply grateful for his brother's selfless helping hand and wonderfully spent time in warmth and joy.

As they were standing at the doorstep, Russell handed Ivan the heavy backpack and said, "Take care of yourself, brother. I was very blessed to meet you today, and I hope we'll play some chess more often."

"I find no words to express how grateful I am, Russell. You were as if sent from heavens to help me."

"God be glorified, Ivan. To him is all the praise!"

He departed minutes later, and now Russell was again alone in his house.

While waiting for Ludwig to come back, he made himself some pancakes, lit up the fireplace again to keep the warmth alive, and turned on the television to have at least cartoons talk to him. Later, he took his guitar and played some Christmas melodies, although this time he wasn't in a mood to sing. The chessboard was ready to be used again, although an opponent was missing. There were also two mugs standing next to it, waiting to be filled with some hot chocolate. However, Ludwig didn't come back until almost midnight, all weary and slightly angry. As many times before, he found Russell sedately sleeping on the couch with television on and fireplace already fading away. Immeasurably irritated, he managed to take control of his fury and went upstairs into his room, where he would pray for about twenty minutes for his brother's lost and lazy soul.

22

Christmas joy and merry feelings were increasing and becoming bigger every day. Russell's house was already decorated, and the Christmas tree was already standing next to his fireplace—the only possible salvation during those cold winter evenings. However, while Russell was taking care of his house and the joy within, his brother was taking care of the villagers and their souls. Daily, he was walking from one house to the other, preaching and teaching everyone who was not arrogant enough to listen with attentiveness and understanding. Treated as a holy one from God in everywhere he went, Ludwig also prayed for the sick and oppressed, bringing light into every single heart—both believing and unfaithful, both weak and strong. Many were standing in the lines to hear his stories about a monk's life, about true religion and essence of Christmas time. Many believed and certainly all who heard him were astonished at his preaching. Most people invited him for dinner, while others were willing to pay him to just come and tell them more about God and real Catholic life. He refused money each time he was offered some, which only increased others' worship and marvel.

"Truly, you are a saint, brother Ludwig!" some would often say after he prayed for certain people in need of spiritual or financial help.

"Stay with us forever, brother. Blessings of God are upon us as long as you are here!" others shouted with joy.

Parents began teaching their children in the same manner they had been instructed by Ludwig, telling them about a saint which protects them all with his prayers and holiness. Everyone in the village was talking about him and his sacred life, also inevitably muttering a few words about his evil brother.

"See how one brother grew up to be a saint, while the other takes care only for himself," people often said. Being spoken of with derision, however, Russell never responded, unceasingly dreaming only of his little orange farm and a happy life with Ruth.

One day, while Ludwig was visiting one poor family for dinner, a woman named Laura took the monk's hand and said, "Brother Ludwig, our family is in great need of your prayers. We don't have enough money to feed our children, and my husband and I barely eat ourselves. Pray for us, brother Ludwig. We need your help."

"Do not worry, Laura," replied the monk, gently putting his hand on her shoulder. "God will provide. Only pray and never doubt." Then he closed his eyes and prayed for them, asking God to grant them peace and everything they needed in their daily life. After his long prayer was finished, he again looked at Laura and said calmly, "God will never leave his children. He will give you everything you ask, only seek happiness in him first, sister."

"Your words are full of truth and light, brother Ludwig," she said. "You should speak on mountains so that thousands of children of God could hear you."

"I don't seek to be seen or heard by others, sister. I just want everyone to live holy lives, thus making God happy."

"People listen to you here, and they indeed exert themselves to try to live a godly life. You changed us all, brother Ludwig. For this, we shall be eternally grateful, for this village will never be the same."

"Thank you," he said, bowing down his head. "But thank God instead. He is the one to be glorified and worshipped and thanked."

"I think I'll speak to our priest and a few ladies to arrange an event for you in the church, brother Ludwig. We've already heard you preach, but I cannot say we don't want to hear more. It would be great if we could gather the entire village to hear your speech."

"I believe this is really necessary, sister," said Ludwig in reply. "People don't need to go anywhere to hear me. I come to people. All they need to do is listen and believe. Besides, speaking of your priest, I've heard your church doesn't have a permanent one. Many come and go, and no priest stays here for long, am I right?"

"It is as you say, brother Ludwig. It's been very difficult for us, but now we have a consolation—you."

"I'm afraid I will not be here for long. Just a few more weeks at most, Laura. I have to go back to the monastery for that's where I belong. However, I think I can help you with this problem. I can speak to my senior monks and several priests I know and see if they can help."

"Thank you, brother Ludwig. Thank you from the bottom of my heart!" said Laura, brimful of happiness and amazement. Looking at him as some divine revelation or an angel, she kissed his cold hand and then asked him to pray for her family some more.

A day later, Ludwig, as usual, came to the church where he met Monica, his faithful sister and supportive friend, and several other believers, among whom was Martha, the old lady which always dressed in her best clothes and was never modest as far as bracelets, rings, and necklaces were concerned. Her little shining purse was in her hand, and the scent of perfumes she had sprayed upon herself could reach even those standing many miles off. They were all waiting for Ludwig to come, for there was a serious matter to be discussed.

As Ludwig approached them, he hugged each of them tightly and said happily, "God bless you, my friends, my dear brothers and sisters! I'm so happy to see you all here."

"Thank you for coming, Ludwig," said Monica hastily, looking as joyful as always whenever Ludwig's face was before her eyes.

"Ludwig, my dear," said Martha, rubbing her cold hands, "let's go to the sacristy where we can talk."

And off they went.

The sacristy was a small room where all the sacred relics and various holy items were kept. It was probably the warmest corner in the church, which is why it was perfect for having an undisturbed discussion.

When they all sat down in a circle, Martha took off her pretty yellow scarf, put it on her knees along with her purse, and, leaning a little bit forward, said, "This morning, Ludwig, I was suggested to arrange an event dedicated only to you."

"Please, Martha, I'm not worthy the attention you give me," Ludwig interrupted her.

"I was not asking for your opinion, my dear," said the old lady politely. "Firstly, this is the most wonderful time of the years. Christmas is coming and the fact that you are with us makes it twice as precious and important. Now, what we want to do is give you a present, Ludwig—an evening when you could address the villagers and say anything you want. I believe you still have a lot to tell us about religion and following Jesus, don't you? As you told us before, you'll be leaving us soon, so I think this would be your farewell speech. People here need someone like you to save and guide them. Your words heal and enlighten, Ludwig. We need your instructions and opinion, which is why that evening would be of great importance to all of us."

"Besides," said a young man about twenty-five years old, sitting next to Monica, "I'm sure the entire village would come, for all adore you here, Ludwig. This'd be like a Christmas miracle to us all."

"Don't exaggerate, Vlad. I am just a human."

"So can we ask for that final speech, Ludwig?" continued Martha. "This would mean a lot to us. Agree, my boy, for this may change the hearts of these people."

"I truly have much to share, brothers and sisters," said the monk. "And I'd lie if I said that I don't want this."

"It's decided then!" exclaimed Monica cheerfully. "We'll begin arranging it! When is it more comfortable for you, brother Ludwig?"

"Anytime is great," he replied. "Whenever you tell me, I'll be here."

"I assume the entire village will come. Will you tell your brother?"

"I must. He's just like us. The only difference is that his soul is lost," said the monk rather sadly and thoughtfully.

"And ours are saved?" asked Vlad.

"Only those who believe are saved."

"Isn't there anything we can do for him?" inquired Monica worriedly.

"He watches cartoons, eats burgers during advent time, and occasionally drinks beer, is that an example of a holy life? Unfortunately, he doesn't care for others. Only for himself. Perhaps the only person he had ever taken care of was our mother, but after she entered the kingdom of God, I presume he reckons he doesn't have anyone to take care for anymore. He once mentioned that he has a girlfriend, but I doubt it. Who would ever want to marry a man like him?"

"He does have a girlfriend," interrupted Martha. "Her names is Ruth, and she lives not far from me. From what I've heard, I can tell for sure that she is also irresponsible and careless. She doesn't go to church and takes no part in our community life. I think they are a wonderful couple, Ludwig," she tittered.

"Even if it is as you say, I think that deep inside his heart, my brother is greatly unhappy. He helps no one, although he earns thousands every month by doing nothing but signing a few papers. Had I so much money, I'd doubtlessly give them all away to the poor. However, he prefers to spend them on modern technologies, tasty though unhealthy food, and devilish movies. He listens to rock music, and he reads literature which I am even intimidated to speak of. What else do you need to know about my lost brother's soul? Will he come to my evening? I'd probably die to see him sitting at least in the back of the church, but I know for certain that he will not show up. He'll probably watch an animated movie in the meantime."

"Have you tried to talk to him and get him back on the right path?" asked Vlad.

"Numerous times. I've prayed for him day and night, but perhaps my prayers were not coming from my heart, which is why they didn't work. My heart is too brimful of rancor and vexation to produce holy prayers for my brother. Even when I think of him, I feel disgrace and pique. My soul aches when I try to send some good thoughts into his mind. Our brotherly connection is strong, although, I believe, none of us wants to be a part of it. We'd rather prefer to fly in different skies without touching or seeing each other. If that was my will, I'd leave him at this same minute for I think this'd be for the better."

"But you will leave him, Ludwig. You will soon leave us all, won't you?"

"Regardless of whether I want this or not, our spirits are connected, and there is little, if anything, I can do about it. I do not know how to fix it. The least and the only thing that I can do is pray."

"We will pray for you, then," said Monica, taking him by the hand, "so you would have strength to pray for him. Our prayers will be united, and the power of it will increase."

"I thank you, my brothers and sisters. You are the only family I have left. I am in need of your prayers and spiritual support, and I thank you for being with me in this time of struggle."

"We shall never leave you, brother Ludwig. You are our saint, and we will always be by your side."

Then he hugged each of them, thanking for their kindness and brotherly love.

Thus it was decided. The evening which everyone awaited with anticipation was to take place one week until Christmas day—that miraculous moment filled with kindness, forgiveness, sense of salvation, and gifts of eternity. Everyone was quickly informed of the exact date and time of the event. It was one of those news that spread around and reached every ear in the village in no time. Being aware that the monk would leave soon after his final speech, the villagers, in secret, started preparing presents for him, willing to make that night as memorable as possible. Women started organizing their choir, which regrettably was a long forgotten subject in their church, in order to greet the monk with songs of glory and praise. Other believers commenced to decorate the church, bringing Christmas cheer and magic inside those grey walls. They put various joyful garlands around the white, frightful-looking pillars, and hung a green chaplet on the front door, letting everyone know that Christmas spirit was already reigning in their church.

Among their loud and noticeable preparations, barely a few managed to notice how quickly the long awaited evening had come. The time was overfilled with mystery, anxiety, and wonder. People were imbued with anticipation, to say the least. There were no thoughts of evil, no anger or jealousy between the villagers—that was at least for a while, in expectation of something none of them knew what. Some waited for a miracle to take place, others—to be healed, and some—to be given a gift to believe. On that glorious evening, the villagers were going into the church with different intentions and expectations, each dreaming of his own.

23

Hours before Ludwig left his house and was bound for the church, Russell, who was already aware of the big event which was to take place shortly, was in his room, wrapping presents for Ruth and Ludwig in papers of red and green colors. Silent Christmas music was on, echoing here and there as though slowly and thoughtfully perambulating from one corner of the room to the other. It brought some special cheerful atmosphere into the air, which Russell enjoyed with all his heart. This was his first Christmas without his mother, and although he wasn't entirely alone, he couldn't make himself admit that he was satisfied and happy living with his brother under one roof again. Wrapping the presents was the most entertaining part of the time before Christmas for him; that was when he thought of and reconsidered various matters numerous times, both remembering what could never be brought back and dreaming of what was probably never come to pass. At the moment, the only thing he found himself thinking of was what would take place in a few hours in their local church.

Images of what the entire event would look like and what his brother would say were constantly appearing in his mind, every now and then forcing him to make a few mistakes in the way he was wrapping the presents. After making a pause in order to stop thinking about the upcoming evening, Russell looked through the window on his right and saw a cold evening filled with freezing wind and a dark, cloudless sky. There was not even a star above them—only a lonely moon, hanging there in a mysterious and somewhat ghastly mode. Despite of how the world looked like through his window, Russell's thoughts were touched or disturbed neither by the frosty weather, nor by the intimidating night, whose inner voice, for an unknown reason, was as though shrieking with terror and instilled, irrevocable fright. Nevertheless, allowing the triumphant Christmas hymns coming from his radio to overcome the darkness of the night, Russell, still deeply staring through the window into the abyss of the distance, started slowly, somewhat fearing to face the consequences of the step, thinking of his mother, whose soul was now probably singing the endless songs of praise and glory along with other saints in heaven. Taken by sadness and regrets, he recalled all those Christmases spent with her, decorating Christmas trees, hiding presents from each other in different parts of the house before it was time to put them under the tree, and playing chess every evening of the advent time, drinking hot chocolate and listening to Christmas songs on the radio. Those were times of bliss and miracles, although Russell managed to fully comprehend it only now. Grief was attempting to enter his heart and there abide, but the cheerful memories of those good moments flashing before his eyes would not allow it to. Cheerfulness and grace of that past life was as great as biblical mountains and blessings of the Lord. He could only be grateful for all those past Christmases, looking forward to those still to come.

Minutes later, when he returned to wrapping the presents and again started hearing the continuous Christmas music, a knock at the closed door disturbed his moment of reverie and pleasant nostalgia. He quickly took a blanket and covered all the presents with it. Not saying a word, he approached the door and opened it just a little bit.

"I'm sorry, Ludwig, but I am a little bit busy at the moment. Could you wait for me downstairs? I'll be there in a minute."

"Actually, that's not necessary. I just came to say that I am leaving now," said the monk, looking serious and focused.

"Oh, right, the big event," commented Russell with a grin. "Well, good luck to you today. I wish you many applause and praises."

"As a matter of fact, I'd like you to come with me," he said as if feeling guilty. "This evening would mean much more to me if you were there."

"What for? To listen to how educated and wise you are? I know that, and I don't need any proof," he said, opening the door a little bit more, remembering that all the presents on his bed were safely covered with a blanket. "Actually, I know you so well that I could ever dare to foresee every single word you will say standing before all the believers of the village."

"I know that deep inside your heart, you are a good man, Russell. Please, do not be angry with your brother, even if there is a cause. If I did something wrong in your eyes, I apologize and ask for your forgiveness," he said sincerely, bowing down his head. "I never meant to hurt you in any way. You are my brother, Russell, and I love you with all my heart."

Touched by the unexpected speech, Russell sighed with relief and opened the door completely to approach his brother and hug him.

"Thank you," said Russell, resting his chin on Ludwig's shoulder. "I forgive you, brother."

"You can't imagine how much that means to me."

"Will you forgive me?"

"I'm afraid I won't. Forgive, and you shall be forgiven, remember?"

At this, the brothers chuckled a little, unwilling to let each other go. This was a moment of grace for both of them, which needed no philosophies about life or formulations of modern religions. Their brotherly love was their religion at the moment, and not a term, not a theory in the world could prove it wrong.

"Will you come with me?" asked Ludwig one more time, after they let each other go. "Allow me to believe in God in my own way, brother. I have no willingness whatsoever to go to that church. I wish all the best for you today, and maybe after you return, we could play some chess?"

"I'd be happy to, Russell," said the monk, smiling. "I'll try to get back as quickly as possible."

"I'll be here waiting with the chessboard ready and some nice, uplifting music on."

"God bless you, brother," said Ludwig, and was off.

Ten minutes later, assuming that his brother had already come to the church, Russell, wearing only a white T-shirt, quickly took his black coat, a very big scarf to hide his face with, and a black winter hat. The way he chose his clothes was based entirely on a belief that the more modest he appeared, the less attention he would attract. Dressed all in black, he was bound for the church, driven by pure curiosity and desire to hear his brother's last speech addressed to the villagers before he was indefinitely gone again.

This was probably the coldest evening of all, and wearing just a T-shirt and a coat on top of it was not the wisest of ideas. However, fearing to be late, Russell resolved not to get back home. Putting his arms into his coat pocket and hiding his face under the thick scarf, he was quickly running toward the church, thinking of ways how to stay unnoticed and sneak into the church without attracting much attention. He didn't want to be seen either by his brother or by anyone else. He was even afraid to imagine what would be if he was accidentally recognized by some watchful old lady, who was familiar with every face in the village. In fact, Russell was daunted by all Catholics in general—their way of living and believing was horrifying in his eyes, sometimes causing nightmares to visit him at nights.

The unendurable cold mercilessly piercing his body and making it hurt was forcing Russell to run faster. The streets were already empty, and not a light in any window was seen; everybody was in the church, which made Russell think that he might be late. The streets covered with snow and cold were as though deserted, for not a soul was there and not a single sound, save that of the wind's, was heard. Russell's ears were reached by some frail noises only when he saw the church standing in the distance. That was also the only source of light in the village on that frosty evening. The closer he came, the clearer he saw dozens of people trying to get inside; some were shouting, a few babies were crying, while several young people with green bands around their arms were strenuously trying to keep everything in order and get everyone a seat. At first, the church seemed too small for everyone to get in, but five or six minutes later, the door was shut, and not a soul was left outside. Russell was also among those who now were desperately trying to find a seat.

"We should've come three hours prior to the beginning!" he heard some woman shout on her husband. "That way we would've found a seat!"

"Stop pushing, young men!" others would yell.

"People, you're in the church. Be quiet please," said one man with a green band around his arm, who was probably one of those responsible for the order of the event.

Seeing all the hustle and chaos made Russell feel uncomfortable and frightened; however, he was at least glad that the believers were so busy finding a vacant seat that no one noticed his presence. His winter hat was still on him as well as his scarf, which was concealing his face up to his eyes. Becoming aware that there were no chances for him to be recognized or noticed, he quickly managed to find an empty spot under the shadow of a tall white pillar decorated with a few red garlands. Breaking his way through the crowd, he sat there and sighed with relief and satisfaction, for he got what he wanted—to be present and invisible at the same time.

Everything settled down in merely twenty minutes, although sounds and annoying noises of murmuring and hustle did not cease for a second. Unable to find a place to sit down, more than ten people were left standing in the back of the church, leaning against either the walls or the pillars. People's faces and their behavior was what Russell eyed with curiosity and wonder; it was greatly queer for him to be present among those in whose eyes he was nothing but an evil spirit, unfit for their sacred community and religion. Seeing happiness in the believers' faces, he tried to understand the way they saw Ludwig and his holiness; summing up all his creativity and imagination, Russell attempted to comprehend what people adored his brother for, and what exactly was it that made others consider him to be a saint. It was a matter without an answer or an end—the cause of all the worship and adoration remained an enigma to him.

About five minutes later, Ludwig walked in and took his place where priests usually preached the sermons. Correcting the microphone a little bit, he looked at the audience, which now was drowning in complete silence and stillness and said, "Good evening, brothers and sisters. I see some of you are standing there in the back. Can someone please bring the chairs from the sacristy and other rooms?" As the four men with the green bands around their arms left to take the chairs, he quickly added, "Bring as many as you can find, my friends. Okay, we shall wait a couple more minutes and then we'll start. Now I'd like to use this moment and thank you all for coming. This means a great deal to me, and I cannot even express how happy and grateful I am seeing you all here." A few brief minutes later, the chairs were brought and now every single believer was comfortably sitting. "Thank you, dear brothers," said Ludwig, grinning. Then he sighed and continued, "Before I begin telling you all about the matters which are most important in our Catholic lives, I'd like to devout a couple of minutes to prayer." Then he bowed down his head and most of the believers did the same. At the meantime, Russell preferred to watch everything with diligence and attentiveness, memorizing anything he could lay his eyes on. "Dear God, Creator of heaven and earth," Ludwig began, "we thank you for this moment, for your grace, blessings, and mercy. I thank you for bringing all these children of yours to this church this evening. May they experience your love and tenderness, and may their faith be strengthened. Mary, Mother of Jesus, protect us and guide us with your loving hand. We beseech you to never leave us, for we are your children and we trust in you." Then he opened his eyes and looked at the believers, whose eyes were glittering with anticipation and pleas to be to spoken to.

Russell, who was happy knowing that his presence there was known only to him, was looking at his brother without even blinking and barely breathing, also anxiously waiting for him to start speaking. Unlike the believers, perhaps it wasn't the words of prophecies or a speech of divine revelations that he was expecting; Russell firmly believed that his own character and spirit was doubtlessly supposed to be included in Ludwig's speech, and that was what he reckoned to hear.

"If I may," began Ludwig in a serious tone, "I'd like to begin by telling you a story about two different men: a rich Catholic and a poor atheist. Once, a rich Catholic was walking down a street and noticed a poor man sitting on the ground begging for money. As an obedient servant of God, the Catholic took out his huge wallet, and, before giving the poor man a couple of cents, he asked, 'Do you believe in God?' The poor man said he didn't. 'That's why you are so poor,' said the Catholic. 'If you believed in God, you wouldn't be here sitting on the ground and begging for money, because everyone who believes in God is rich and happy, both in this life and in the one to come.' 'Tell me about this God, good man,' said the poor man in reply. Then, instead of giving him some worthless cents, the rich Catholic told him about God and Jesus and prayed for him. The poor man's soul was healed. That's what he needed the most, even though he didn't know that. Prayers, and not the money, is what people are in need of, brothers and sisters."

"Ludwig, what a clown you are," muttered Russell silently, almost laughing in his heart.

"The rich Catholic could've given him enough money to start his own business or live happily for many years, but instead he preferred to give him something what the world could not offer him. Forget things that are useless, brothers and sisters. Pay attention to the things that last forever, for this world is coming to its end, and soon there will be no more sadness, computers, or worthless money. All we, as believers, need to do is support each other with prayers, strengthen the weak with our faith, and enlighten the brokenhearted with our love. Sometimes, giving money is easy and comfortable to us, isn't it? However, it would be a lot better if we fed the souls, not the mouths, my friends.

"I must say that throughout this time since I came back, I've learned more than in many years of studies. I've seen things—outside this church, of course—which seriously tested both my faith and my firmness. At first, I was convinced that the way I understood religion and this life was right and leading to holiness and spiritual perfection. However, having met a brother whose stiff-necked convictions were literally leading him to spiritual death, I understood that my knowledge would not be enough. Until then, I thought that all I needed was peace in my heart and wisdom in my mind. I must I admit that I was wrong. The brother, whose selfishness and lies had closed his eyes and taken his soul into the abyss of darkness, unconsciously showed me that wisdom and understanding was not enough for salvation to take place. Regardless of how desperately I tried to preach to him, his soul and attitude would not change nor bend. He lived according to his own law and religion, unwilling to accept the truth. Such stubbornness and foolishness was something I had never seen before. It is then when I reckoned that mercy is better than knowledge, and the power of forgiveness exceeds that of wisdom's. I did something I want to strongly encourage each and every one of you to do not only daily, but hourly, brothers and sisters. Though I was offended and insulted not once, I fell in love with that poor brother of mine, for that's what Jesus would've done. Do not love only those who love you. We are true followers and believers only when we love, not seeking love in return. Along with love came forgiveness and final peace between us. Although I cannot change anyone's perspectives or beliefs, I still can spread love through my own actions of kindness and mercy. Touched by my love, this poor soul asked for forgiveness and I forgave him. Maybe his stubborn mind didn't change whatsoever, but I do believe that his soul was enlightened at least for a while.

"Moreover, I cannot say I could've endured all these difficult days without prayers. This is where we go back to the story about the Catholic and the poor atheist. A few words of a prayer said with the heart are more precious and valuable than four million euros, my friends. We can help the poor as much as we want, but if we do not feed their souls and refuse to sow a seed of Christianity in their hearts, then I must say our financial sacrifices are of absolutely no use. Maybe they bring some piteous happiness for a short while, but they have no eternal value whatsoever. The world is overfilled with money and generosity, but what it lacks is spiritual food which redeems a soul and grants it eternal joy.

"During my stay in here, I've also learned that community is more important than any kind of friendship or brotherhood in the world. It is like a family which entirely belongs to God Almighty, and is guided by the loving hand of Mary, Mother of Jesus. I think there is nothing better in the life of a religious person than when he comes to the church and is greeted like a brother, a friend, and a saint. This is a kind of feeling which only a community can bring. It is a sacred and greatly blessed gift, which, I dare to say, is one of the greatest of all."

"I can't believe my ears," muttered Russell again, shaking his head. His eyes were brimful of frightful astonishment and shades of hatred as his soul was shivering with displeasure and mutely yelling with tears.

"Some say," resumed Ludwig proudly, "that family is a bliss, and that real friendship is a gift from heaven. However, is not community both the family and the unity of friends and brothers? What else could we ask for, save the grace of being a part of such a family divine? Worldly brothers will betray you, and friends may turn away anytime, but those who share the bread of life with you will always be there to pray for you and not to let you stumble and fall. I look at you, dear brothers and sisters, and I thank God for this wonderful community which is full of unity and love. You, as one big family, need nothing more but each other: pray together, share the Eucharist, and do not despise those who are not given to understand what community is all about.

Remember that the devil is always at work, and the last thing he wants to see is people praying and being together. Some will not comprehend what it means. Lost in their selfishness and hypocrisy, they will continue to ferociously attack you, seeking only one thing—to destroy the unity of communities in the world. Stay strong, pray, and never doubt, my friends. The day will come when never again will we be attacked, mocked, beaten, or stoned. We must pass this age of darkness together, supporting each other by any means possible, in order to reach that heavenly place where we shall be united once more!" he shouted enthusiastically, what was followed by loud applause.

Unable to continue listening to his brother's speech, Russell stood up, and left the church as quickly as he could. He reckoned this was the best time for him to leave unnoticed, busy praising and applauding to Ludwig, none seemed to care about some man dressed in black, passing by with velocity. Even Ludwig didn't seem to notice. Russell was as a phantom, as a ghost—no one saw him, no one knew he had been there.

24

The weather was viciously cold, making Russell's entire body ache as he was quickly walking back home. Wearing only a T-shirt and a coat on top of it, he soon was unable to feel his arms, which had become as cold as ice. Hiding his face under the scarf was helpful only for a while until his lips and nostrils started hurting. His hands were in his coat pockets, although that too was of little use. His entire body was utterly imbued with the torturing frost, which managed to cool down even the fiery anger in his soul.

"Community, sure!" he muttered angrily. "What about family values, Ludwig? Have you forgotten all those wonderful Christmases spent with your family in warmth and love? Don't you feel ashamed before your mother in heaven? Community is your new family, eh? In that case, I give you my blessing—live happily with your new family, for I see I can find no place among your happy and highly blessed brotherhood of saints. Poor Ludwig, you've been offended by your evil brother so greatly that now you even had to complain about it before this entire village! Well done, dear saint, now everyone will know how unchristian and possessed by darkness your brother really is. At least now, people will have something to talk about until their tongues fall off. You think I care? I do not," he mumbled. "Live and believe the way you think is right, but I ask you just one thing—leave me alone, for I wish neither to see nor hear you. Be a saint, be anyone you want, but do not dare touch me with your holiness and perfection. Now, I reckon, you've achieved what you've always wanted—you are loved and glorified by all, dear monk. Now you are seen and heard, you live under a shadow no more. How does that feel, monk? Are you enjoying your minutes of fame?"

Most likely, his deep discussion with himself would've continued hadn't he been stopped for a second by an astounding view before him. Two little birds, sitting on an edge of a trash can, were calmly and thoughtfully staring at Russell talking to himself, not moving, not making a sound. The tiny birds made Russell's unending speech cease, though all they did was watch him with attentiveness and wonder. Taken by modest shame and an uncomfortable feeling, Russell, speechlessly this time, continued walking home, passing by the two little birds without looking at them. The birds left sitting in the same place, following Russell with their tiny eyes until he disappeared in the darkness and was seen no more.

The streets were deserted as before—not a shadow, not a light seemed to exist. There were no street lamps whatsoever. The village was too small to be noticed by the government and be taken care of. The only source of light that unbearably cold evening was the decorated Christmas tree, humbly standing next to the only supermarket in the village. Garlands and lamps were proudly shining on the rather poorly dressed Christmas tree, which apparently was also suffering from the surprises of the weather. The snow was innocently, depending entirely on the wind, lying on top of the tree's branches, bringing miraculous and entirely convivial look into the square. Hadn't it been for the weather, the atmosphere would've been entirely cheerful, filling the blessed time with louder celebrations and more joyous sounds of glorious music, and enlightening the sky with a greater amount of sacred stars than it was at the moment.

Although it was dark and not even the lands covered in snow were able to illuminate the village at least a little, Russell knew very well the path leading him to his house, where his consciousness and soul were already lighting up the fireplace and making some hot green tea. Irritated and angered by what he had seen and heard in the church, he exerted himself to try to forget and ignore all that, thinking only of the number of warm blankets he would wrap himself into as soon as he got back.

"I should've never come there," he murmured as his fast walking turned into running. "Warm blankets, five cups of hot green tea with lemon, fireplace, music," he said repeatedly. "Warm blankets, hot drinks, woolen clothes, fireplace, and nice music…" Then, as he realized, he was about ten minutes away from his doorstep, Russell saw something what didn't belong to the gloomy night. He managed to distinguish an obscure image, which looked more like a slightly moving silhouette of something what was not supposed to be there. Russell instantly stopped running and slowly walked toward the mysterious thing in the distance. It was lifelessly lying on the ground, and only when Russell approached it, he saw that it was a human. He blinked a couple of times to convince himself that that was truly a man in his late forties lying on the ground with nothing but a sweater and jeans on him. The unconscious man was barefoot, and for a second, it occurred to Russell that the poor man already might've been in some place else. Also greatly frightened, he, not wasting any time, kneeled down next to him and grabbed his wrist to see if there was anyone left to save. Feeling the pulse, Russell also felt the strong odor of alcohol coming from the poor man on the ground. His clothes and perhaps even the snow which he was lying on were saturated with the sharp smell of spirited drinks. This revealed the probable cause of why the man was unconscious, although reasons and explanation was what Russell sought for the least at the moment.

"Sir!" said Russell as loudly as he could, for speaking was also difficult in such a cold. His throat was as if seized by some invisible barbed wire, making it hardly possible to utter at least a shortest noun. "Speak to me, sir!" he said, shaking the man.

The wind was rising and the cold increased with every second. Seeing a barefoot man dressed only in a sweater and jeans almost made Russell lose his consciousness as well. Nevertheless, assuming he had to act fast since every second could be the poor man's last, he quickly took off his black coat and put it on the unconscious man, who fortunately happened to be twice smaller and lighter than Russell. Without long hesitations and considerations what to do, he took off his scarf, his winter hat, and also his shoes, and put it all on the lifeless-looking drunkard. Realizing that the church was too far away now, and not a soul was around them since everyone was in the holy place listening to Ludwig's preachings, Russell came to realize that he was the man's last and only hope. With nothing else but a T-shirt and jeans on him, he took the man, put him on his shoulder, and, feeling as his body was about to fall down any moment, continued walking home.

"Help!" he tried to shout as he walked in hope that someone would hear and come.

Walking on the snow, his white socks quickly got wet, but Russell couldn't feel that—his hands and feet were something he was able to control or feel no longer. The cold was so great that even dreams of hot coffee or warm woolen blankets weren't consoling enough anymore to fill his mind and frozen eyes. Neither his soul nor any part of his body seemed to contain life in it; he didn't even have strength to think how he was able to keep on walking.

"Hold on, brother," he said silently without moving his lips, which by that time were as blue as the sky on a sunny summer day. "Don't you dare to die, you hear me? God, give me strength. I love you, Lord. Give me strength." Perhaps at that moment, Russell would've said more, but there was not enough energy in him to do so.

Hoping to meet at least someone on his way home, Russell felt his body was becoming more lifeless with every step he took. No one was there to help him or call an ambulance—not a soul, not a sound, not a movement. Barely able to breathe, he didn't even feel how tears started uncontrollably rolling down his already frozen cheeks. Those weren't the tears of pain or sorrow; wind and the deathly cold were what caused those tears to start dropping down. Notwithstanding, feeling nothing, Russell continued walking further and beseeching God not to let him fall, for then he wasn't sure if he would be strong enough to stand back up. The fact that the drunkard was getting heavier with every step he took didn't seem to bother Russell, for he was tall and strong, used to carrying even heavier things.

After a couple of more minutes, he began to reckon that they would never reach the house. The road seemed to be as long and endless as none other in the world. Perhaps it would've been a great idea to enter any house he was passing by, but there were no lights in them, and despite how loudly Russell tried to cry for help, no one heard and no one came. Soon he started feeling how his legs commenced to bend at his knees, and at that moment, Russell realized that he would fall any instant now. His feet started slipping a little, and his lower back began to unendurably ache from the cold. Yet, supported by nothing but miracle only, he did not fall. An image, more precious and divine than any masterpiece of art, had suddenly appeared before his eyes. His little house was visible in the distance, and that was when his legs were given their strength back and possibilities of giving up and falling were now left behind. Russell would've shouted with joy, he would've cried out the words of gratitude toward the heavens, but he could not. Though his feet were moving forward, his spirit was fading and his eyes were slowly approaching their last blink. He knew not which breath would be his final, although now, when the house was just a few more minutes away in the distance, his fate did not concern him at all, for all he cared about was reaching the doorstep and finding enough strength to say his ultimate, conclusive thank you.

While moving toward the house, Russell's eyes were brimful of the only thing in the world which kept him alive and strong at the moment. Looking at his house in the distance, he saw a picture different from the surrounding places and the cruel reality in which both he and the unconscious drunkard on his shoulder were most likely eternally trapped in. This time, full of sorrow and regrets, Russell's eyes saw what at that moment was as far away from him as never before. It was an image full of hope, happiness, and eternity. An orange farm somewhere deep in sunny Spain with a little humble hut standing independently next to it were before Russell's eyes, which now wanted nothing but weep. Instead of the house which was as if coming closer with every struggling step he took, Russell saw himself plucking oranges from the trees and putting them into a basket; also, in the divine image, there was a woman playing with at least four children, having fun and modestly laughing. Inside that picture, hanging in the air before his eyes, there was also freedom and everlasting sense of happiness. No evil in the world could reach them there, no one could dare to influence their time or dictate their choices in faith and life. They all were like angels, enjoying every second of being together under the sun somewhere in the middle of an orange farm. Ruth's, his future wife's, smile and her beautiful eyes were encouraging his heart to carry on beating, and the laughter of all those children running in circles next to the field of dreams was the only thing moving his legs and giving him the strength not to stumble or fall down. Though barely paralyzed by the extreme cold, Russell, standing in the middle of that orange farm and hearing his family giggling and playing, could still feel the warmth of the sun and the freedom in the air. He could smell the oranges and touch the trees. He could also smile and unstoppably laugh.

However, the picture rapidly disappeared as he finally reached the front door of his house, which never before seemed so dear and precious. By the time he approached the doorstep, even the hellish pain in his entire body had ceased. There were as if no more lively places left in him, which is why even the ache had gone, having fulfilled its torturing purpose, its duty.

As happy as a child, he, still holding the unconscious drunkard, who was as if impregnated with the sharp odor of alcohol which Russell's frozen nose could sense no more, using his other hand, took the keys from his jeans pocket, and slowly, scarcely able to move at all, unlocked the door and stepped inside, leaving the door open behind him. Summoning his last sparkles of energy and strength, he walked into the sitting room, laid the drunkard on the sofa and thinking only of lighting up the fireplace. He approached it, took some matches which were on a log beside it, and, utterly seized by disability to move at least a finger, fell down on the ground, all shivering and hardly breathing. With his eyes closed, Russell kept lying by the empty fireplace both unwilling and unable to either go somewhere or do something worth taking a risk.

The fireplace was left as cold as the atmosphere of that dreadful evening, and nothing but the wind, entering the house through the open door, was able to make a noise among the dead silence in the air. The two bodies were left environed by darkness with no one in the world to warm them up or save them. The fireplace was cold as death, the matches lying next to Russell's body were of no use anymore, and hope had eventually, and most likely eternally, faded away.

25

Ludwig's loud and effective speech in the church lasted another hour after Russell had left unnoticed. A lot of applause and praises were generously granted to Ludwig as almost everyone in the church that evening was being influenced and deeply touched by his words of wisdom and love.

"Right now, for instance," said Ludwig as his glorious speech was supposed to approach its ending, "my dear brother Russell, whom I love with all my heart, is waiting for me to come back home as soon as possible. Do you want to know the reason, my friends? He wants to play chess with me." Instantly, echoes of laughter entered the air, as well as a few frail noises of murmurings. "This is no joke. The world is in need of God's Word, a helping hand, a loaf of bread, and salvation, but some, like my poor brother, don't seem to care. I'm sure that a warm fireplace, hot tea, nice music, and a ready chessboard are waiting for me at home—and who could ask for more on such a cold winter evening! But let me tell you something, right here, in this cold church, I am already at home, because I am with my brothers and sisters who are bold enough not to belong to this sinful world. We should never seek pleasures which this world is offering. Seek the kingdom of God first, for this is all we need! I want to encourage you all, brothers and sisters, instead of playing chess, watching a movie, or skiing, better help the poor, feed the hungry, and clothe the naked. This is the essence of Christianity—simple, inconvenient and true, leading us all to the heaven, where we shall be united once again forevermore."

"What a holy man you are!" some shouted from the back of the church.

"Holiness is exactly the thing that each and every one of us should also seek with patience and diligence," said Ludwig in reply, enjoying every single minute of the evening. "Who are we without holiness? How would we be able to live if purity and sainthood were absent in our easily influenceable lives? Could we be called Christians and followers of Jesus if we were not pursuing to be saints? I tell you, brothers and sisters, that holiness is the only thing which forces us to do good, to help others, and to sacrifice ourselves for the sake of strangers. Some of you may think that only those who love unconditionally can selflessly sacrifice their lives for others, but I tell you that holiness is not possible without love. Only saints' love does not depend

on others. If one doesn't love, one cannot be called a saint."
He chuckled. "Saints are not those who wear monk's apparel
or a cassock. Love and selflessly live for others, that's how
you will achieve sainthood and Christian perfection. You
don't need to travel across the world to find happiness and
holiness inside yourselves, my dear ones. Right here, in this
small village, do good deeds, pray without ceasing, and help
your neighbors at all times. Then you shall come to realize
that sainthood is not as far away from you as you may think.

"Now, allow me to thank you once more for your
generosity, kindness, and unity which are before my eyes
at this very moment. Love and faith abide among you, and
these are the most important gifts of all. This community
before which I stand is greatly blessed. Never doubt in each
other, unconditionally help your neighbors, and let love
keep reigning among you, my brothers and sisters!"

The speech was finally over, although the believers, both
rich and poor, both ill and healthy, were willing to hear a
little bit more. They were applauding loudly, but there they
were still feeling hungry.

"I want you to know that I love you, my dear ones,"
added Ludwig, returning to the microphone. "I am always
with you in prayers and thoughts!"

Afterwards, entirely surrounded by hustle, whispers, and
noises impossible to be recognized or named, most of the
Catholics, led by Martha—the old lady in charge of much as
far as the well-being of the community was concerned, went
into a room in the same building, where hot tea and snacks

were already waiting. It was warm in there. The cold was left outside, desperately knocking at the windows and thus occasionally reminding of itself. As those who wished to see and hear a little bit more (for couples with small children and many other believers who had to rush home, apologizing and expressing their gratitude for bringing peace and faith into their hearts, left soon after the speech was over) came in and rushed to take their seats on the chairs which were standing in no particular order, Ludwig entered the room, and closed the door behind him with a smile. That was the moment which gloriously announced that the main part of the evening's event was just about to begin.

With eyes hopefully and joyfully glowing, all the believers who had left wished to speak to the holy monk. They wanted to touch him, to hear him preach, and to never see him leave. As soon as he walked in, everyone stopped talking and looked at their own saint, expecting him to utter at least the most silent of consoling words.

"Dear Ludwig!" exclaimed Martha, approaching him with widely opened arms, hugging him tightly afterwards. "Make yourself at home, my child! You better drink some tea and have a snack, for a long night is ahead of us. We will not let you go until we all have a word with you!"

"I'm sorry, Martha, but I'm afraid I don't have much time," he said in a whisper, as the hustle in the room slowly increased.

"Nonsense!" she said loudly in reply. "Here, have some tea and eat some cookies!" She gave him a cup of hot green tea and a small plate of different tasty-looking biscuits and showed him a chair to sit on. Witnessing the immeasurable kindness in the old lady's face and her deeds, Ludwig could nothing but childishly obey, giving thanks in every step he took.

The monk was sitting in loneliness for not more than two seconds until a lady in her late fifties, whom he had never met before, came to him with happiness encompassing her entire being, took a seat right next to him, and, boldly stretching forth her hand, said, "Good evening, brother Ludwig. My name is Clara, and I just wanted to thank you for literally changing my life and saving my soul!"

"Hello, Clara," said Ludwig, at the moment lacking words to say anything more. "I'm very happy for you, but I am sure it is Jesus Christ who saved your soul, not me. To him alone be all the glory and praise."

"Of course!" said the woman emotionally, willing to hug him tightly and thus be blessed and eternally redeemed. "Your words are full of truth and power, brother Ludwig. Thank you for your love and holiness. It inspires us all to live in kindness and humbleness."

"I am just a human, Clara."

"But a holy human," she corrected. A minute later, she leaned toward him a little, and, in low voice tone, as if about to reveal the most mysterious secret of all, said, "Brother, I want to ask you a favor. I don't actually know how to put it in words." She was talking rather nervously, which made Ludwig assume that the matter was indeed serious. "I am desperate, brother," she continued in a whisper. "I need your prayers, because I don't know how to continue living this life."

"I listen to you, sister," said the monk, beginning to feel worried.

"I am single," she said, looking at him as if expecting him to fix her marital status. "My children live abroad, and I am all alone in this little village. I know your prayers reach God's ears because you're a true saint, bother, and that's why I want to ask you to pray for me and this little issue."

"I see," muttered Ludwig, hardly believing in what the whole intensity and suspense was about. "Well," he resumed, slightly relieved, "I will surely pray for you, sister. I reckon this is the best I can do." He shrugged with a forced smile, doubting whether there was anything else he could say in addition.

"Oh, that's more than enough for me, Ludwig!" exclaimed Clara joyfully in her normal tone. "I thank you from the bottom of my heart!"

"Don't worry, Clara," he said, putting his hand on her surprisingly firm shoulder. "God never wants anyone to be alone."

"I believe your words, but I am afraid, Ludwig," she confessed again anxiously, leaning closer to him. "I cannot live alone any longer!"

"I'll pray for you, Clara. Do not worry or doubt. I'm sure one day God will send you a perfect man who will love you more than anything in this big and crazy world."

"Thank you," she said and kissed his hand, what greatly displeased the meek and submissive monk.

"May the blessings of the Lord be upon you, sister."

Afterwards, she stood up and disappeared in the crowd of believers, whose presence in that large room was utterly based upon their willingness to speak to the monk and through his words be filled with love and sense of salvation. All were talking to each other, sharing different funny stories and enjoying the bliss of the heavenly Christmas time. Somewhere in the deepest corner of the place, there was even a radio turned on, from which silent Christmas melodies and carols were coming. The cheer of the moment could never be described. No words of poetry were rich enough in their essence to even come close to the blessedness and joy which reigned both in the atmosphere and in each believing soul in the room.

Once Clara left, Ludwig found himself having a minute of freedom since no one seemed to notice that he was sitting without attention and a companion. While no one was looking at him, and no one approaching, the happy monk let himself admire the community while he still had a minute to spare. He looked at the believers, who were talking and tittering unceasingly, and thought of what great gift and honor it was to be their brother—someone whom they loved, and whom the monk could unconditionally love in return. In his blue eyes, it was nothing but the very core of Christianity and life itself. He found brotherhood more important than faith, patience, or any spiritual virtue at all.

Slowly perambulating in the room, there was also a silhouette, a personage of Russell, every now and then glancing at Ludwig thus letting him know he's also present. The monk, still modestly sitting and waiting to be talked to, noticed the figure of his brother as soon as it appeared. It talked to no one, and it didn't do anything but slowly walk around with a smile. Ludwig wanted to come closer to him and ask what he was doing there, but he instantly reckoned that Russell's figure, which looked as real, would not be able to reply. *Were it real, it wouldn't be here*, Ludwig thought. Rather sadly, he blinked a couple of times and slightly shook his head to be able to see those illusions of his dreams no more. The figure was gone as well as any unwelcome thought about Russell and things which could never take place.

"Brother Ludwig," silently said a young woman, standing right next to the monk, who was deeply immersed into his thoughts and reveries and hadn't noticed how and exactly when the woman approached him. A little surprised, he, with a smile on his face, quickly stood up in front of her. "I'm sorry if I have disturbed you, brother," she continued. "I saw you were somewhere else."

"My apologizes, sister," he replied, bowing down his head a little. "My mind has a tendency to abandon my body."

"If this is a bad time, we can talk later," she said, feeling guilty and uncomfortable.

"By no means! This is a perfect time, sister! I apologize, but I don't seem to know your name," he said after a short pause.

"I'm Maria," said the young woman shyly. "My husband and I are not from here. My aunt who lives in this village invited us to come."

"I am very happy to see you here, Maria. It is an honor to me," he added.

"Please, brother Ludwig, do not say that. I've heard many things about you, and I cannot even believe I'm standing now in front of you!" said the young woman, excitedly looking at the monk as at some angel divine.

"Well, people are fond of exaggerating things," he said with a sigh. "Perhaps the life of village is not well known to you, is it?"

"Just a little," answered Maria. "I remember a few peculiar and unforgettable details of village life from when I was a child. I must say there is indeed beauty in all the gossips and eyes watching every move of yours." She chuckled modestly.

"You're not a stranger in these dangerous waters, are you?" asked Ludwig also with a titter.

"Although I live in a big city, where eternal turmoil and interminable chaos are so familiar and habitual that it is barely noticeable anymore, I still recall my childhood years spent in this village with nostalgia and gratitude to God. I do prefer peace, but I cannot help but miss this place of bliss."

"I agree with you, sister," he said, nodding with a smile. "There is something special in a village life, which is usually inhospitable to those who don't accept its customs and routine."

"That is true," she said, also smiling amiably. "Brother Ludwig, I must thank you for such a powerful and inspiring speech you gave us. My soul shivered when I heard your voice, and I could've never imagined that saints like you could be real."

"I'm just a man, Maria. None of us is a true saint, but that doesn't mean we shouldn't try to be one, right? Aim and pursuit for Christian perfection is what usually makes us saints, for such endeavors are often based upon love, kindness, and mercy."

"Your words are true and blessed, brother," she said, looking him deep in the eyes, attempting to make herself believe that this was just a man. "Will you be here tomorrow? I'd be glad to come and talk to you a little bit more."

"Yes, I will come here first thing in the morning."

"That is wonderful! I'm afraid I must go now for my husband is waiting for me outside, but I will come here tomorrow if you don't mind."

"And I'll be here waiting, then. May the blessings of the Lord be upon you, Maria!" he said, gently taking her hand. "I'll pray for you and your husband."

"We are thankful for that, brother Ludwig," she said, bowing down her head. "God bless you!"

After the young woman left, Ludwig was as though noticed again by the believers, which quickly approached him with requests to pray for them and to bless them. Spending there another hour, Ludwig did not leave until he talked to most of his brothers and sisters. When he reckoned it was time he went home, he apologized and said, "I will still be here a couple more days, and this is not the last time you see me, my friends. I must be off now, but I'll come back here tomorrow, and I hope to see you all after the morning mass."

"We cannot allow you to do that, my dear!" Martha said loudly, approaching him with a little box wrapped in green paper. It looked like a present, and somewhere deep inside him, Ludwig knew that it was for him. As silence filled the place, Martha looked around and continued in the same loud voice. "You, brother Ludwig, have given us what we've never had, peace in our hearts and in our lives. You prayed for us, healed the sick, and blessed the brokenhearted. You've shown us that community and love are the greatest gifts of all without which life would be as meaningless as dust. We will be eternally grateful to you, Ludwig, for bringing faith and heavenly light into this uneasy village life. Since you've come back to us, not once have we doubted or stumbled. You've always helped us and prayed for our souls." After a brief pause, she continued even louder. "I know that there is nothing on this earth what can be esteemed worthy to be given to you in return for everything you've done for us! However, we cannot let you leave with empty hands. Therefore, may this little box," she said, handing him the box wrapped in green, "always remind you of your holiness and influential love, which has illuminated and saved many souls including mine, my son. This community will never forget you, Ludwig. You are our brother, and our prayers and hearts will always be with you!"

Then she approached him, and, saying not a single word more, hugged him tightly as her own dear child. All other believers did the same. They came closer to Martha and Ludwig, and lovingly hugged them both. Gathering around in a circle, they embraced each other from the back, with their eyes closed and hearts uniting into one beat and rhythm. Not a single soul was left indifferently standing outside the circle of hugs. Every believer was hugging someone and being warmly hugged in return. In the middle of it were Ludwig and Martha. Their figures were lost among all those who were brotherly hugging them from right and from left. No one was talking at the moment. The words were of no use. The only sounds faintly traveling in the air were those produced by hand movements while brothers and sisters were embracing each other as if welcoming them into the eternal kingdom of heaven. Warmth and kindness reigned in the atmosphere without any conditions or time limits. Neither the towers of cold nor castles of temporariness happened to be firm enough not to eventually collapse and disappear from the sight of that evening's blessed eyes.

The image of true brotherhood and glimpses of pure sainthood lasted long enough for everyone not to feel the same after they let each other go. Not much was said after that either. Ludwig only humbly bowed down before the community which was as dear to him as the Word of God, and was off, tightly holding his present in his hand. The promise to meet again after the following morning's masses was made, although this was not the matter concerning Ludwig's thoughtful mind as he walked home with velocity. He thought neither of the gift, which was still unopened, nor of the community, which he had left somewhere behind him now. Although unwillingly, the monk was as though forced to think of Russell and try to assume what he was doing at the moment. He could not comprehend why it should concern him and what was the reason behind those gloomy doubts and peculiarly real fears that had so instantly appeared in his heart. He commenced to walk faster, passing one street after the other. He felt how the cold was beginning to seize his body and prevent it from making additional and unnecessary movements. Moments later, driven by his thoughts and the unbearable cold, Ludwig started running. Although it was not very convenient to do in his monk's long robe, but it was nevertheless wiser than to become utterly frozen both in soul and body.

While running recklessly and fast, he, as well as his brother a few hours earlier that evening, passed by two little birds who were still sitting on the edge of a trashcan as before. The two birds, in the same stillness and curiosity, gazed upon the running figure of the monk with wonder and diligent attentiveness. Ludwig didn't seem to notice them, but as for the tiny birds, they saw his every move and seemed to have counted his every exhale. As the running silhouette disappeared in the distance, the birds, as if recollecting and carefully pondering over what they had just seen, continued sitting calmly as two moveless little statues made of cold and lifeless stone.

Once his house was faintly seen in the distance, Ludwig saw a man, who had been in the church to hear his speech, on his right, carrying some logs into his house. On seeing the running monk, the man said loudly, "Good night, brother! Make sure to light up the fireplace! It's probably the coldest night ever!"

"God bless you, Tim!" said Ludwig in reply, slowing his pace. "Do you need a hand with those?"

"I'm fine, thank you! God bless you! Good night!"

"Good night!" he said and continued running toward his house, whence, as far as his eyes could see, not a single light was coming.

The wind was rising, spreading the cold wherever it wished, but neither time nor the hellish frost bothered his already worried heart anymore. Having only the picture of the house drowning in darkness before his eyes, Ludwig started running even faster, not able to feel his legs anymore.

When he finally reached the house, his heart started beating faster and the fear captured his entire being, filling him with doubts and haze. Standing before an open front door, Ludwig was afraid to go inside. Various horrible speculations started passing through his frozen mind, making him tremble with fear even more. He knew not what he would find inside or whether there was someone at all; in fact, he was too scared to even presume. Unable to stand in the cold any longer, Ludwig took out his wooden rosary from out of his jacket pocket as some kind of sword, which he was ready to use to protect himself from enemies more dangerous and darker than those visible ones. Looking around, he slowly, making as little noise as possible, went in. Trying to hear or see something, he turned on the light in the corridor, which is when his tumultuous fear somewhat ceased, for he saw nothing worth panicking about. Then, on his left, he slowly entered the dark sitting room and turned on the light there as well.

Momentarily Russell's rosary fell from his hand on the ground as his heart almost stopped beating. He saw two grown men lying lifelessly in different sides of the room: one on the sofa, and the other, his brother, by the fireplace with a box of matches next to him. Not hesitating a second and without even looking at the man on the sofa, Ludwig immediately fell on his knees next to his brother's body and took him in his arms. Russell's body was frozen as ice, and it showed no signs of life whatsoever. Seeing his brother wearing only a white T-shirt and jeans, almost made him faint with fright and horror. He had no idea what had happened there whatsoever or who was the man on the sofa. The terror made it hard for him to breathe at all. However, wasting no precious time, he quickly took Russell's wrist in hope to feel the beat of life and hope. Willing to weep with sorrow and regrets, Ludwig looked at his closed eyes and screamed out, "Brother!"

26

The night by the other side of the window was as dark as it could be; in fact, those more used to the light and brightness would've easily deemed the night to be an abyss of despair, vanity, and utter nothingness. Listening closely, one could hear vague screams echoing in the silent air as soon as the wind ceased to blow for a couple of short seconds. Then, as it slowly but surely rose again, the yelling and weeping voices were silenced, as if eternally lost in the infinite depth of the wind without a name. The entire lifeless atmosphere that night was also lost in its hopelessness and blackness. If not for the wildly beating heart, even the monk, strong in his faith and stubbornness, could be possessed by doubts whether life continued to exist, or whether the people of the earth were still meant to be loved and be free.

Now, as he was holding his brother Russell in his hands and screaming with teardrops falling down, he hoped that everything he believed in—mercy, miracles, power of prayer and love, power of kindness and forgiveness—would not fail him. With fear as old as the world overwhelming his hope, he kissed his unconscious brother's forehead twice, speechlessly asking him to wake up and prove that darkness was never supposed to be stronger than light. Russell was lying as dead, although his pulse was not yet eternally silenced and calmed. Once a few more attempts, made clearly out of despair and confusion, to wake up his brother appeared to be to no avail, Ludwig gently laid his brother back on the ground, wiped his face from the tears, and started slowly figuring out what to do next.

Lost in his emotions and thoughts, he quickly ran to the front door and firmly closed it. There was so much to do at the moment that the monk knew not where to begin or how to keep on standing on his feet. Frozen as ice himself, he, counting every precious second, ran upstairs, and took as many blankets as he could find. Commencing to think spontaneously, he took any warm things he could lay his eyes upon—woolen sweaters, pillows, a few warm socks. Taken by fears which continued appearing in his mind with every frail moment coming and going, Ludwig started panicking deep inside his shivering heart. The cold resumed controlling his body, what made it complicated for him to move freely and without pain. His legs were as paralyzed, and his back was one of those things it ached to even think of. Breathing heavily, he ran downstairs, losing a couple of woolen socks just before entering the sitting room. He wished the bodies had been gone. Before entering the room again, there was nothing he wanted more than to know this was all just a horrible, temporary nightmare, which now had passed, signifying that a new day was dawning. Yet, the bodies were in their places just as the monk had left them. Seeing them lying without a sign of life, this time he was completely frightened and almost convinced by a doubt that neither of the men were still unconsciously hoping to be waken up. Hardly bearing the pain in his entire body and soul, caused by nothing but severe cold of the cruel night, he, as before, fell on his knees next to his brother's body, put a warm pillow under his surprisingly light head, and, unable to control his tears and emotions this time, covered him carefully with as many warm woolen blankets as he had managed to find. "Come on," he muttered as if praying some long litany. "Wake up, my brother. I beseech you. Wake up!" Kneeling next to him, he found himself in a position which was unfamiliar to him. Nothing in the world—neither the riches nor the community nor the future nor the past nor the mysterious drunkard lying on the sofa behind him— seemed to be of any importance at the moment at all. His eyes were fixed upon Russell's frozen face, and his heart and soul were united like many times before in the unique power of prayer. "If you leave me now, brother, my heart will never continue beating. Along with yours, it will stop existing until the day of the Lord finally comes. I do not know what happened here, and, frankly, I do not care. Not this time, brother. I admit I was a fool, and that I've offended you more times than I can recall. I am guilty!" he shouted, beating with his fist upon his chest and weeping bitterly. "I admit, Russell! I've never wished you or anyone any harm! I apologize! Forgive me, brother, please forgive this poor and lonely sinner!" Then he, crying as loudly and regretfully as never before in his life, fell down on his brother and hugged him as his last hope to be heard by God and be forgiven. He said not a word more. He just kept crying, not comprehending how or when he would stop.

A minute later, divinely illuminated by a thought that his tears were incapable of helping his brother to open his eyes and stand up, he rapidly took his cellphone which was in his jacket pocket, and, again wiping his eyes to be able to see the screen and the tiny buttons, dialed the number of the senior monk who by that time had probably gone to sleep. Politeness and humbleness, however, were merits to be forgotten on that unforgettable and ghastly night, since all Ludwig had left was quick and unafraid of the consequences thinking and unceasing, silent prayers, continuously being recited in a secret chamber of his trembling and loudly beating heart. "Please, pick up," he said repeatedly for a while, until a sleepy voice was vaguely heard on the other line of the phone.

"Hello, this is brother Paul. Who is this?" said a thick manly voice, obviously displeased by the very late call.

"Paul!" shouted Ludwig. "This is brother Ludwig! I'm sorry for calling this late, but the matter is urgent, and we cannot waste any time."

"Ludwig? Brother, what happened?" asked the voice, becoming clearer and more lively with every word he said. "Calm down…Your brother? How…Okay, just don't panic. You want what? Fine, I think that can be arranged. Just keep on praying while I send a car for you. No! I said keep on praying, and the car will arrive very soon. God is with you. Do not be afraid, brother. Of course, I will be praying too. Just do not be afraid and try to calm down. I'm going to hang up the phone now because I need to inform other brothers and send the car. Pray, brother."

They both hung up, and a minute or more later united in prayers for Russell's icy soul. The car from the monastery was sent, and all the monks, most of whom were still a little sleepy, had gathered in their church to pray for Ludwig's dying brother.

From the side of Ludwig himself, however, the prayers didn't last long, for numerous things were still troubling his doubtful mind. Checking Russell's pulse every two minutes, he also didn't forget to keep glancing at the stranger, whose presence in their sitting room was surrounded with more questions than Russell's current state. The drunkard, from which the strong odor of alcohol was spreading faster than the usual and unending gossips in their village, was still lying unconscious and slightly, though little bit less than Russell, congealed as well. As a true monk and a brother to all, Ludwig found himself concerned about the poor stranger's soul and fate as well; dedicating him a few extra blankets and several prayers, Ludwig became less intrigued in the mystery of the night, and therefore, less scared. After a few vain attempts to wake up the drunkard in Russell's clothes, Ludwig left him be. With questions and speculations blinding his eyes full of tears, the monk, whispering the words of gratitude to the Almighty for giving him such a wonderful idea, lit up the fireplace in hope that at least a frailly burning fire would not allow his brother, and also the stranger, to completely freeze in silence and darkness. The fire, as it was expected, brought not only trustful light or sounds of sparks ensouling the entire place, but also warmth, able to heal, resurrect, and seal. Afterwards, he closed the door of the sitting room, not letting the warmth out. Diligently thinking of what he might do next, Ludwig again kneeled down on the ground, desperately sighed a few times, and, tossed by doubts into any direction imaginable, continued praying slowly and thoughtfully, looking at his brother's stony face. Amiably staring at Russell, he thought of the irony of the feelings, fighting for survival somewhere in his soul, which, at the moment, he could feel no more. He smiled at God's sense of humor, covering his grin with sorrows and sincere confession, which was in no need of words. After reconsidering the matter a few more times, Ludwig admitted that this was the only time in his entire life when he wished to save a body more than a soul; moreover, this was not caused by his despair or incredible pain. It was nothing but truth, overcoming any philosophies and fancy manners of preaching, which he was used to. While praying for Russell, he found himself saying no words about his brother's soul. All he wished for was to see his eyes again, to feel his warm embrace, and to hear him say anything he wanted, even the most insulting words of all. Ludwig didn't care about trifles like that. He just wanted to see his brother alive. If not for as long as he'd want to, then at least for as short as a blink of an eye.

Hour and a half later, when Ludwig already began reciting the holy rosary for the third time without a break, a knock at the front door visited the house. The monk rushed to open, and when he did, he saw two tall monks in black robes, reaching down up to their shoes, standing in front of him. He knew them very well. They were his trustful brothers and friends, with whom he could fearlessly share not only his past or personal, carefully cherished beliefs, but also the deepest secrets which were never meant to be brought into light or reach the ears of strangers. Now, they were standing as two angels, suffering from the acridity of the icy night and willing to sacrifice as much as themselves for the sake of their brother, who this time happened to be not a monk.

Wasting no time on unnecessary familiarities, Ludwig showed them his brother, and afterwards all three monks carried Russell and safely laid them into the minivan, which had been parked as close to the front door as possible. All the blankets and the pillows were taken as well, except for those which were warming up the stranger lying on the sofa.

"What about the other guy, Ludwig. I think he is unconscious too. Who is he by the way?" asked one monk as he and the other brother from the monastery were getting into the car.

"I have no idea. Wait a minute, please," said Ludwig hastily and rushed back home.

He came back into the sitting room, where fire in the fireplace was slowly dying and the air becoming cooler. Having approached the unconscious stranger, he shook him up a little, and said loudly enough to wake the entire village, "Sir, wake up!" The man did not reply. He neither blinked nor moved nor grinned. One more time checking his pulse, it occurred to Ludwig that the man had just drunk too much, and neither prayers nor unceasing loud shoutings would help. Why he was dressed in Russell's clothes, and what he was doing in the house at all, remained a mystery—a question which most likely was not supposed to be answered by Ludwig. The latter, finding himself in an utmost complicated situation, could neither throw him out of the house, for the stranger could freeze to death in just a couple of hours, nor could he leave him inside, not knowing what he might do. "Why have you done this to me, Russell?" muttered Ludwig, standing still in the middle of the room, completely unaware where to run or what to do. The monks and dying Russell were waiting for him in the car, but Ludwig was just caught up in a trap of his own doubts and lack of inner strength.

Afraid that, any minute could be Russell's ultimate bridge leading him into a better world and a better life, Ludwig, after contemplating a few more seconds, took a blank sheet of paper and a pen. This was, in all probability, the best option he could come up with, considering the intensity and sense of risk, which by all means had prevented him from acting as any pious man would do.

Hastily, he took the pen, and on the bank sheet of paper wrote:

Dear Stranger,

This is Ludwig Preston writing. I do not know what happened to you and to my brother Russell, but he is dying and I take him with me to the place where he can be healed. I do not know when, and if, we will be back, but I would like to ask you, whenever you wake up, to go home. I leave the door unlocked. I trust your kindness, sir. Ludwig

Then he left the note on the small table standing next to the sofa, and left, closing the door behind him. As quickly as his still frozen and slightly paralyzed legs let him, he got into the car, and they were off, hoping that the dawn of the following morning would shine on all of them.

27

The road back to the monastery was long enough to feel how hard and tiresome it was. The snow was a great obstacle, often forcing the car to slow down; here and there it was slippery, and at other times, it happened to be too dark to drive as fast as they needed. The only thing supporting them throughout their seemingly endless journey was prayer. The monks (two of them sitting in front, and Ludwig in the back, with his brother's head lying on his legs) were praying without ceasing, changing prayer after prayer, not giving themselves a minute to discuss what exactly happened or why. Sitting in the back and praying along with his brothers, Ludwig was looking down at Russell's moveless face and, using his words of prayer, asking him to wake up and smile. A few more tears dropped down, but certainly not more. Now, since they were on their way to the place which happened to be their only hope, Ludwig was as calm as a summer sea, refusing to allow himself to fall into regrets, vain contemplations, or sorrow. Surely, there was pain, but not strong enough to overwhelm the everlasting, miraculous power of prayer.

As soon as they arrived, all the monks belonging to the sacredness and silence of the monastery went outside to meet them. They all, carefully and respectfully maintaining the silence in which the prayers, which continued to be recited, were immersed, took Russell, and quickly brought him inside. There, as they passed a long corridor on the first floor, the walls of which were adorned by a few modest religious icons depicting a few well-familiar saints and the Holy Trinity, they carried Russell into a typical cell where no one currently lived. There was a lonely and rather frightful-looking bed standing by the window, a wooden table with nothing put on it, a small closet, and, most importantly, a wooden crucifix, hanging on the white and vastly cold wall. Though there were no possibilities to escape the hustle which had appeared as all the monks followed those who were carrying Russell into his cell, the sounds of prayers, echoing from one wall to the other, were nevertheless stronger than any sounds in the world at the moment. The men, lifting up their voices with dignity and courage, prayed without a pause to at least take a breath or yawn. More voices joined the glorious and heavenly prayer as they walked; and by the time they had reached the cell and lay lifeless Russell on the bed, all the monks were loudly praying, glorifying God and imploring to grant the gift of healing. The voices and the echo was so loud that it seemed even the concrete walls were joining in the holy prayer. No part, no corner of the monastery was not touched by those unimaginable, assonant sounds of prayers—every monk, every heart and thought were tied together as one into a sacred voice, which was certainly able to encompass the entire world and fill it with nothing but forgiveness, mercy, and grace.

The prayers continued even when Russell, covered with many warm blankets, was lying helplessly on the rather uncomfortable bed, and Ludwig was kneeling on the floor beside him, praying with others in holiness and monastic mightiness. All the monks, whose exact number was unknown, gathered around the bed on which Russell lay, and prayed continuously with their eyes closed and voices reaching even unto the heavens. Some of them knew not who the man they were praying for was or what had happened to him; even not all were aware that the man on the bed was Ludwig's real brother. Nevertheless, their voices were not weaker because of lack of information. Each monk praying as for his own brother, they didn't stop to ask questions, they didn't stumble in doubts, and, as it has become clear, they did not cease asking God to heal the dying man.

As the dawn shyly approached, the picture in the monastery remained the same as many hours before. Nothing changed, except for the light of the morning sun eagerly breaking its way into the room through a tiny window in a concrete, cold, and greatly lonesome wall. The brightly shining light of the sun was an unexpected guest in the room, which instantly was regarded as an additional and vastly important ingredient in their medicine called prayer. Those whose heads were bent down and eyes closed could not see the rays or a new day dawning; meditating upon their recitations and mysteries lying behind them, the monks, forgetting and abandoning their own wills and wishes, asked God only for one—to heal and resurrect the dying man and not to let him leave.

Two more hours later, monks started getting up and leaving the room still mindfully muttering the words of prayers along with others—both those who were leaving and those who earnestly kept on kneeling. The senior monk, who had also been present in the room beside Russell's bed all this time, was also about to leave it for an unknown length of time. He looked at Ludwig but the latter's head was bent down and he could not see him. Then he came closer to him and gently touched his shoulder. Speechlessly, they looked at each other with eyes which had nothing to say in addition to the prayers still sounding in the air. Ludwig's pale face and weary eyes spoke for themselves. The senior monk didn't dare to ask any questions or command his brother to have an hour of rest. The most he could do was look at him with worry and plea not to forget himself; but, in reply, Ludwig only shook his head, refusing to leave his brother. The senior monk nodded with understanding and left, followed by all other monks in the room. The door of the cell was silently closed and now only two brothers, one of which belonged neither to those monastery walls nor to the sacred brotherhood of those who prayed for him, were left in it.

Tightly holding his wooden rosary, Ludwig looked at his brother's face with regretful and sorrowful eyes. Having forced himself to stop reciting the prayers for a moment, he silently said, "We are under the wings of angels, brother. Those who claim there is no God are fools, for who else could ever bring us together in a place where, blessed by mother, I lived for many years selflessly praying for you and your soul. Maybe this does not bring you much joy, but you are here now, and all these prayers which your soul has just heard were for you. The monks, my brothers, pray for you, and, God willing, I am sure you will get well pretty soon. You've been always accusing me of devoting more time to prayers than to true Christianity or helping others. Yet now, brother, as you can see, prayer is the only way from darkness to light. No medicine, no fireplace in the world will warm up this frozen body. I know that you wouldn't allow me to, but I will be praying for you until the moment your eyes open."

And so he did as he said, reciting the well known Catholic prayers, one after the other, nonstop.

Later in the afternoon, a few monks entered the cell where they were warmly greeted by the same image they had seen when they left it many hours ago. Ludwig was still kneeling by the bed as if rooted, moving only his fingers as they were squeezing and passing each bead of his wooden rosary. Complete silence was in the air. All prayers were said in the monk's mind, where only he and still unconscious Russell could witness and feel them. The only disturbance that was discourteously attempting to ruin the utter peace of the picture was the usual winter's breeze, knocking at the tiny cell window as if annoyingly asking to be let in. When the door was opened and the monks, as quietly as they could, to what they had been accustomed, went in, Ludwig didn't react whatsoever; his eyes remained indefinitely closed as his fingers continued slowly going over the beads of the rosary, which he held over the bed, next to his brother's body.

Astonished at what they saw, the monks went inside, carrying a lot of something in their hands. One of them came to Ludwig and whispered into his ear, "We brought the holy Water, the cross, and a few icons. Also the holy rosary for your brother." Receiving no reply expect a nod in return, the monks put everything on the table next to the bed, and, almost making no sounds, left the cell, closing the door.

Ludwig finally opened his eyes and stood up not until a few more hours later. Continuing to murmur the prayers, he went to the table on which the monks had put the religious protections against the evil and, in its own point of view, its sarcastic way of darkening the souls. Firstly, he took a tiny glass bottle, as big as a finger of a grown man, in which was the holy water. Upon opening it, he leaned over his brother, spilled a few drops on his thumb, and made a sign of a cross on Russell's forehead. "May your soul be blessed and cleansed, my brother," he said while making the sign. He repeated the act two more times and then closed the bottle and put it back aside.

Afterwards, while the prayers kept coming out of his mouth, he took a wooden cross hanging on a tiny cotton rope as a necklace. Blessing it with words of the Hail Mary prayer, he hung it around Russell's neck. Ludwig believed that it would help them heal not only his body, but also his inner wounds which, regrettably, were known only to the unconscious man. The cross around one's neck was always considered to be a protective shield from fiendish enemies of darkness, which had myriad joy in hurting either a man's soul or his body. Once this was done, gently and brotherly, Ludwig raised Russell's head a little bit and slid two religious images under his pillow—one of them depicted Virgin Mary, the Mother of Jesus, with her right hand pointing to her open and brightly glowing heart, and with her left, motherly pointing above. The other image represented the power of Michael, the archangel. Standing over an enemy familiar to many, he was gloriously holding a long and unconquerable sword, protecting the children of God from any kinds of threats, dangers, and temptations. The images, often regarded as substantial reminders of the magnificent mightiness of God and his kingdom, were put under the pillow, upon which Russell's head rested, as two shining candles, expected to enlighten and warm up the dying man's body and soul. The rosary, which had also been brought by the two monks along with the holy water, the cross, and the images was to be used with divine purpose. Ludwig wrapped it around Russell's left hand and gently hid it back under the blankets.

Sighing with relief, Ludwig found himself calmed and eased from the unknown fears and doubts resembling his temporary weakness. Seeing his brother resting under the protecting and healing objects pertaining to the God Almighty's hand itself, Ludwig, grinning with delight, kneeled back on the ground, put his arms on the bed next to Russell's body, and continued reciting the Hail Mary prayer, fingering the rosary in his hand.

Meanwhile, coming from the church that was in the other side of the building, Ludwig heard the words of psalms loudly and gloriously being sung by the monks. He knew the sacred purpose it served, to which he only grinned one more time, and said, having stopped reciting the rosary. "You hear that, brother? Those psalms are sung for your soul. Do not leave us, brother. Please, do not. We still have a chess game to play, remember?" Then he suddenly burst into tears. "I'm sorry I was late!" he cried. "I'm sorry I was stubborn and didn't listen. Come back to play chess with me, brother! Do not leave me entirely alone in this vain and foolish world!" Then he emotionally bowed down his head and continued praying without a pause.

The sounds of psalms lasted until around midnight, but Russell's brother's soul never ceased persistently reciting one prayer after another. Soon, the dawn of the next day started approaching, but the picture of the cell with two brothers in it never changed. The door was never opened after the two monks left, and Ludwig's mouth never stopped uttering words of love and earnest pleas, supported by his meekness and humbleness before God. Russell was still not showing any hopeful signs of life, lying as dead, though still miraculously alive.

Until the next day came, speculations had arisen outside the cell where the two brothers were. Some monks began to doubt whether it wouldn't be wiser to call a doctor or do something more for the dying man. A few started to question their method of praying, being sincerely worried for the one whom they barely knew.

"Maybe some medicine would help," said one monk, as he and his monastic brother were going in a corridor to their cells. "Prayer is good, but don't you think putting our entire trust in it is not wise?"

"I must agree, Jacob," answered the monk thoughtfully. "Yet, since our senior and brother Ludwig have decided to use only prayer as our medicine, I presume there is little we can do. Besides, speaking of Ludwig, have you noticed how devout he is? He prays continuously kneeling by the bed, and he hadn't gone to the bathroom and hadn't had as sip of water for more than twenty hours now!"

"Indeed. The fact that he trusts fully in the Lord is what astounds me the most. His faith is something I've never seen before. However, I still believe that tomorrow we should suggest our senior to call a doctor."

Such and many other conversations took place in many cells that night. The monks had a lot to talk about, marveling at how selfless and holy was Ludwig's love for his brother. Some found it hard to believe that a man could entirely trust in his prayers, while there were found a few who secretly were angered with the fact that all the attention was directed to the dying man. In general, despite the fact that daily and commonplace schedule in the monastery was utterly out of order, the prayers for Russell's soul were ascending into the heavens from most of the cells along with the pleas to heal and save Ludwig's brother.

In such a spirit of prayers, the morning of the following day finally broke in. Though the hope had not yet faded away, the rays of the sun, slightly tickling Russell's face, did not make any changes in the atmosphere of hope mingled with sorrow. That was supposed to be the irrevocable truth, but suddenly everything changed with a move of a finger, with a blink of an eye. The air recovered its light, and the walls surrounding the two brothers were not cold anymore. Warmth was what instantly filled the place, and it had absolutely nothing to do with the sun, whose brightness was entering the room through a tiny window. Whether it was a brotherly sense, or an accidental coincidence, not even the angels could tell. It happened so suddenly that the fact itself was left unnoticed, being followed by emotional stillness and silence in the air. Ludwig, touched by a feeling that something had just happened, opened his red and weary eyes, and, with his mouth open and no words coming out of it, looked at his brother, fearing to doubt in the moment's reality. Russell's eyes were open, and they were looking straight at the shining sun and its rays enlightening and warming up his face. His fingers were moving, and face was as though telling that now it would all be all right.

"Thank you, God. Thank you," Ludwig silently muttered, weeping as a child. "Brother," he said, drawing closer to Russell, who was staring at the sun and its light. "It is me, Ludwig. Do you hear me, brother?" he asked, wiping his face, although he still could not stop crying.

In reply, Ludwig received only a tiny grin on his brother's face, and that was enough for the monk whose soul, too, had been saved—saved from eternal sense of misery and guilt. He burst into tears, kissed Russell's forehead as many as at least ten times, and kneeled down again to thank the Lord for this grace and salvation.

Afterwards, about a minute later, Ludwig quickly left the room and went to tell all the monks, who at the time were in the church praying for Russell, that his brother was alive, that he had woken up. There were no more prayers being recited, no more worries taking place; curiosity about a miracle unseen was what hastily carried the monks into the cell, where, regrettably, they found nothing worth calling a wonder. It was a surprise to Ludwig as well, for he could dare to swear that he had seen his brother open his eyes and smile. Russell was lying lifelessly like many hours before—his fingers didn't move, and his face showed no hopeful signs of life.

"But he opened his eyes just minutes ago!" said Ludwig in disbelief, approaching his brother as some ghost full of mysteries and inevitable unpredictabilities.

"You are tired, brother Ludwig," said one monk courteously, feeling rather sorry for the weary and desperate man. "I know it is not my business, but you should have a few hours of rest."

"I will not rest until I see my brother's eyes," retorted Ludwig, questionably gazing upon Russell's lifeless face. Again kneeling down on the ground to continue praying, he said, "Please, be with me in prayer. All we need is prayer now. I need your support, brothers."

While Ludwig secretly started recalling what truly happened in the cell a few minutes earlier, one of the monks came to him, and, gently putting his hand on his brother's shoulder, said, "We will pray for you even if it takes us ten years, but it will be a lot easier if we put everything into the Almighty's hands, Ludwig. Sometimes our wishes do not match those of God's."

"Are you saying we should stop praying for my brother who can die any second?" he exclaimed, turning his red and exhausted eyes to the monk, who now had felt quite guilty and embarrassed.

"God forbid, I never said that," he replied, turning red. "We will pray with you, brother, but let us keep in mind that our Lord's will is greater than ours."

On hearing this, Ludwig stood up and angrily replied, "Ask and you will receive, seek and you will find, knock and the door will be opened to you. Do these lines sound familiar to you? God can open a door, but first we must knock."

"Please don't tell me I am where I think I am," suddenly said a voice, interrupting the unholy dispute, and scattering the intensity in the heavy air. Momentarily, everyone's, who was lucky enough to be present in the cell at the precious and miraculous moment, eyes were opened widely, and not one dared to utter a word. The voice that spoke was familiar only to Ludwig, who happened to be the first one to react. With eyes as red as a rose, and his face pale, he, driven by happiness unspeakable, burst into tears once again, and fell on his knees next to Russell's bed. The dying man's eyes were slightly opened as he was slowly eyeing every monk standing around him. Enveloped in displeasure with the fact that he was utterly surrounded by monks, Russell was as though ready to get up and leave that same instant. The fact that he could barely move a finger did not bother him; realizing where he was and frightfully imagining what had probably been done unto him while he was unconscious, Russell glanced at his weeping brother on his right, speechlessly, in their own brotherly language, begging him to tell that this was not real. Understanding his brother's plea, Ludwig only smiled with a nod in return.

In ten minutes or less after Russell finally woke up, all the brothers in the monastery were on their feet, carrying all kinds of helpful things into the cell. Jams of raspberries and cranberries, two jars of honey, and different porridges to help recover the strength faster, were brought into the cell were Russell lay. Moreover, the entire process of healing could not possibly take place without an electric kettle, which was also brought along with various herbal teas; drinking as much hot herbal tea as possible was greatly beneficial for the still frozen body to recover its warmth and liveliness.

The burdensome hours of prayers were behind now, and a new time had begun—a time of taking care for Russell's moveless body, feeding him, and strengthening his soul with encouraging words of true brotherhood and love. This part was of course Ludwig's responsibility, and he had taken it with honor and a sense of duty. Each day, he fed his helpless and still weary brother every now and then, telling him of what had really happened. Although having plenty of questions himself, Ludwig didn't dare to bother Russell with any of them; not until five days later, when he had recovered at least some of his strength, and was ready to leave the monastery where his life had been miraculously saved.

28

A day before Russell eventually left the monastery, Ludwig, for the first time since the night when he found Russell lying on the floor by the fireplace, had gone back to their house in order to take some warm clothes for his brother, who was slowly getting well. He was going there with a jumbled mind, fearing to think what he might find there. Although thoughts about the drunkard never left him, all he cared about was taking some new clothes for Russell and leaving the house for good. To his surprise, the house was empty, and not even an odor of alcohol was present. To convince himself of that, however, Ludwig went to every room, every closet and bathroom to check if the astonishing fact was verily true. It was, but along with it came even more doubtful questions, which, luckily, Ludwig had found too negligible to be answered.

The following day, Russell, carrying a bag with his old clothes in it, left the cell with Ludwig, his brother, walking by his side. Russell was dressed in warm winter boots, a woolen scarf, sweater, and a brown winter coat on top. Keeping the body in warmth was the most important task now, and Ludwig had taken a good care of the matter. Now, they were walking down a long and empty corridor toward the main entrance door, both feeling rather tensed up about the fact that they were about to separate again, for the second time in their lives.

Slowly marching and passing windows on their right side, which opened a view into the monastery's inner garden which now was all covered in snow and utter frost, Ludwig said, "I've asked one of our brothers to get you safely home, brother. The car is already waiting."

"I don't think I'll need that. A little walk will do me no harm," said Russell silently, for his voice had the hardest time of recovering. It was still sounding quite hoarse, and even the tickling woolen scarf around his neck was unable to change that.

"Don't be foolish, brother," insisted Ludwig. "Cold will not help you recover faster."

"Still, I refuse. Thank you for the concern," he said kindly with a smile.

With a weary sigh, Ludwig, after a few seconds, said, "You never really told me what exactly happened that night. I know it is painful for you to remember, but to hear the entire story would be great."

"There's nothing to tell, Ludwig. Nothing worth mentioning."

"When I returned home yesterday, I didn't find the drunkard. Who is he?"

"I have no idea," he said thoughtfully, recalling each second of the night when he carried the unconscious man on his shoulder. "Was he there when you found me?"

"Yes, unconscious and drunk," replied Ludwig. "Sure you don't want to share what really happened?" After receiving silence, which was accompanied by the sounds of their steps, in reply, Ludwig said, "Before I left the house, I wrote a note to him, asking him to leave once he wakes up. When I returned there yesterday, right beneath my message on the same note, I found two more words written. He thanked you for something. Besides, your black coat was left on the sofa."

"Interesting," said Russell, looking at the entrance door which was before them in the distance.

"I have many questions about what happened and don't blame me for that. You almost died, brother. When I found you lying lifeless by the fireplace, I thought I had lost you. Your body was freezing, and for a second, it occurred to me that your soul was no more in that room."

"I'd tell you everything about that night, but the fact is that even I, who went through all that horror and unspeakable pain, begin to doubt whether it really happened to me."

"Horror? Please, stop torturing me, brother. Tell me what happened," said Ludwig, anxious to hear the truth.

"All I can tell you," said Russell, stopping and turning toward Ludwig, "is that this cross"—he took the wooden cross hanging around his neck from beneath his clothes—"will be hanging around my neck. I promise. I will not take it off."

"That's a surprise. I thought you'd throw it away the minute you wake up," said Ludwig kindly with a smile.

"I know, this is a miracle to me as well. I usually don't believe in such idols as this piece of wood, but I think I can make an exception."

"This is supposed to be a reminder, not an idol. Pictures of Jesus and wooden crosses are to remind us of whose we are, and who is always by our side, loving and forgiving us our sins. When we look at photos of our dear ones, and, moreover, when we kiss them, we do not praise or worship the image itself. We just honor the memories and the precious moments they contain. The essence behind a picture, a statue, or a small wooden cross is what we praise."

Hiding his cross under the clothes with a sigh, Russell replied, "I never thought of it this way."

"And I never thought that I would see you standing inside the monastery walls," said Ludwig, also smiling.

"Indeed. Neither did I."

Suddenly, as they were standing in front of each other with wide smiles on their faces and talking, a monk passed by them rather quickly. "Good to see you, brother! I'm very happy that you got well!" he said gladly and went away.

"Thank you!" replied Ludwig to the monk. Turning to his brother, he said, "I know you don't like being here, but you should be thankful to these monks, for they prayed for you and their prayers were answered."

"I choose to thank God instead," he answered. "Besides, I thought only you were praying by my bed."

"The entire monastery was praying in one voice day and night, Russell. Now you see that unity in prayers can do wonderful things, amazing things. When people pray together, anything is possible. The devil is clever and sly. He knows what can save the world and destroy his reign. Look around, Russell, communities separate, the unity among the Christians is weakening. What we need is brotherhood and prayers, reaching the throne of God in one chord and sound. You are the example of what I am saying. Whenever you look at the mirror, remember my words, because it was the prayers of united Christians that saved you."

"You know," said Russell, continuing to walk forward, "what you say does make sense, and, at some point, I admit that I agree with you. But why loneliness?" he asked suddenly.

"Loneliness?"

"This whole monastery thing and living apart from the world and civilization. How does that help you to be a better Christian? I always thought that we, followers of Jesus, should be among the unfaithful, not among those who think they are saved."

"I can hardly understand your words," said Ludwig, frowning.

"I know." A moment later, he resumed, "Why not have a family and make the world a better place by educating your children and teaching them the ways of the Lord? Praying in a lonely cell will not save the world."

"Yet it saved you, didn't it? Likewise, we pray for the entire world, asking God to grant us peace, mercy, healing, and forgiveness." Then he put his arm on Russell's shoulder and added, "Let us have no more vain disputes, brother. God leads us all in different ways, yet toward the same goal. Some are meant to be good fathers, others to be honorable politicians, and some, like me, pious monks, whose purpose is not always clear. Now, however, I know that nothing in this world happens in vain."

A moment later, they finally approached the front door, which looked as frightfully as never before, whispering into their ears that this was where they would part. They stopped, and both were afraid to open it and say their last, ultimate good-byes. They looked at each other with eyes full of love and pleas to be forgiven, allowing the moment of utter silence to torture their souls just a little bit more.

"Tomorrow is Christmas," said Ludwig finally. "If you have no one to celebrate with, you can come here and spend the day with us."

"Thank you, brother," replied Russell, "but I don't think I will ever be coming back. Besides, I think Ruth has already called the police, which is searching for me all around the village. I must be going, my life is waiting for me to come back."

"Where are you bound for now? What is the plan for your future?"

"To love the woman I cannot live without, to live with her in a small hut next to a huge orange farm somewhere in Spain, and to spend my days in love and gratitude to God."

"Is this where I can find you in case I miss you?"

"Yes. Of course, I do not forbid you to come into my dreams every now and then," he said with a smile.

Then Ludwig took a rosary from his pocket, and, without asking any questions, slowly put it into Russell's coat pocket.

"You know, I am not going to pray it," said Russell rather sarcastically.

"I know," replied he with a modest smile. Minutes later, he looked at him and said, "Before we part, Russell, I want you to tell me something. I want you to answer my last question to you." After a brief pause, he said, "You are not humble, not obedient to God's commands. You drink beer, you seldom curse, and you often get angry without any reason; it is not a secret that you are not modest or a true prayer warrior. However, a voice within me forces me to call you a saint. Why?"

"I'll tell you that when I become what you just called me," replied Russell, and he opened the front door. "This is where we part, brother. I want you to know that I always loved you and I always will. There are many brothers behind these doors, but I have only one." Then they brotherly and tightly hugged each other, holding their emotions behind manly firmness, which was beginning to fade. "Do not worry, my dear saint, we shall meet again one day."

"Shall we?" asked Ludwig, as a couple of tears dropped on Russell's shoulder.

"I promise. If not in this world, then in the one to come for sure."

Although the car was waiting outside, Russell apologized to the driver and told him he would go home by bus. The weather was not as freezing as on the night when Russell's soul and faith were tested. There was a straight, long, all covered in snow road before him, and, not turning around to wave or see his brother one last time, Russell started walking forward, with his head lowered and heart intricately wrapped in thoughts belonging to the time which was long past. Ludwig, on the other hand, kept standing by the open front door, gazing upon his brother until the latter's figure completely disappeared in the distance, enlightened by the winter sun from above.

Having reached the lonely bus station standing near an empty road, Russell noticed that he wasn't alone. A man of fifty was sitting on a bench with a beer can in his hand, probably also waiting for the bus to arrive. Glancing a few times at the man, Russell saw that he was dressed poorly, not to mention the unpleasant smell coming from him.

He stood aside, leaned against a bus stop sign post, and continued recalling everything whatever was on his mind, beginning with his childhood years and ending with the night when he helped the poor drunkard and carried him to his home.

A few minutes later, when still no sign of a bus was visible in the distance, the man with a beer can stood up and slowly, with his left leg limping, approached Russell, who was looking at him with suspicion and caution, and said, "Have some money to spare, brother?"

Looking at the poor man with ragged clothes and a desperate expression on his face, Russell smiled at him, took a rosary, which Ludwig had given him, from his pocket and handed it to the man. "Are you cold?" he asked afterwards.

"Yes I am, good man," replied the man.

Then Russell took off his coat, put it on the man and said, "Would you like to come with me for a warm cup of tea, brother?"

"Would you let me, good sir?" the man humbly asked in astonishment and inexpressible gratitude.

"I insist," said Russell, and a second later, the bus finally arrived.

CPSIA information can be obtained
at www.ICGtesting.com
Printed in the USA
FSOW03n1439140816
23670FS

9 781681 874555